NIKOLAI
KLIMONTOVICH

THE
ROAD
TO
ROME

*Naughty reminiscences
about the late Soviet years*

Translated by Frank Williams

glas

The Editors of the Glas series:
Natasha Perova & Joanne Turnbull
Publicity director: Peter Tegel
Camera-ready copy: Tatiana Shaposhnikova

Front cover design: Anastasia Perova

GLAS Publishers
tel./fax: +7(095)441-9157
perova@glas.msk.su
www.russianpress.com/glas

Glas is distributed in North America by
NORTHWESTERN UNIVERSITY PRESS
Chicago Distribution Center,
tel: 1-800-621-2736 or (773) 702-7000
fax: 1-800-621-8476 or (773)-702-7212
pubnet@202-5280
www.nupress.northwestern.edu

in the UK and Europe by
INPRESS LTD.
52 Harpur Street, Bedford, MK40 2QT, UK
tel: 01234 330023
fax: 01234 330024
www.inpressbooks.co.uk

Published in cooperation with Harbord Press

ISBN 5-7172-0068-4

© Glas New Russian Writing 2004
No part of this book may be used or reproduced in any
manner without the written permission of the publisher.

Contents

Klimontovich's Road to Rome   *6*

Liberty Island   *10*
The Berlin Wall   *27*
Czech Spring   *40*
Soft Blues   *50*
Japan   *59*
Viola   *76*
Gulya   *91*
Round Dance   *129*
Anna and the Fountain   *157*
Girls on the Way Back   *176*
Navigating a Fjord   *193*
Ksenia   216
The Mystery of the New York Ichthyology   *229*
Full Moon at Halloween   *244*
To Paris   *253*
Return To Rome   *260*

Klimontovich's Road to Rome

"A veritable Moscow Decameron," "the Soviet Casanova of Russian literature" — these appellations were given to the naughty autobiographical narratives penned by Nikolai Klimontovich during the 1990s, of which *The Road to Rome*, stands out.

Born in 1951, he made a living as a reporter before becoming the prize-winning novelist and playwright he is today. The son of a famous physicist, an Academician, he was also trained as a physicist while writing stories and plays from the age of nineteen. In 1977 he was lucky to have a collection of his early stories published by a big Soviet publishing house (as part of their short-lived campaign of "encouraging young talent"). Although the reviews criticized the book for its lack of "ideological position", Klimontovich was able to join the Writers' Union, which gave him the official status of a professional writer, a great convenience at the time, opening many doors. However, his subsequent works never passed the Soviet censors and were invariably rejected by publishers and journals alike on grounds of their "erroneous aesthetic and ideological views." Instead he was widely circulated in samizdat (in the USSR) and published by tamizdat (abroad). Because of this he was constantly under KGB scrutiny – appearance in émigré periodicals was considered a crime in the USSR.

Opposed to the dominant ideology Klimontovich with some fellow-writers — well-educated, nihilistic, ironic, oriented at Western culture — founded an independent writers' group called the "Belle-Lettres Club" in the spring of 1980. The almanac *Katalog* was the first and only output of the Club, which included some of the young and talented but unpublished writers, such as Evgeny Popov, Evgeny Kharitonov, Dmitry Prigov. They decided to legalize their almanac by applying to the Communist Party Central Committee for official permission to publish it. The same day the writers' homes were searched by the KGB and their manuscripts and books confiscated while the club was dissolved. In one day Klimontovich lost all his manuscripts, including an unfinished novel, a play, several short stories and his notebooks. In 1982 the *Katalog* was published by Ardis in the USA.

Klimontovich, like most intellectuals of his generation, suffered from a "confinement complex", lacking the freedom to travel and see the world. This is the subject of his best-selling book *The Road to Rome* relating his picaresque encounters with women from the West as his way of breaking out of stifling Soviet reality and into an exotic and forbidden world.

Eventually able to travel abroad, he ends up spending a year in America and returns to Moscow – the Third Rome – with firm conviction that his place is in Russia for better or for worse. However, as a result of his Odyssey, both existential — during his internal exile within Soviet Russia

— and real travels to foreign lands, he attains the desired self-liberation.

The appeal of this book is not only in its infectious eroticism, its wit and humor, but mainly in its masterful portrayal of Soviet Russia in the 1970s and '80s through a multitude of cleverly observed details.

Although *The Road to Rome* is actually a collection of reminiscences about real events, it is structured as a plot-driven narrative and was in fact nominated for the Booker Prize as a novel in 1995.

And finally, why Rome? "The Third Rome", a catch-phrase referring to Moscow, comes from the 15th-century political doctrine first formulated by the Pskov monk and writer Filofei in his correspondence with the Moscow Grand Duke Vassily III: "Moscow is the Third Rome... Two Romes fell, the Third Rome stands, and there will never be a fourth." The Moscow rulers aspired to establish the importance of Moscow as Russia's political and religious centre and establish claims to the Roman and Byzantine thrones. The saying "All roads lead to Rome" is reinterpreted by Russians in this sense as well.

The editors

"Moscow is the Third Rome...
Two Romes fell, the Third Rome stands,
and there will never be a fourth."
From a 15th-century Russian chronicle

Liberty Island

A healthy adolescence: football in the yard, picture books about pirates, puerile mucking about between lessons and the constant itch to get under a girl's skirt and at her knickers — try and remember where exactly on this latter voyage of discovery my odyssey began. But even supposing I did have some kind of hazy dreams about her, what could I have dreamt of? The smell of coconut milk, tangles of sugar cane, peaceful pink sands at the ebb tide, the fretwork silhouettes of palm trees, and out in the lagoon a schooner riding at anchor? All so unlike the unpretentious northern landscape in the area of the knickers of my classmates Tanya, Olga and Lyuba, a region I had explored pretty thoroughly.

These expeditions around home territory were not short of a sense of excitement, of course, but it bore no comparison with the feeling she aroused in me, forcing me to run the other way, down the stairs from our classroom as soon as her slender figure appeared in the dusty and shabby reaches of our corridor. Yet I wasn't really in love with her, the way I was with Tanya or Olga or a dozen other girls — on and off and with all of them at once; and to be frank, she didn't strike me as beautiful: she was skinny, half a head taller than me — for though I might have been shy, I was still a strapping lad; she was swarthy, with a thin, sharp face, and eyes very dark and small, a bit rodent-like, and a year older than me, too, which could have been a huge plus for her if she had been in the class above, but she had been put in our year which cancelled out her advantage in age. Not that she had been made to repeat a year, no, she was Cuban, or as I would have liked to think, a mestizo, because at that time I was more than just a soccer-mad Lothario, I was a voracious reader, devouring verbose Dickens, tedious Daudet, heroic Captain Blood and the enthralling Mayne Reid.

She had been born during Batista's rule (*The Young Pioneer Pravda* had run a series about the horrors of his regime), and was the daughter of a Cuban ambassador, apparently from the old aristocracy which the fearless, but pragmatic Fidel had partially won over to his side. She despised Russians — perhaps because she reckoned all Russians were communists, which in those days wasn't far from the truth — and her contempt showed in her cool manner, if you can talk about manners in a thirteen-year-old girl, and in her independent opinions, and in a standoffishness, which killed any willingness on the part of our teachers to teach her anything. The other girls treated her with no more than a twinge of superstitious revulsion, though not without curiosity, as if she were an over-intelligent house-trained monkey, so they were not at all envious of either her clothes or her things — actually, she was modest and ascetic in this respect; as for the boys, they called her Tarzan's ape and on the whole ignored her. Anyway, Moscow in the twilight of the Khruschev era was full of foreigners, for the most part dark-complexioned like her, or even plain black. My more enterprising friends used to trade badges for chewing gum with them, and get arrested for it, picked up briefly either by the police or by the student volunteers from the University patrol at the Lenin Hills viewpoint from where you still get the best view of our awkward, sprawling, charming monstrosity of a city.

For months we never said a word to each other, but then I began to detect an inquisitive glance, very direct, and one day she gave me a fright when, after our eyes had met briefly, a smile appeared on her usually glum face, a smile quite without playfulness, reserve or come-on. I had been watching her quietly before that, and discovered much that was seriously enticing. She had unspoken permission not to wear the school uniform, and mostly she wore tight-fitting jeans, which, incidentally, at that time looked like ordinary sports gear, they weren't a symbol or a fetish; naturally, she didn't wear the red pioneer neck scarf, since she wasn't formally a Soviet Pioneer. I was captivated by her voice, husky in comparison with the shrillness of the other girls, by her accent, by her obvious foreign pronunciation and by the way she almost completely ignored declensions, even though she spoke Russian tolerably well compared to the other foreigner in our class, a Hungarian girl who was fat and slovenly, but still game for a laugh. Secretly, I watched her walk — she moved lightly, on the balls of her feet, she didn't shuffle, didn't sway like some of the older girls; she had very pink nails on her dark fingers that were always clean and neat, and I guessed she manicured them every day; in each translucent lobe of her golden ears gleamed the almost invisible silver dot of an earring, her shiny straight black hair was always combed smooth and pulled back into a knot, while her blouse was taut across the mounds of her breasts with their claret-coloured nipples. She was different in every way, and this in itself evoked dangerously mixed feelings. She was more perfect than all the others around her, including me of course, and any intimacy with her would demand strenuous effort and perfection on my part.

What could I do to impress her — perform prodigious feats during a game of football; offer her a nibble of my jam doughnut during break, which always worked with the Olgas and Tanyas; take the piss out of our class tutor, a hysterical old maid of a civics teacher who was always looking for any excuse to call my parents to the school; name off by heart a couple of dozen writers — that only worked on the Russian teacher, Alevtina, she of the hooked nose and moustache, who would call me out of lessons to the staff room under the pretext of helping her with the wall newspaper, stroke my hair and talk breathlessly about her summer love affair with a flight lieutenant. There was probably only one time I could have won her admiration — at a Pioneers' meeting, which censured my habit of keeping my pioneer scarf in my pocket instead of around my neck — but she never went to meetings. How could I win her over, make her weep with gratitude, write me notes, breathe into the phone, blush when I caught her sneaking a look at me? It was unthinkable to lure her to my place some grim winter day while my parents were at work, or up to an April attic with the cooing of doves and mounds of droppings, or to May-time bushes by the volleyball court for a solitary kiss and a fumble. It was quite impossible to imagine her in a collective grope in the locker room, like Lyuba, the best endowed and most generously proportioned girl in the class, overflowing with such seductive juices that even the least prepossessing boys swarmed like flies around her big thighs and sateen slacks.

The more I spied, the more I realized the degree of courage to reject home, habits and the peaceful joys of a cosy and carefree existence that adventure requires, since even a chance exchange of looks with her seemed an adventure to me. Of course, a real pirate captain, were she captured by his men, would have ordered her taken to his cabin and, true gentleman that he was, guaranteed her total inviolability — to do that, though, you would have needed to hang a dozen or so mutinous swabs from the yardarm and to have at least two permanently loaded pistols, not to speak of other arms and accoutrements, about your person. But it wasn't just the lack of practice at quelling mutiny and scanty ammunition that made chatting her up such a difficult thing to do — caution, fear of rejection, and an unwillingness to risk my hard-won leadership of the class also played a part, since my emotional state, despite my friends' dim-wittedness in affairs of the heart, threatened to become all too obvious at any moment. Furthermore, there was something else — something women regard in men as chicken-heartedness — a vague presentiment that, besides a simple urge to get into their knickers, girls can sometimes provoke, by use of their powers of bewitchment, a mysterious, dangerous and irresistible feeling in your soul, which, to quote a Scandinavian novelist of high emotional charge whom I did not read until later when it happened to me for the first time, inclines even the heads of kings to the ground.

Meanwhile, I discovered other details about her, which in my eyes placed her at an even more insuperable distance. First of all, it turned out she spoke other languages besides Russian. That she knew Spanish was not too hard to figure out, but one day during an English lesson, when we were struggling with irregular verbs and the teacher asked a question, she suddenly came up with, *I don't like Mondays*. She shut up immediately, realising she'd said too much and given the game away, that her earlier pretence and fake efforts to learn like any other beginner had been exposed. A little later we found out she played tennis; someone met her on the street carrying a racket, not that it was a big deal, in foreign movies they often played tennis, then kissed, rich people as a rule — we didn't like rich people much, but we tolerated them as a relic of the past, especially in the movies. Besides, we had rackets and balls at home; true, I'd never seen my father play tennis, though he tried to get me to play against the wall a couple of times, but it was boring just belting a ball, there was no obvious purpose or competitive spirit. Anyway it wasn't so much the tennis as the fact that, when I heard about her interest in it, I instantly saw her, with a stab of pain that surprised me, all of her, from her head to her toes, dashing to pick up a low shot and the vision was so gracious that for a long time afterwards I went about obsessed by an image that was purely the product of my own imagination. Then one day I was walking past the apartment building for diplomats where she lived, the dipdom as we used to call it, because I lived on the other side of the street in a block which was its identical twin in appearance — the same brick, the same eight-storey box, the same Khruschev-era utilitarianism and abhorrence of architectural flourishes — I was coming up to the entrance to her yard, glanced at the guard perched in his glass booth on the pavement, and was forced back by a gleaming car flying a brightly coloured flag on its bonnet as it pulled very slowly out of the entrance. She was sitting in the front seat, looking supremely aloof. The man at the wheel was, presumably, a chauffeur, because in the either silk- or velvet-upholstered rear I glimpsed a swarthy gentleman with an unbelievable moustache, though not as long as I remember it now, and not as pointed as in the photographs of Salvador Dali. I don't think she saw me.

The car drove off, I didn't even look round, but I was filled with such an unbearably sweet longing for the unattainable that that very evening I picked a fight, and drew blood, with the boy next door. The next morning she was the one who made the first move.

She walked over and took out of her satchel a big, shiny, gaudy record like I'd never seen before and I didn't see another until two years later when my dad brought me one from Belgium, when they let him go there for a conference. She offered me the record and asked: Listen? It was so unexpected I didn't really catch on to what she meant, but nodded anyway. You listen Bill Haley? The second time around her question sounded more like an order. I took the record obediently, trying to hold it so my sweaty fingers wouldn't leave marks all over the sleeve. Listen! She repeated the order, turned and walked off down the corridor, not with the satchel on her back, but carrying it by one strap and swinging it just above the floor.

I had a record player. It could play Soviet-produced records of two different diameters, both of them smaller than this disk, which turned out to be American, that is, of almost astronomical value — even I understood that, though I was never a music freak, either then or later. I used to listen to Soviet records from series like *Sing Along, Friends* or *Spread the Circle Wider*, the most daring things in them, I remember, were versions of the twist by Arno Babadjanyan, though you could detect something vaguely akin to rock n' roll in the music to *Amphibian Man*, a movie, locally produced of course, which had a song that went: we all, we all, we all, we all want to live in the slime — which summed up the debauchery of some hypothetical, un-Soviet, foreign way of life. Speaking of which, some of my friends had big brothers or sisters, even I had an older cousin, and if you gate-crashed their parties you could hear bootleg boogie-woogie recordings cut on exposed X-ray plates, ribs and all. And here I was with a genuine western record, *Rock Around The Clock* — that it was a Top Ten hit, I had absolutely no doubt, she would never palm me off with something second best. As soon as I put it on, I was seduced by the seeming casualness of Bill's delivery, but above all by the beat, so crisp, so tight it set your feet tapping of their own accord.

I played the record once, twice, three times, jumping around the record player, in a hurry to carry out her instructions and have the chance to report back and, possibly, get something in return. I wasn't that naive, I understood that Bill was just an excuse for closer acquaintance, though I hadn't a clue what, exactly, our acquaintance might consist of. I was so impatient I was late for school, and when I flew into class, she was already at her desk — in the middle row. During break I went over and silently handed her the record. She looked at me quite impassively: You can dance this? Thanks for, yeah, I can, I mean no, I can't rock — was sort of what came out. I learn you, she said. When? — I managed to ask, without hesitating. Today possible, she said after a pause to work it out. You know where live? Know where live, I replied, not intending to take the mickey in any way, just anxious we might not have understood each other fully — in other words, not know. I realised I'd put my foot in it, but it was too late. You know, she affirmed, I wait four...

What did she mean, wait? Because even if she had told me what number her flat was, I still couldn't get into a dipdom, the guard would probably detain me. Explaining wouldn't be any use, it was forbidden to pester foreigners, so my friends who liked to barter for chewing gum told me. The guard would hold me and make out a detention notice, though Letuchev had three of them and still seemed fine; true he didn't have a dad and had had to repeat a year. I could try not going past the guard in his booth, by climbing over the wall at the far side of the yard, but — and I'd heard of stunts like this — there was probably some invisible wire stretched along the top, which would either strike you dead if you touched it, or, at best, set off an alarm, the guards would come running and you'd end up in a colony for juvenile offenders for attempted breaking and entering. However, by half past three I'd already completed one circuit of the outside wall of her courtyard, trying to check out the best place for committing the putative crime — no doubt defectors paid just as careful attention looking for the weak spots in the defences of the Soviet Union's inviolable borders. I slipped past the gates twice, trying not to look at the guard who was reading a newspaper anyway. At the far end of the apartment building there was a solid concrete wall twice my height and absolutely smooth, whichever way I craned to look, I couldn't make out any wire along the top, I calculated it wouldn't be too hard to scale the obstacle — it was a matter of technique — but spotted in time that the guard's booth was positioned so he could see everything going on in the yard, which meant I had to find the exact spot to climb over where I could use some kind of cover inside, otherwise I'd be trapped, and with these thoughts in mind I was wandering along the fence, making my third circuit, when I saw her walking along the pavement. She waved, and as soon as I came close, grabbed my sleeve and pulled me past the guard, who gave us no more than a perfunctory glance.

My preparations for committing a crime had somewhat dulled the sense of anticipation before a date, but now instead of being pleased to see her, I felt vaguely humiliated — she was in my class, after all, and I wasn't used to having girls lead me by the hand to places where I couldn't go; but there was another feeling, too — of slightly stupid pride: if only my friends could see me going somewhere they had no chance of getting into; but there was also, of course, fear from the knowledge that what was going on was illegal. The one thing that was absent was the question: why, actually, should what I was doing be against the law?

Meanwhile, I was surprised to notice that the dipdom was scarcely any different from ours — the same pathetic trees planted any old how, the same cracked asphalt, except the kids in the sandpit were black. The only difference was the lobby, which had a different smell and tiled walls for some reason, otherwise the metal lift was just as noisy and just as scratched inside. The miracles began on her floor, where instead of the obligatory four doors per landing, there were only two. She drew me to the right, didn't have to ring, the door just opened, and in front of us stood an absolutely black woman in a white apron and cap, and I was caught off balance by the contrast between starched sugar white and the blackness of her skin — she smiled a no less dazzlingly white smile and with a slight bow gestured me inside, but my escort paid her not the slightest heed and drew me on down the corridor. On the way past the dining room I caught a glimpse through the open door of some unusual furniture, polished chrome legs and bright blue surfaces. To sit on chairs like that, eat at a table like that you'd surely need a lot of practice.

Her room struck me as actually pretty simple: semi-transparent curtains at the window, books with Latin script on the spine lying open face down on a chest, here and there the usual soft girlie things, dolls and straw mats everywhere. At last she let go of my hand and the first thing she did was switch on the record player. I was completely thrown when the sound came not from where I expected, but from the other side of the room — the only record player on the Soviet market in those days had the speaker mounted in the lid.

A dark-skinned woman, resembling the gentleman in the car in some intangible way, only without the moustache, came into the room. She pulled funny faces and moved her lips silently, smiling and looking at me, and I understood she was saying she was sorry she didn't speak Russian. She put down a little tray with two bottles and a bowl full of shelled nuts, and with the same mimed smiles and gestures went out, looking at me all the while. Coca, my friend said the way she always did, half question, half order. I shrugged my shoulders. I had never tasted Coca-Cola before, but wanted to try. Dance, she decided, without giving me the chance. She pulled me out into the middle of the room, chanting; one, two, free, one, two, free... She was already dancing, jerking my arm, and I tried to copy her, to overcome my awkwardness. She found my clumsiness funny, I felt. The music played, drums beat, Bill Haley urged me on. Finally she burst out laughing and collapsed onto a narrow divan, poured herself some coke, drank thirstily, stopped laughing, put her glass down, looked me in the eye, beckoned and pouted: Kiss!

The word was new to me, but I put my lips to hers. She was taking too much of the initiative for my taste, but on the other hand I was pleasantly surprised she wasn't a tease. As soon as my lips touched hers, her expression changed — her smile became radiant, tender, I didn't know she could smile that way, she took off her blouse and dress, kicked away her sandals, leaving only her knickers on. I must have looked really stupid, because I was riveted by those knickers, I couldn't take my eyes off them. Not there, she said, intercepting my gaze, and for emphasis pointed between her legs. It was all pretty weird, but strangely enough it was her knickers I found most amazing. I'd never seen anything like them — they weren't some scrap of fabric, but seemed to be of transparent human skin. You could see everything under them, even the moles in the hollow of her skinny thigh, right beneath her hipbone, the fit was so tight and smooth across her flat little tummy, except for between her legs where they were heavily embroidered in a pattern like dense, hoarfrosted grass, and in this place there was nothing to be seen. And so I understood her words and her gesture to mean not so much that getting under her knickers was forbidden, as that knickers like that were impossible to take off, and if they were taken off they would be more like a plaster cast, grown to the shape of her body. I couldn't think straight any longer and decided that probably over there, on Cuba, girls wore knickers like that as a precaution, so nobody'd try getting into them, and was astonished at the subtlety of their foresight. I sat down next her, almost naked, on the divan. She leant over and pressed her mounds against my sweater. In this act, too, I felt there was something exotic — I'd heard that on some islands people kissed by rubbing noses. She took my hand and brushed it against her cheek, then her neck, then put it on her swellings, and suddenly I wanted to take it away, I felt something akin to disgust, as if I was being forced to touch somebody's inflammation. But when she began unbuttoning my shirt, saying over and over kiss me, kiss me, I even began to pull away and resist. Then she did something I really had not anticipated: she slipped her hand down and put it on my zip. No girl had ever put her hand there before. I didn't even feel embarrassed — I felt wilted, and my wilting appendage also acted the puppy dog — too young to come to whistle and do as he was told. It was limp, like a felt Father Christmas on a tree, like Father Christmas with a sniffle, because its nose was dripping — from overexcitement and overstimulation — a steady drip from goodness knows where of sweet and sticky juice. Boy, she said with her usual semi-interrogative intonation, and carried on persuasively, but without a shadow of irritation or disappointment: You are boy. And she left the room, her quick bare feet not touching the floor, and I realised to my horror that all that time the door hadn't been shut. It had been left half open.

She left it half open as well. I was still trying to figure out where she had gone dressed like that when I heard the unmistakable gurgling sound. At this point I got upset, really upset: it meant she hadn't had to loose any bonds! Her knickers came off quickly and easily, there was no ban from which she herself was exempt... I was blind with fury when I quit the dipdom and walked past the guard. Probably, if he'd called me over, I'd have thumped him, and that would have been suicidal, they'd have put me in a juvenile penal colony, but at that moment I would probably have been glad to suffer for my freedom, for freedom in general. But the guard didn't even look at me.

Yes, I was hurt at the time, but not that gut-wrenching hurt which longs for an opportunity for apologies, forgiveness and reconciliation; it was that everlasting and most bitter of emotions which the proud call disappointment and for which there can be no forgiveness. But now, though we never spoke after that and in the autumn she disappeared from the class — now I can, strangely enough, remember her hands, and transparent earlobes, and even her smell, it seems. Because I've forgotten nothing. I remember that golden era, Fidel's beard on posters midway between Marx and Engels in size, I recall the chipped five-pointed star made of opaque red glass we put on top of the Christmas tree, Christmas trees had just been allowed again, remember the newsreel pictures of Khruschev's bald head bobbing peacefully, like a buoy, in the Black Sea just before Brezhnev's coup... My God, what a lot of good things there were: Wonderworker soda, the first and last strike I ever led (the class I was in, 4-A, wasn't taken to the welcome parade for Yuri Gagarin), the fat yellow volumes of the Children's Encyclopaedia with colour gatefolds of dinosaurs, the food processor (GDR made) which could even juice carrots. And the first bottle of Trifeshti drunk in the entrance to our block, and Indian cigarettes — brown with a gold band, and Krakow sausage, and duffel bags, and loose hiking trousers, and the weeds' song from a cartoon about maize, and Chinese Two Balls brand juggling clubs, and the movie *If This Is Love*, and the happy taste of childhood's semi-freedom, and my father's Norwegian skis, and the dacha at Skhodnya, and the university swimming pool, and the exercise book with songs copied in by hand, and pineapples in mid-April — in time for my birthday, and apple trees on Mars...

___The Berlin Wall___

    Continuing in the communist nostalgia vein, I can't help but introduce at this point an episode that robbed me of yet another sweet illusion. It took place in the later sixties, ninth class coming to an end, springtime, round about our sixteenth birthdays. Let's have a *bardak*, we used to say, if somebody's parents had gone off to the country and there was a flat free. Not a party, because that implied something much more insipid. A *bardak* had the same ingredients — music, booze and girls — the difference was in the quantity and quality.

    For a full-blown *bardak* booze was obtained in copious amounts, plonk was very cheap in those days and came in many different varieties, most of them called *portvein*, an appellation that figured as a sort of postscript on the label as a generic description of the contents' type, though it had absolutely nothing to do with real port, no more than *shampanskoye* has to Champagne or *kon'yak* to the spirit from that distant French province. It was fortified, sweetened filth, called by a wealth of names which sonorously illustrated the broad expanses of a multi-national power: Ukrainian Belo Mitsne (popularly known as Biomicin), Turkmenian Agdam and Sakhra, the old Slavonic Solntsedar, labels with an Azeri accent — Kardanakhi and Alabashli, Armenian Aigeshat and

Arevshat, Moldavian Fraga and Gratiesti, Arabic numerals — 777 and 33, fruit-and-berry wines from Central Russia such as the cloying Zapekanka or the tender Vishenka, pepper and citrus vodkas, and also stuff exotically described as liqueur — apricot, lemon, anis, strawberry, jubilee and even Benedictine, even Chartreuse, all priced roughly the same, between a rouble and two roubles fifty. Lord, where have those golden and magic days gone, when for such a reasonable price you could buy a bottle of some bright green fluid. And how could they have called this sticky mentholated stuff Chartreuse? And some poisonous sugar-based swill, port? Was it because somebody, somewhere in our then Great Power still retained the music of these names in his memory? I remember going into a village shop near Smolensk one day and buying a whole rucksack of wine just because of its enchanting name, Chateau d'Yquem. It was the usual portvein, of course, but what streak of linguistic tenacity had retained these thrilling outlandish sounds all those many years? How strong the dream of paying homage to the pure springs of the land of holy miracles must be, how deep-rooted the need for variety in life, how responsive the soul to a dim and distant appeal that is borne inaudibly from an alien geography and a past that long ago ceased to be part of ours...

To go with the drink there was music, all imported, but under the foreign cover the sounds were pretty basic, the Beatles' rock-n'-roll, their dizzy miss lizzie, the unpretentious go jonny go, the obscure hippy hippy shake and speedy gonzales and tutti frutti — all of it recorded on disgusting quality thick brown tape which was always breaking — you stuck it back together with acetone or nail varnish thinner — and played on antediluvian Yauza or Kometa tape recorders, which had the dubious virtue of a choice of two speeds, so you could record at either nine and a half or eighteen if you wanted. That year we did the shake to everything. It didn't involve any special steps, just stamping, writhing, jerking and hopping, and the one who got the most body parts twitching most convincingly was the winner.

These two components of the *bardak* were subsidiary to the main purpose, and it was the girls available that determined the choice of drinks and music. You never see their like today, except maybe on Moscow suburban trains or in some bar out in the sticks, but at that time Moscow was full of them, our age, fifteen or so, usually studying in a trade school, excitingly different to the prissy girls in our class.

The scenario of the *bardak* was astonishingly consistent, as if it were some ancient rustic festival or mystic rite, though, regrettably, there was no sub-text, the aim being no more than the pursuit of not very subtle carnal pleasures — swilling portvein, spewing in a corner, dancing in a clinch, groping under a skirt and ejaculation — frequently into your own trousers. First of all the male half had a drink to boost their courage, then sent someone to fetch the girls who were waiting in a strictly pre-arranged quantity — matching the number of sabres mustered by the male contingent — at a cinema or tram stop, and while waiting debated whether they'd show up, but then the bell rang, the girls squeezed into the hall, crowded round the coat hangers, jostled giggling by the mirror, filtered into the main room, though never singly, settled in a bunch, village-style, on the divan, sipped at the portvein, went pink in the face, the sassy ones, who'd already paired-off last time, were dancing by now, a burst or two of swearing, the light went out, solo dancing gave way to dancing close, when the girls were squeezed and groped without mercy, some couples were already snogging in the corners, and so the desired atmosphere of alcohol-fuelled exhilaration and idiotic bravado was achieved, producing those little incidents which added spice to the evening and for the sake of which the whole business was, in fact, undertaken. Either somebody, after performing rigoletto in the toilet, passed out on the floor, curled foetus-like around the porcelain, or one of the tousled and dishevelled girls was so drunk she forgot her knickers on the bed and they were found by the next couple, or one of the girls had her period and the owners' bedcovers had to be soaked in the bath, another created a jealous scene, or ran out into the street without her blouse and had to be dragged back. It was all discussed afterwards — which of the girls went all the way, who scored, even though he had got off with somebody else last time, who played tight, and was she really a virgin? — until the next *bardak*. Actually, all these confessions, consultations and commentaries were mostly talk, coitus took place infrequently and was a real event. Basically, physical relations with the ladies were confined to relatively innocent petting, but whatever happened, there was always a taste of adventure to savour, since neither the invitations extended to street girls nor the consumption of large quantities of alcohol figured in the edited version of events presented to the parents, who returned from the dacha and couldn't understand where the hairpins in the marital bed came from, or the peroxide blonde hair in mother's comb, why the number of matching glasses had shrunk, what had happened to mother's lipstick from the dressing table, father's dry wine from the fridge and grandmother's favourite books from the bookcase (they'd been taken to the second-hand bookshop before the event, to raise the funds for the booze).

If the truth be known, fundamentally we were swottish little homebodies, and our criminal inclinations were masochistically exaggerated by the more anxious of our parents. We probably lacked some essential vitamin, a fourth dimension to the naked three-dimensional world, and neither books nor sport were a substitute. Secretly fearful, our bravado a pose, we were trying to get a taste of a life that was different to our school world, but only succeeded in catching a glimpse of life on the other side of the windowpane, not realising that only too soon we would have to live in it. The street provided that window, and so there was actually little erotic about the *bardak*. The girls from our class were mostly as homebound as us, but were more grown up. What we saw were snooty, unbearably pretentious, two-faced goody-goodies who had no concept of our other life. In fact it was all the other way round, the most single-minded of them were preparing for that other life, and we were only practising how to be irresponsible, growing a shell of infantilism which would help us survive later.

And then, incredibly, a group of German girls turned up at one of our events. Yes, a whole gang of them, more or less presentable, in Moscow as part of a youth exchange with the GDR, our age, and every last one wearing a blue neckscarf, pioneer scarves we discovered later. Maybe you stayed a pioneer in the GDR until you married, or maybe they were young pioneer leaders on socialist training in the USSR? One way or another, one day in May they turned up at our school just before what promised to be a very lively *bardak* — Seryozha's mum had gone away on a business trip and his grandma had plans to stay with a friend in the country. To digress a moment, Seryozha's family was living at the time in a flat that was tiny, but had three rooms, two of them adjoining, one separate, which was just perfect for the needs of a *bardak*, and equipped with heavy furniture — all that was left from Seryozha's industrialist grandfather, as great a legend in their family as the monarchy. The women's team had not yet been named, but the booze money had been collected, the only threat lay in the changeableness of the weather, some stupid shower or idiotic fall in the barometer could frighten off the old birds. But the weather was consistently May-like, here and there you caught a scent of lilac, grandmother's ailments retreated, Seryozha's behaviour was model and even I, so used to urging him down the road to the ruin of a dissolute body and the destruction of an already parlous state of health, temporarily backed off.

In actual fact, the idea of inviting the German girls was mine. And it was not an idea you could ever dismiss as uninspired. It was one thing to ask the loose, coarse girls from the new Khruschev-era housing developments and the technical school hostels who liked portvein and a good time, quite another these wholesome over-aged foreign pioneers in their blouses and coloured socks, with their open expressions and indefinable social origins, who had come from the inscrutable West, which only formally counted as socialist, of course, because to our generation even Latvian farm girls and Estonians from the islands seemed European. Looking back, I think somewhere deep down there was a certainty that it wasn't just the obvious behavioural differences, the greater openness and readiness to smile, there was, in the subtleties of a foreign girl's inner make-up, something intangible that made her different to the local models. No adolescent can imagine the object of his adoration pissing or shitting, and it was similarly inconceivable to us that one of these unearthly German girls in a blue pioneer scarf might bonk or fuck, they had to have some kind of substitute for these functions, and most probably our schoolboy joke about Martians who reproduced by slapping each other on the back was no coincidence. With this in mind, it might be thought the idea of a *bardak* with the German pioneers was blasphemous and cynical, as, actually, any research idea is, because it really only amounts to stepping beyond the boundary and dismembering the object under investigation. Like anybody else standing on the threshold of the unknown, we were timid, but sixteen is the age for daring, and I went up to the most likely looking of the Germans — a slim girl, wearing a short skirt, with a friendly laugh, cropped dark hair and an adult's face, and managed to explain that my friends and I wanted to invite her and her friends to a party where there would be music. Obviously delighted, thanking me profusely, the effect of the European upbringing so lacking in us, she accepted — and we agreed the time and place.

We made conversation somehow, they in their stumbling, broken Russian, we in what passed for English. Though they turned down the offer of portvein, we had been foresighted enough to lay on dry wine and ice cream, but the party really got going as soon as we put on the Beatles. The fact that we listened to She Is A Woman, Baby You Can Drive My Car and Can't Buy Me Love came as a profound surprise. And their surprise, in turn, filled us with pride, and we were happy to make out we were little Europeans, barely touched the portvein, gallantly stroked our partners' backs as we danced, and conversation turned more and more to literature, to Goethe and Heine, though neither of these names meant anything to them the way we pronounced them in Russian.

The dry wine worked as well on the abstemious German girls as fortified portvein, and one of them, a little shorter than the others and with a big bum, was already giggly as she danced in Seryozha's long arms, another was in the corner and looked about to burst into tears, a third was drinking bruderschaft with a boy, several more were dancing energetically in a circle. Imperceptibly — eins, zwei, drei — we smooched off to the other room, the grandmother's, with a carved divan embellished with a crown, a bookcase containing a set of the complete works of Sholem Aleichem (sheer size had saved it from the second-hand bookstore), and grandfather's framed portrait watching us carefully. It was as cramped as a broom cupboard in there, dancing was impossible, with bated breath I pressed my German girl gently back against the wall and cautiously kissed her on the cheek. She cautiously kissed me. I put my arms around her, pulled her close, and at the same time squeezed her small taut buttocks under her smooth little skirt with both hands, and with my two others fondled her small tight breasts in the tight bra. But when my hand slipped under her hem and moved up to the top of her stockings, she took fright; she gasped, shook her head, pulled away, I repeated mindlessly: all right, all right, I won't, I won't, my knees so wobbly they'd hardly support me. She believed me, started to kiss me again tenderly, she, too, was trembling, and I knew that with such an inconceivably foreign chick nothing would happen first time, and when she whispered in her accent that sentence which I was to hear so many times later in just that instrumentation *ya lyu-b-lyu te-bya*, I love you, I was convinced I would be her faithful suitor, and we would make a great couple, I would write her tender and crazy letters, and then she would open a window to Europe for me, and a huge world would burst open, and I could physically feel the pressure of the wind against my face, the way you can on only the tightest bends.

Next day they left for Leningrad — there was no sense in seeing them off at the station, they were an official delegation and their leader had only let them go that evening after they'd said who they were going to see, the address and phone number. I was left with the impression that I was on the verge of an otherworldly love and with her promise she would write to me from Berlin.

No letter came for three weeks, and then I was called to see the headmaster. I was often called to his office — either for smoking in the toilets or for drinking behind the garage — we only did it out of sheer bravado it was so uncomfortable there — but today the headmaster was beside himself. He told me to sit down, while he remained standing, which meant things were really bad, for him, probably, as well as for me. I sat down on a chair by the wall, while he paced up and down and checked twice that the door was properly shut. Then he looked at me with a look of real anguish. Many thoughts flashed through my mind: he suspects me of setting fire to the sports hall, though it was still intact when I came to school this morning; he reckons I'm involved in a bank robbery, the police rang and told him; somebody had grassed me up for reading samizdat — and this was the only accusation that had any truth in it.

To my astonishment he started on about the German girls. He told me who had invited them — it was me, which I admitted, but he just brushed it aside. He told me what we'd drunk and what music we'd danced to. He even knew I'd got off with one them, and she happened to be the one in charge, and that Seryozha had suggested they raise the question of the GDR joining the Soviet Union as the sixteenth republic, something even I didn't know of. He was extremely upset, stumbled over words, and it wasn't difficult to tell that his version of events hadn't come from one of my friends, every one of whom I was as sure of in those days as I was of myself. This rather spiteful and neurotic man, a chemistry teacher, could only have been as upset as he was because of a signal received from somewhere on high. I realised quite quickly what he actually wanted me to do — keep quiet. "Why, oh why did you have to do it?" he repeated a number of times, then blurted: "Don't you know they write reports?"

I had no clear notion of the mechanics: most likely, each of the pioneers had described what happened in a report to the group leader, who in turn reported to the Embassy, from where a memo went to the Ministry of Education and from there down to the school. Actually it wasn't so much the trajectory of the report that interested me. I was dumbfounded by the revelation that they squealed over there as well.

I found this simple fact so amazing because it was absolute proof positive — they were just like us. It was a remarkable discovery: in the heart of Europe, in Berlin and Budapest, in Prague and Warsaw — people were doing just the same, informing and squealing on one another. And if that was so, then everything else was undoubtedly the same there as here, too.

"Why, why," the headmaster kept saying as he wiped his forehead, "Couldn't you get enough of your own?" This was a mistake, shifting from the plane of morality to the level of politics. This left the field wide open, and I began shouting at him, it was them, our teachers, who'd taught us to dare, to seek and not to yield. He flapped at me with his handkerchief as though I were a wasp.

"Enough of your own..." Even if there were five times fewer of them it would still be enough for everybody. But what about the first half of the question — why? Is it really that to convince yourself you are with a truly different being, the fact of a hole in the place where you have an appendage is insufficient? Or that a different skin colour, a different language, foreign citizenship and different habits are more arousing? And if this difference also happens to be forbidden... But at that time I couldn't have explained that to the headmaster, or to myself.

Czech Spring

Actually, I would have found her attractive even if she'd been a Serb or a Bulgarian — there was no doubting her Slavic origins — though I don't usually like big girls, and she was big, my height, powerful thighs, strong arms, legs and shoulders, heavy boned, a mighty bosom, a long, albeit sturdy neck, and it was her neck, shining above the opening of her blouse, dazzlingly exposed, that attracted your attention most. It was an instant pointer to the bloom of her luxurious flesh, to the vital sheen of her skin, to the tenderness of her bosom, to the hot generosity of her loins. In addition she had a radiance, tasty rustic lips, brows of thick glossy fur joined by a barely detectable thin dark growth, clear prominent hazel eyes and a long sweep of black hair that gleamed dark copper in the sunlight.

But since I found out just a minute or two after we met that she was Czech, I didn't just want her, which anybody would have done in my place, I instantly fell in love, saying to myself that if the Czechs ever thought of choosing their own Marianna, they would never find anyone better suited than this eighteen year old history student — in that year of clouded freedom I felt the Czechs could do with such a symbol as never before.

It happened sometime during the spring term, we

met on the Lenin Hills, I walked her home, since we were practically neighbours, she was living with other first year students in a wing of the University skyscraper, while I wasn't far away, in a faculty residence, and less than a year had passed since *that August*. I can still remember how we heard about the tanks moving into Prague, and remember that no matter how dumb I was at seventeen, I realised immediately the Soviet trap had snapped shut — the circles my family moved in set great store by the Prague spring, as they did by Poland later, in August '81; my parents' generation, fooled by the liberalism of the Khrushchev era, felt that the warm wind blowing from Czechoslovakia would delay the onset of frost after that pretty insipid thaw. But besides fear, I remember also feeling relief — later I experienced this strangely mixed feeling more than once. You do when your worst expectations come true.

The news was brought by transistor radio, it found us in a camp on the river Oka, and despite the seriousness of what was happening, it would be too much to say that the BBC report, sought so avidly through the racket of the jammers, instantly put paid to our mood of frivolous high spirits. We had just left school, we had passed entrance exams at university or college, and our trip was the climax of a carefree adolescence that we were bidding good-bye to with all the enthusiasm of ignorance. Matters were improved further for me because I was beginning to tire of my affair with Tanechka, a girl from another class. It had carried on all that last school year, though not long enough to make me altogether lose the appetite for her declarations of love, which became all the more passionate the further we drifted apart — I was making a break for the big wide world, and she was concerned, not without reason, that it would have no place for her schoolgirl love.

In short, I was a successful lover, I was full of wild young strength, the future promised to be one long fiesta of student licentiousness — in fact my parents belonged to the category that doesn't impose restrictions, and for all of us the tanks were purely abstract, while the reality was Vysotsky's songs, which we belted out by heart, girlfriends, our little group itself — at the time we had this romantic sense of the bonds of our friendship being indestructible, for not one of us had felt the grip of the state around his throat yet. That is probably how young people feel at the outbreak of war — they put off thinking about it till later.

However, when I was on my own in Moscow, this first pinprick, made by that information through the jamming, grew gradually into a steady, nagging depression and a persistent, unpleasant premonition — the basic ingredients of fear, in fact — that the juggernaut that had crushed freedom in Czechoslovakia would sooner or later get me, and this idea wasn't so far-fetched. The seven brave souls who went out to protest on Red Square and were then packed off to the camps were friends of friends. In the not-so-wide circles of the dissident intelligentsia everybody knew everybody else. Not forgetting to include in the mix young people's intolerance for skulduggery, and what else besides skulduggery could I have called what our rulers did then, we didn't know the language of geopolitics, we only read Pasternak and Mandelstam. And all this taken together — secret fear, liberal passion, the music of Akhmatova's *Requiem* (read in manuscript), and most potent of all — the deep-down feeling of inevitable servitude, that dark voice of prison/exile melancholy which seems to be in the blood of even the most prosperous Russians — could not but evoke sympathy for the Czechs.

I well remember there was an ice hockey international that September between the Soviet Union and Czechoslovakia, and even though I had never ever been to a sporting event, I cheered on the Czechs and was so happy when they won, it was as if I'd been on the barricades fighting communism myself. Obviously my Czech girl with her coarse beauty touched my heart, and it wasn't the usual lust, but an incredible tenderness that was fuelled by my guilt complex about the actions of my compatriots, about the Soviet lout who'd beat himself drunkenly on the chest in bars, beer halls or trains and insist it was him in the leading tank that day, and this selfless bloodthirsty bullshit was actually in a general sense absolutely true.

This pneumatic, ample-bosomed Czech girl seemed older than her years, she looked quite the young lady, and it would have been stupid to pursue her like a schoolboy, take her for a walk in the park, put my arm round her on a bench and then squeeze her hand in the seclusion of a darkened cinema. Of course, I should do what they did in Europe and invite her to dine, and if she accepted, it would be a positive signal that my hopes were not without foundation and the attraction was mutual. I had no money for a restaurant, anyway a restaurant would not allow for immediate recompense, so I waited for a day when my parents had gone out and there was only my grandmother in the far room, and she was always very understanding and stayed in her room.

I made ready as follows: candles, napkins, wine, Cuban rum, lemon juice — in case she wanted a cocktail, fruit, but the centrepiece was chicken *tabaka* which I had made myself. I set the table in my room, made up the bed in readiness, and threw a tartan blanket invitingly over it — it didn't even enter my head how offensive such obvious planning might be. It's only with age that we acquire a healthy fatalism, and regard failures with the same scepticism as we do easy victories.

She rang the doorbell at exactly the second I sat down to look at my watch, still flushed from my exertions in the kitchen: when we agreed the date, she smiled as she refused my offer to meet her — it's simple, I'll find it. She was all dressed up, and I can remember her outfit to this day: a pale lightweight skirt that hung loosely around her big round knees, a matching silk blouse that was a creamy pink, almost the colour of pear drops, and a black velvet bolero with folk style red and gold embroidery. Her shoes were black, too, and her black hair was held at the back with a big black and gold hairclip; she was wearing lipstick and eye shadow — the girls put it on thickly and with a little flick at the side in those days, to lengthen the eye — she smelt of a perfume I'd not encountered before and looked impossibly elegant, fresh and inaccessible, exactly the way attractive women know how to look when they go on a date but haven't made up their mind yet. I didn't understand these subtleties then, however, I merely admitted meekly to myself that to start kissing her, looking like that, was as inconceivable as making a pass at a woman in silk in the foyer of the Bolshoi; she was a work of art, she could only be looked at, not touched, and the fact that she happened to be in my shabby room could only be described as a miracle. My culinary efforts were gross, my table wretched, my own fussing pathetic, but she put her black bag on the tartan blanket, as if she did not notice the made-up bed, and sat down in the arm chair I offered her, rather clumsily crossing one leg over the other. She asked for a cigarette. I fumbled to give her one and lit it. She didn't inhale, but I was even charmed by this and I — in an attempt to hide my infatuation — fussed and fawned on her.

She accepted my attentions with a slight smile, but her obvious satisfaction with the effect she produced should itself have suggested to me that she had made an effort in part for my sake.

Fortunately she lived in a hostel and had a first class

appetite, so she didn't stand on ceremony and tucked into the chicken and the wine — I was so nervous I started out on rum — soon she had gone a bit pink, her curls began to escape the comb, her lipstick became smeared, and then she abandoned the folksy bolero; the silk revealed the full power of her shoulders and the might of her breasts restrained by her bra. Chicken fat trickled down her big fingers with the red-varnished nails. She laughed at my jokes, tipping her head back, gripped the chicken in both hands — holding it away from her blouse — she bent forward and gnawed at it neatly, putting the bones on her napkin, and wiped her mouth with the back of her hand when she thought I wasn't looking. We moved on to dessert; I noticed she'd kicked her shoes off under the table, and poured her a glass of rum — neat, she tossed it back, nibbling a segment of orange I'd peeled.

She spoke Russian like a native, with hardly an accent, only occasionally she couldn't find the right word, and then almost without pausing she'd use the Czech one, which also gave her speech a kind of folksy touch. Gradually she unwound, told me how many Czechs there were in her group, and that she had to share a room with an old bag of twenty-one, from the GDR — goodness, I hoped it wasn't the one from the previous chapter, because the world is much smaller than we like to think — and that she had a little sister in Prague...

I went to brew an espresso — one of the incredible trophies my father returned with from his conquest of

Europe, and came back to find her going through my records — she was standing on the parquet in stockinged feet and looked so stocky, homely somehow, it took me by surprise. She didn't turn around, and putting all my tenderness into *do you want coffee*, I embraced her from behind and kissed her somewhere under the ear. She laughed and shook herself free: put this one on — only then did she turn to me, her eyes glinting a little tipsily, and handed me an Adamo record. I put it on, lit candles, turned out the light, poured coffee, added rum, trembling inside with anticipation, having placed my own interpretation on the eager look in her eyes, she in her turn, a little steamed up, excited, suddenly began telling me heatedly about the boyfriend she'd left behind in Prague, without skipping even the intimate details. She even told me he'd made her have an abortion, while I couldn't contain my disappointment, unaware that there is a certain type of rather unintelligent woman who uses every new lover as a psychoanalyst before going to bed with him. She was boringly detailed, one moment looking into my eyes to see my reaction, and the next drifting off into her gynaecological past, and a couple of times she brushed aside my tentative attempts to cut the flow or at least squeeze her hand in sympathy. In its own way it was a song, but all inspiration dries up eventually, she began to flag noticeably, her head drooped slightly, I put my arm around her shoulder, she murmured she was glad, glad she came to Moscow, and I, partly touched, actually, by her misfortunes which she had so trustingly confided to me, and realising with regret that a postponement was inevitable, and that after such an outburst it would be tactless to seize a woman by the bosom, so I kissed her hands and decided to play my trump card.

Interrupting Adamo, I began whispering intensely how guilty we all here were towards her country, that not all Russians were the same, yes, there were those who gave the orders and rode in the tanks, but there were others, others, too... At this I felt the silk stiffen under my quivering lips, felt her back grow tense and her shoulders draw back; her hands, stiff now, withdrew from under my nose. I looked up and in the semi-darkness could see the unpleasant set of her large lips, just a moment ago so sweetly slack from the rum and reminiscences. She spoke, and her voice sounded pretty coarse now. From out of the stream of sound, which surprised me with its unexpected vulgarity, I caught that those fascists wanted to shoot her father, that her father and the entire family were on those fascists' black list...

Lord, why hadn't I thought of it sooner? Of course, who could the new government send to study in Moscow after the August events, particularly to the History Department, considered to be an ideological one? Only young people with unimpeachable backgrounds, her, for example, my would-be girlfriend, daughter of a general in the Czech KGB.

To her credit, she didn't grass, though she knew what

faculty I was in, and my name, of course. More than that, she wasn't even cross with me for very long, apparently, because when I saw her once sitting in a restaurant with some very wealthy-looking young men from the Caucasus she gave me a friendly wave. Another time, in the international club, where I used to go sometimes as well, she was dancing with someone and blew me a flirtatious kiss from behind his back.

Soft Blues

*W*e discussed it a lot, Sergei and I, from every conceivable angle, but whichever way you looked at it, it was all strictly theoretical, although we had met blacks at student hops and at one point we'd been friends with a Ugandan — he'd been at the Sorbonne before coming to Moscow, he played the sax as well and asked us to find him a russky gel — alas, he couldn't or wouldn't find someone for us, though we suggested a swap, one Russian girl for two black chicks. From Leonid Andreev's sad little story we got the message that even the most modest specimen of manhood at any moment lusts after females of the opposite race, how else would there be so many mixed race people in the world. Dialectical materialism is a discipline unjustifiably neglected today, though we were force-fed it then, but it did say that contradictions must come together, but where in Moscow in the late sixties and early seventies were we going to find sufficiently convincing contradictions. I remember, we even made a friendly bet of a bottle of Bulgarian brandy to the first one to sleep with a black, but that was all front and swank, a piss-take, because our situation seemed pretty hopeless at the time. So when I did score, by pure fluke, it seemed even more incredible.

It couldn't have been simpler: Sergei and I were

walking across the bridge from the Comecon building to the Ukraine Hotel, she was walking towards us and I said *khau du yu du*. How do you do, she said back, flashing this amazing smile as though her mouth were full of ivory. We made friends with her on the spot, took her by the arm — to show her moskow vues, and dragged her off to the Metelitsa, where — as well as the brisk trade in weed in the bogs — they served a greenish Italian cocktail vermouth dirt cheap, even for those days. We drank vermouth on the rocks, chatted in our crippled English, and I suddenly remembered a long sentence *ai vant to spend mai laif viz a gerl laik you* from some song or other, I couldn't have come up with anything like that myself, and I leant over and said it to her. And she flashed a smile so surprised, so grateful and tender, that it was probably from this moment our fleeting romance began.

Besides the fact she was black as night — a superb, exemplary, classical black — she had one incredible characteristic — she was impossibly slender, like a long-stemmed wine glass, and anybody with even the slightest awareness of anatomy couldn't imagine how all the various organs fitted in there. She wasn't tall, up to my shoulder, but because of her improbable build seemed very long, though without looking at all skinny; it wasn't skinniness, rather a gorgeously artistic play of nature which had carved her in proportion from one piece. I never saw, before or since, such a miniature waist, such delicate, elongated thighs, such hands and ankles, ears and neck. She came from Jamaica, but lived in London, and she was in Moscow as a tour rep for an English travel company, accompanying a group of rich old English ladies.

I think she was about twenty-two. By our standards it would have been hard to describe her as beautiful — a real Negro face, like the drawings in children's books to show them their Papuan friends, big protruding lips, broad flattish nose and small, shining, dark hazel eyes below her tightly curled black hair, pulled together in what they call corn rows in America. She was surely pure Negro, her ancestors' African blood had had no interaction with Indian or Spanish, but to me she was a whole Cooke's tour in one — London sounded just as exotic to us then as Jamaica.

As we left the Metelitsa, we agreed to meet again that evening, just the two of us. I remember how I rushed home — to get changed and prepare for a date — my first ever — with a genuine representative, in all respects, of another tribe — here you had Great Britain and the Caribbean, and the West, and her colour, and not the least hint of the ghost of socialism wandering endlessly through my own country and our neighbours — except that I was faced with one huge, complicating problem — where to get the necessaries to give my black windfall a good time. In the old days one would have said that one's resources were sorely depleted. I was far too casual a student to have a stipend, but I still kept partying, and I hung out nearly every day in bars — most of the time we brought our own wine. Of course it was my father's money on the whole, but from time to time I did have to go out and make some, though I had absolutely no aptitude for business of any sort. Sergei had an exceptional gift for commerce, and I can remember us outside a shoe shop flogging some kind of cheap tack a Polish woman supplied us with and putting on a profit margin of up to three hundred percent. There were other ventures. That spring we'd been part of a student team concreting the basement of an unfinished building in Chertanovo. The work was hard and extremely nasty, but at the end of the job it was cash in hand. And since I was a regular member of the team, while Sergei poured concrete only when he felt like it, his share was given to me to pass on, and this was the money, which for some reason hadn't found its way to him, I pounced on in my excitement at my new adventure.

It's funny, thinking back to what was the fashion then. When I was going out I dressed like this: dark corduroy trousers, green socks, pale fake buckskin shoes with a fringe, ditto jacket, but the crowning glory of the outfit was my shirt — black, with a tiny yellow floral design and a high collar with enormous points that buttoned down below the collar bones. It was quite the wide-boy style, and considering my hair was nearly shoulder length, the overall look should have satisfied the most exacting black taste. That evening I took my black girlfriend to an expensive cafe, the Adriatika: then it was fashionable with the Moscow hipsters — there were hardly any prostitutes, the service was OK and they did pate in ramekins, cocktails and cold champagne. We sat on a soft curved divan in a shallow niche, drank brut and chatted away — her English by some miracle was like what we'd been taught. I asked if she'd been to a Rolling Stones gig, as it struck me that if you lived in London that was as natural as going for a swim in Odessa. In fact she'd never seen the Stones, but I immediately joined her in a whispered chorus of *ai ken't get no setisfekshon*, and then she asked me had I been where you keep that dead leader, and was astonished in her turn that there were Russians who had never once been to Lenin's Tomb. I launched with gusto into an anti-communist sermon, and she remarked that she wasn't a communist, either, which struck me as odd — I thought it went without saying that a girl like her couldn't possibly be a communist, seeing she'd been born in Jamaica, but lived in London. So I then immediately confided I wasn't even a member of the Communist Youth League, the Kom-so-mol, but it didn't produce the requisite effect — she had no idea that in our country from the age of fourteen everybody had to be a Komsomol member — though she did conscientiously repeat after me *koum-sou-moul*. Soon we were kissing, and what she did was to take a sip of champagne and pass it into my mouth, which was, I confess, something unusual, but extremely pleasant, though the champagne was a bit warmed, and I wasn't the least put off by the difference in race. Our behaviour was, in a way, a challenge — maybe people did that in London pubs, pour wine into each other's mouths, but in the Moscow of those years it was kind of extravagant, though at the neighbouring tables they chose to pretend not to notice. Of course, kissing a black girl that way under the full gaze of the Soviet state, I experienced that flush of heroic enthusiasm that comes over you when you make a stand for freedom — her London residence doubling up with the colour of her skin, and I knew full well that the first could attract the close scrutiny of the organs of law and order, while the second would be no less offensive to our racist-inclined public opinion — I knew what my fellow-countrymen felt about the Russian tarts who got into taxis with coal-tar, negatives and blackarses. A sense of danger, we know, only heightens sexual arousal. We picked up another bottle of brut and took a taxi up to the Lenin Hills, figuring that all cats are black in the dark, and that in the park we could indulge in African lovemaking without interference.

Admiring the view took about three minutes. Then I took her elbow and led the way down a steep path to a relatively horizontal glade, dimly lit by the moon and distant streetlights, — backing into the shadow of some bushes, I took her in my arms and the response was such sweet tenderness as I had never experienced before and that was generally in short supply in our hasty and frosty times. I unbuttoned her top, fondled her gorgeous little breasts with their rather large, very hard nipples that were like taut rubber. Her slender, fragile body bent back, as if we were dancing. Then it was her turn to unbutton my shirt, her hot tongue licked my skin, and her thighs worked back and forth. It was so secluded here, everything pointed to immediate intimacy, but there was just one thing holding me back — I had just finished a course of antibiotics, after a dose of the clap I'd caught from a girl at the selfsame Metelitsa. I probably couldn't have infected her, but anyway — I'd been made to sign this undertaking by a doctor with a Beelzebub beard and very strong glasses, which made his Jewish eyes look truly horrendous behind the thick lenses. I can remember him, as he ordered me to pull back the foreskin, show me the tip, squeeze the base, saying crossly you're a student, you should be using your brains, not your prick, and then, after examining the source of the infection, remarking pensively: well, I can see your point...

I felt and caressed her all over, dotted her black skin with a thousand kisses, held her close, crushed her buttocks with both hands, my loins were ablaze, my member was ready to spring from my fly like a thoroughbred from a starting gate, but prohibition was stronger than desire, and as we clambered back up that same path she was, no doubt, pondering the enigma of the Slavic soul, thinking there was nothing more wondrous than this Russian tenderness and mysterious sexual delicacy, though it was she who had sounded the signal to retreat, saying her ladies might get upset if they needed something, and she wasn't there.

The kissing, hugging, fondling all continued in the

back seat of the taxi, much to the irritation, I could sense if not see, of the driver. She kissed me passionately on the steps of the Ukraine Hotel, her luxurious mouth taking my lips, even my cheeks, it seemed, but out here you needed no extrasensory perception to tell that dozens of pairs of eyes of scores of the KGB watchers and minders who always swarmed around Intourist hotels were upon us. I tried to restrain her excessive affection, but maybe she saw that as reticence, too, because it was her first time in Moscow and, naturally, she had no concept of our ways. She asked for my address and I had to explain, furious at both the Soviet regime and myself, that it would be dangerous for me to get letters from her. Even correspondence from my father, on exclusively academic matters, came strictly through his university department. Then she asked: But if you ever come to London, will you give me a call? And she handed me her business card.

What was I supposed to say to that? She walked backwards, blowing me kisses all the way to the revolving doors of the Ukraine until they swallowed her up. I repeated her last words: *ai'll rait yu a letter*... I kept that card of hers a long time. Her name was Elizabeth Smith. I never did write to her. And not because a letter without a return address never left the country, and a letter with one was to denounce yourself. It wasn't just that. Really I had nothing to say to that black girl who — and I was absolutely certain of that — I would never see again. What was I to say: that I'd made a full recovery from the clap;

that I still wanted her and remembered how she kissed; that *ai vant to spend mai laif viz a gerl laik you*, but I lived in a country where people couldn't choose the routes they travelled and that even inside the country other people kept deciding which way they went; and that I'd never get to see London because I wasn't in the *koum-sou-moul*, and also because I never went to Lenin's Tomb.

Japan

A chronicle of the semi-criminal _dolce vita_ could take a seasonal approach, a time of the year would correspond to the name of the bar where at that moment the hard-currency dealers, the prostitutes, and the golden youth, so to speak, of the criminal world preferred to relax, because the godfathers preferred the Sandunovsky Public Baths on Mondays, out-of-town saunas, dinners in private rooms at the Uzbekistan or the Berlin — the other more prominent landmarks being: the Zolotoi Kolos at the Exhibition of National Economic Achievements, the cooperative restaurant at Tarasovka, a dreary glass-walled cafe in Ismailovo Park, the motel on Mozhaika, Rus', Izba, Iveria, Russkaya skazka, the motel Solnechny, the restaurant in the Soyuz Hotel. Well, if you know the geography of Moscow's watering holes you will observe that fashion, supposedly fickle, is far from haphazard; it systematically selected places a little way from the centre, away from the eyes of the uninitiated public and the forces of law and order. The small hall at the huge restaurant in the Druzhba Hotel on Vernadsky Avenue, where Vitold invited me once, was no exception in this regard. But before going any further, who was Vitold? I met him through one of the girls from Kalininsky, "from the system", as they said at the time.

He was known pretty much throughout the criminal world by the nickname Mongol, though there was nothing mongoloid about him, and despite the fact that there was another underworld celebrity, the Jap's mentor no less, with the same moniker. So Victor, to give him his secular name, was known at the centre as Vitold, and preferred when on tip-top form to introduce himself as Vitold von Goernich. That was his sense of criminal chic, him trying to be elegant, though it was he who once let drop, quite without irony, how they see freedom in the camp zone — a fine quiff, a leather jacket and soup with lemon. He wasn't a fully paid-up member of the criminal fraternity, of course, but he'd spent half of his thirty years in jail, starting off in a juvenile colony at fifteen, and the intervals between his stretches were brief — but inspired. Actually, it was when we were introduced — he a recidivist who had done time for burglary, theft and extortion, and I a professor's son and rookie journalist — that Vitold decided seriously, it seems, to go straight, but I have to say, this good intention paved him a road straight to hell. This wasn't a case of lack of character or weakness of will, Vitold had real balls, but once unleashed, his wolf's instinct, now no more than a set of animal reflexes, would never let him go, and he ended badly. He was killed in a cell of the remand wing of Butyrki prison. At the motel, which at that time was the only late night restaurant (not counting the hard currency places), he bumped into a former chick of his and took a diamond ring from her which happened to be a present — he was not to know this, and she didn't say, because that would only have added fuel to the fire — from her present lover, a man of authority, for which Vitold caught two bullets right there, was picked up by the police, patched up in the prison hospital in order to have his throat slit by his cellmates, presumably on orders from outside.

But that was later; that summer Vitold was working in some artists' studios ninety kilometres from Moscow, for he could not obtain a permit to live in Moscow with his strangely respectable-looking mother. He had some ability, his own peculiar artistic sense and taste, and at weekends he would travel to Moscow to see his girlfriend, and my acquaintance from the Metelitsa — Tanka the Drum.

Tanka was actually as thin as a rake, and had obviously acquired her nickname from a perverse kind of reverse logic. Anyway, for her it was a case of true love, she waited for Vitold all through his last stretch, and when he was released she went to fetch him. I'd caught a glimpse of him then, the long leather greatcoat, the animal suppleness and quickness of movements, the scars on his thin, vulpine face with its long, fleshy nose, bent slightly to one side, and little gimlet eyes of a very unusual colour — a reddish brown. Tanka was not a prostitute in today's sense, though of course she slept around from time to time. And anyway, compared with today, the entire system in Moscow then was completely unprofessional. Prostitution, currency dealing, dope — it was all disorganised and spontaneous, spheres of influence weren't divided up, there were no hard and fast methods of bribing the cops, nobody was paying a cut even from the most lucrative pitches, and in this sense it was all a bit reminiscent of the official economy today, whereas then the shadow economy was only just getting on its feet and under way. In any case, it wasn't even business back then, more like a way of life that developed spontaneously, in which the boundary between work and leisure for prostitutes, say, was very hazy. The whole system was not so much a set of groups, which might have their differences but are tightly organised, but more of a patriarchal community with elements of a socialist phalanstery, but also its own very romantic ideology of brotherhood, opposition to authority and a Rabelaisian approach to the baser functions, including all kinds of bodily affliction. And the people themselves who made up the system, with the exception of a few maestros, were an open-hearted and astonishingly motley crew: alcoholic actors and failed dancers, inspired whores who didn't take money but slept with whoever they fancied, in other words with everybody in turn; *zelyonki* — greenies, who went with foreigners not so much for bucks as for clothes; and they weren't controlled by professional pimps, they had young lovers, very often from the Caucasus, who made their own turn by reselling the things their girls had been given; good natured queers — quite unlike today's aggressive lot, kids from good families gone to the bad, singers who hadn't quite made it, petty speculators, artists' models who, of course, only worked sporadically, would-be artists, and idle and curious young people — like myself, who enjoyed sharing the naive pleasures of life in the fast lane and justified what they were doing on the grounds that someday the experience will come in handy. Today only a few faces from that crowd come floating up into my memory — a tall, gangly, street prostitute nicknamed Luna who'd screw anyone in a gateway for a shot if a hangover threatened, but when sober went around with an unbelievably high and mighty expression on her rotund face (hence the nickname) — she had syphilis, and probably drank herself to death; Anka, who grew up in an orphanage, a mercurial, pretty little chick, her love of theatre was touching and she slept with actors for free; Lida Sh., who used to case joints for burglars in Sochi, an incredibly beautiful girl, who had an even more remarkable inner strength, and if I had the space I'd describe the brief affair we had on the basis of my idea of writing her memoirs; Gennady, a tragic drunk, a charming and utterly reasonable individual in his late thirties, his beard already greying, an unsuccessful theatre director, never emotional, never trying to get off with anybody until after he'd had a few, when he'd always be after the youngest and prettiest girl in the room; then there was a whole swarm of bright young things — like Grandson, whose parents were abroad and left him a flat on Kalininsky, and because of that everybody loved him, bought him drinks and made a fuss over him, and Luna made him a present of syph; or Yurochka, already hitting twenty three, son of an actress from the Puppet Theatre who'd been in the movies once upon a time. By a quirk of fate we'd once been to a summer camp together, we'd made friends, run off into the woods and built a fire, but it wasn't him I was interested in, I used to wait for his mother to arrive on Sundays, always in a car and with a new man, a dazzling mother who I was exhaustingly and mournfully in love with...

The introduction happened like this: my parents had gone off on their summer holidays and I had been left on my own (my grandmother was dead by then) to enjoy the pleasures of a large flat when Tanka phoned, and when she heard how things stood, she said she would come round with a friend. We didn't fix a time, I went off somewhere and was very surprised when next time she called she sounded very anxious — where've you been? They were round within fifteen minutes, Vitold and I shook hands and I was favourably impressed by the cut of his clothes, his quietly dignified demeanour, his moderacy in alcohol consumption, and totally won over by the tone of our conversation at dinner — about literature, and it was only later Tanka told me they'd phoned a few times and Vitold had said he wasn't going to fuck around any longer and was going to burn the place down. And he would have done it, too, Tanka assured me.

They stayed overnight, but the morning didn't pass off quite as stylishly. I woke up and went out into the kitchen to find Vitold standing there in only his boxer shorts, his body covered in vile lead-coloured tattoos. Tanka was sitting there with her skinny legs bare and every vein and wrinkle of her rodent — either squirrel or chipmunk — face straining to follow the least movement of her lord and master. Vitold was slurping the soup my mother had left me straight out of the saucepan, drinking my vodka from the fridge. He gave me a friendly nod and pointed with his spoon — as if to say, take a pew, he even pushed the saucepan into the middle of the table. It must have reminded him of a cauldron in some remote lumber camp. Tanka drank neither soup nor vodka. I have to say I never saw Vitold again in such a cosy domestic mode, relaxed and at ease — it was plain that that morning even he felt some masculine gratitude towards Tanka and maybe even something like tenderness.

It's hard to explain, but from that day Vitold felt some liking for me. It was hardly likely because of Tanka: it must have been obvious to him we'd been sharing her, we were milk brothers, he wasn't that sentimental, though there might be something in it. Maybe it was because, as we discovered later, Vitold secretly wrote poetry, and though I was only a beginner, I was still a writer. Finally, it could have been the usual way thieves are drawn to the intelligentsia, a kind of vague respect for them, something you never get in ordinary people who haven't passed through the zone. Vitold had a simple way of making money — he screwed it out of people who were screwing it out of other people, he engaged in the most basic form of racket — he'd go up to the first black market trader he saw, grab something from him, wait a moment and then offer calmly — do you want to buy this cheap, two hundred roubles? It never failed. The amazing thing was that Vitold lived and operated solo, nobody was behind him, absolutely nobody, and it must never have entered the heads of the people he screwed, otherwise they wouldn't have stood for it, but in case of trouble nobody would have been there to bail him out, he relied entirely on his own powers — always, so was it surprising that sooner or later he would lose out?

He always paid for me in the bars he took me to, there could be no question about it, and to pay him back in some way, I once took him to the house of an acquaintance, a former Komsomol poet and an over-aged wally whom I tolerated because of his touching, sincere devotion to Literature. The poet used to attract a motley assemblage of versifiers, mostly trash, but with some genuinely talented people among them, which was not that strange, since there was no alternative back in those dead years other than get together in a ruck, and some of the people who were at those gatherings did, when the Bolsheviks collapsed, drift up to the surface and emerge into the light of day — some in the big literary magazines, others in parliament. Vitold read his poems there.

I heard those poems then for the first and last time. I wouldn't swear to it that they were actually written by

Vitold and not by the person in the next bunk, but they were brought out from prison, that is a fact. I remember one poignant poem about a hungry camp dog, teased by cruel men — it wasn't clear whether they were prisoners or guards — who got it to stand on its hind legs for hours by holding a piece of meaty sausage above its nose. The poet hadn't a clue who his guest was, and so played the grand maitre, removing and twiddling his glasses, dabbing at the bridge of his nose, he launched into a professional deconstruction of what we had just heard, and you had to see the good-natured calm with which Vitold took it, looking with his brown eyes from the depths of his black experience at this buffoon, turning his nose up and talking about rhyme and alliteration. The scene is imprinted in my memory precisely because it is such a perfect example of the unfathomability of men's ways, the unfathomability and multiplicity of the ways, which lead us all, essentially, to one and the same...

The hall really was small, seating about two hundred, and when we sat down at the big table laden with *zakuski* that had been reserved for Vitold, I looked around and realised that this was a gathering of the system's elite, of those people who caused a wave of whispers to go round the tables in cheap bars on Kalininsky when they appeared. There was the wealthy currency dealer, Hamlet — his real name, by the way, and an indicator of his status, since very few in this world went about under their own name; a forty-year-old Greek woman Lintata, the mama of Moscow's prostitutes, a procuress, gangster and fortune teller all in gold and in a very low cut dress; a whole bevy of tarts surrounding a flamboyant gypsy beauty — the celebrated Shu-Shu, or Shura Sharovaya to give her full name, in a black dress with bare shoulders, but no rose in her black hair, — and around them buzzed young men who looked Armenian, wearing long, spangled magicians' jackets with huge lapels; Lida Sh. was there, I hadn't made her acquaintance yet, but I had heard so many intriguing stories about her. There was a band, which somebody must have ordered and paid for specially, because usually there was only music in the big hall, a girl singer belted out hits like *we ate sweet berries together, the bitter ones I eat alone*, and she didn't just manage to make it sound playful, she was even able to inject a note of deep underworld melancholy, so it was never really clear whether the song was about an unwanted pregnancy or a sentence handed down by a People's Court. And the whole bit — the vodka flowing at the tables, the bar-room hoarseness of the semi-naked singer's voice, the thud of the drums, the outrageous, over-the-top crowd, the girls' make-up beginning to slip and their smiles half-pissed, the men's faces reddening — exuded alcoholic and sexual intoxication.

From time to time Vitold acknowledged somebody with a nod, sometimes even raised a heavy tattooed hand in greeting, but neither the party mood nor the alcohol took hold of him, he — and I had observed this a number of times before — simply withdrew into himself and clammed up, without getting tipsy, and you could feel, almost physically if you were sitting next to him, how the sludge floated up from the bottom of his soul, a poisonous mixture of bitterness, spite and malice, which even he could feel stifling him. It created a physically perceptible field around him, and not everyone had the guts to step out into that field. Meanwhile, he didn't call anybody over, he tossed back glass after glass, in silence, though without ever forgetting to clink glasses with me: bottoms up.

I kept watching the crowd of dancers, hoping to pick out Sh, dreaming she'd come over to our table — I knew she was in deep with Vitold. But who did suddenly come over was Shu-Shu, and she acted with the familiarity reserved for secretaries who've been sleeping with the boss, and haven't been put in their place. She wasn't drunk, but was under the influence, of course, and even tried to sit on Vitold's knee, but he shoved her fairly brusquely onto a neighbouring chair. She was, actually, not stupid. She was cunning and resourceful, and not many other people would have lasted in her position, manoeuvring endlessly between the doormen of Intourist hotels, clients and the KGB. She would have been flawlessly beautiful, were it not for the expression of vulgar disdain on her rapacious mouth — the mark of a moral deficiency, if you want to be highfalutin'. I didn't listen to their conversation, as I was trying to pluck up the courage to ask Lida to dance — and anyway I wasn't too certain how her escort, Vitold or even she would respond to my attentions, though the last was probably the least of my worries, when I detected an unpleasant note in Vitold's voice. Then Shu-Shu's sharp riposte, glancing round at me:

"Mongol, you shouldn't think things like that out loud!"

"I reminded her", Vitold said when Shu-Shu had gone away, "how you and I had a threesome with one of her mates last month." This wasn't his usual style, he didn't normally discuss sex, wasn't inclined to say much at the best of times. I realised he was pissed. I remembered the antics Tanka told me he could get up to: go into some entrance for no rhyme or reason and start hammering on the steel door of the lift: get up you wankers, you're fucked! — he was a dissident of a sort. Here, surely, he was among his own kind, but then who of us can say where his own kind are? Now he was staring at the back of some kid's head. The kid was sitting some distance away, his back to the aisle and the dancers. I followed Vitold's stare: a quite unexceptional back of a head.

"You know him?" I asked.

"Why should I know him," came the reply.

It was Shu-Shu who came to the rescue.

"Look who I've brought to see you."

Two girls stood behind her, shrinking back with fright.

"Dzhapan, Vitya. D'you understand, dzhapan. They're Japanese girls. Yeah? Come on, you sit down, sit down," she said to the girls, pointing to empty chairs.

The two round-faced Japanese girls with their high cheekbones, short black hair, snub noses, short legs and broad, clumsy thighs looked around without smiling. Then as Shu-Shu kept repeating *seet daun pliz* they sat down opposite us.

This was a completely new ball game. Just when we were getting really bored, two Japanese girls appear at our table. They were the genuine article, no doubt about it, yellow skin, slanty eyed, short arsed, and instantly new horizons beckoned. Listen, you ever had a Japanese? Vitold asked me, sizing up our guests. Me neither. There was a Romanian girl once. From Moldavia.

I, too, had to confess I'd never fucked a foreigner, let alone a Japanese, unless a Polish girl who studied in the same group as me counted, which she didn't.

Vitold was transformed, he became courtesy itself. The first thing he did was call the waiter and whisper in his ear. The dishes of red and black caviar increased in number straightaway, the champagne — also suddenly increased in supply — migrated into ice buckets, and there was a superabundance of fish of various kinds, and juliennes and cold cuts. The Japanese girls exchanged glances and had a quiet discussion. "Listen," Vitold asked me when the goblets were foaming, "what are they saying to each other in that mumbo-jumbo of theirs? Say something to them in English, they're bound to understand that."

I said something. I don't know whether the Japanese understood, but they replied in their own gibberish. Not that it stopped them drinking the champagne and stuffing their cheeks with caviar while simultaneously nibbling smoked sausage.

"Listen," said Vitold, "haven't they got tons of caviar of their own out East? What they're being so gutsy for?"

I shrugged. "Homesick for their own food, I suppose, can't get enough of it."

"A-a", said Vitold profoundly and relapsed into silence, scrutinising them, sizing them up and choosing. "Listen, Kolya, give them to me, will you, the pair of them."

This turn of events wasn't what I had planned, I'd already got everything all worked out — it might be a slightly exotic route, but at least I was to get to touch foreign parts. And yet — first off, it was Vitold paying, second, Shu-Shu had brought the Japanese for him, not me, plus I could ride the crest of his passion to grab a little something for myself, ask him for an introduction to the legendary Sh.

"No," Vitold banged the table. "We'll pair off. We need a change of scene. We've got a place to go... Tell 'em we're going to the flat. Listen to myuzik. Myuzik, understand?" He said turning to the Japanese girls.

"Myuzik, da-da", the Japanese girls nodded and pointed towards the band.

"They agree," Vitold said. "We'll take all this with us, the waiter'll wrap it up. Let's get going, beats hanging around here..." He looked at the girls, eyes full of lust, even though neither of them, objectively speaking, could hold a candle to Shu-Shu or Lida Sh., or even Tanka the Drum. The waiter was approaching our table.

"Wrap it all up," said Vitold, "we're taking it with us. Three more shampoos. And cognac..."

"Understood", replied the waiter. "I was asked to give you this." He placed a paper napkin folded in half in front of Vitold.

Vitold unfolded the note. He read it, crumpled it up and threw it in the ashtray. "Where is she?"

"Getting her coat. They're leaving..."

Vitold stood up and made for the exit. I retrieved the note from the ashtray, smoothed it out and read it, scarcely able to decipher the big letters: "Mongol! They're from where you are. Love them and cherish them. Shura".

I looked at the Japanese girls. Of course they were Mongolians, strange we didn't twig it right away. A neat revenge on Shu-Shu's part, but Vitold was unlikely to see the funny side. Where'd she found them? But then this hotel wasn't part of the Intourist chain, the Mongolian girls could well have been living here, and Shu-Shu just scooped them up in the lobby. Vitold came back and I could tell by the way he looked that Shu-Shu wasn't such an idiot as to wait around after a stunt like that. He came up to the Mongolian girls from behind, they — either because they saw the look in my eyes, or because they sensed danger — turned around, but Vitold grabbed one by the right ear, the other by the left ear — hair and all — and began swinging their heads.

"Vitold", I cried.

He stopped dead, but didn't look at me. The Mongolians froze, too, not making a sound. I think he was afraid to look at me, because then he might have felt like killing me, and he didn't want to kill me. His face had gone white, his cheekbones jutted and the skin on them was trembling.

"Vitold", I repeated, and sensed that I was going white, out of fury and fear combined.

He slowly relaxed his fingers. And the two Mongolian heads sprang apart, as if they were clockwork, and one of the girls began to whimper. Still not looking at me, Vitold turned and went into the centre of the hall, where nobody was dancing now and the entire space between the tables was clear. There was a kind of ominous grace in his unhurried walk, but I had no idea what he had in mind. The second girl was still staring at me. They didn't realise how close they'd been to the abyss, hadn't a fucking clue, they owed me, I might have settled for tugriks, or a sheep if it came to that... Something moved in the air, something happened, some instantaneous change, though apparently nothing had changed, except the guy Vitold had been staring at earlier had vanished, and the hanging edge of white tablecloth had turned bright crimson, as if he'd been put through a liquidiser. Vitold carried on walking at an even pace past the table and even the people sitting right next to the guy would have wondered whether their friend hadn't fallen off his horse on his own.

I began to move towards the exit. Perhaps we had something in common; maybe it was an inclination to lone rebellion. After all, I also felt I was in some sense in the zone and dreamt of freedom. And my dream of freedom was much the same when it came down to it: a fine quiff, a leather jacket and soup with lemon. But our ways were to part, each of us had his own road. Farewell, Vitold.

Viola

Still, sooner or later it had to happen, and it did, nor did it feel like a crime, or even an illicit escapade: Moscow University, Zone B, seventh floor, the postgraduate residence of the Philology Department, the usual two room unit, shared shower and toilet, autumn twilight, a bottle of brandy, and it's not important how I came to be there — habit, I suppose, since nobody that evening would have liked to swear that I was quite sober. She had the look of a Finnish country girl, blond straying towards flaxen, with a simple round sweet face and broad low-slung hips. She was friendly and liked a drink, and less than half a bottle later we were in bed. For all the moral laxity that prevailed in university residences and aware though I was of boy talk about the legendary sexual availability of Scandinavian women I was nonetheless astonished at the speed of this encounter. We had known each other just a few minutes. Probably, it was all because of my charm, I concluded in my simple-minded conceit, plus the undemanding ardour of our instant coupling, her sexual attentiveness which had none of our Russian feelings of humiliation or arrogance, just a good-natured carnal hospitality, all these things combined stopped me from understanding quite what had happened to me. Only as I finished the brandy did it dawn on me that I'd stepped out onto the road of my dreams, but no matter how hard I tried, I couldn't find anything unusual in what had happened. I don't know, but maybe if you dream passionately about being in a particular place and the road to it seems difficult and dangerous, yet marvellous, too, and you spend too long anticipating that moment, you're bound to be disappointed when the door finally creaks open. Anticipation is always sweeter than the act. Or maybe to an impulsive nature, too long a preparation makes the thing seem routine. And then the fact that we came together so casually, that she was living in Zone B, just like many of my friends, and that she was Finnish, writing a dissertation on Vassily Shukshin, and spoke near perfect Russian, also put me off my guard and led me astray; after all, when you came to think about it, Finland and Zone B had both been parts of my Empire at some point. One way and another, that first evening I was almost disappointed, and there wasn't the least hint, nothing to suggest that fate might have a way of opening up in the most prosaic manner, luring you in by degrees — that's how people get sucked into a trade or a life of crime, into love or illness, which may and may not be curable and which at best end not with death, but its rehearsal...

We began seeing each other from time to time.

Of course I was chuffed I had my own foreign girlfriend at last. It was *de rigueur* in the bohemian circles I mixed with at that time. Generally speaking, the idea of having your own foreigner didn't have to involve sex; lots of people developed family friendships with their own foreigner, and whether adultery occurred or not was irrelevant; every decent family had to have its foreigner and he/she was valued more highly than a relative who had won the Lenin Prize, was guarded from envious prying eyes more than children or wives and cultivated as assiduously as social climbers boost their status and businessmen value sources of sure and steady profit. Your own foreigner — it didn't matter how disreputable or scruffy, just as long as he wasn't from a Third World country (socialist countries weren't even worth considering) — magically lifted human existence above the humdrum, though the rewards were few — a few packs of Marlboros in exchange for the immense quantity of *shashlyk* and *pelmeny* the average Westerner ate in a Russian home, or packets of herb tea or a few second-hand clothes, which could, if it came to that, always be sold. The sex, profession or nationality of a foreigner were, on the whole, secondary. He played the role of a living amulet, to love him was a happy experience and without sin, and the average gentleman or lady was so busy deluding him or herself, he or she took the disinterested nature of this selfless emotion for incredible Russian hospitality. Very few of them guessed that should they, let's say, take out Soviet citizenship, the relationship would end in disgust and contempt, if not hatred, which is the only end a dream defiled can have. I mean, for a Moscow playboy, having a foreign girlfriend was indisputable proof of his prowess. So I was naturally proud of my trophy and dragged her round to people I knew, opening nights, parties and birthdays, parading her in front of my friends and showing her off to all and sundry — and right now I might be living on some farm in Suomi, if I'd been smarter, more perspicacious and more careful at the time.

Gradually, as our assignations seemed to become more compulsory, I found out more about her and finally realised, to my not inconsiderable surprise, that she had nobody — no fiancé in Helsinki, no lover in the Finnish Embassy, which meant that, in all probability, young women in the West were no different to the girls in our rough-and-ready country in wanting to get married. A vague idea began to grow in me — not a conscious plan, not a more or less precise vision of the future, but a certain luminous image — it grew tenderly, sluggishly, the way only the most fantastic ideas grow, swelling deep down inside, never appearing to me in my dreams in the way charlatans would have a credulous public believe — as ideas that are destined to change a man's life, sometimes change the whole of mankind. In short it came into my head that I could marry her, but I should keep quiet about it so as to not ruin everything. For if it were to happen — do I really have to explain what would have happened next: we'd get on a train called the Tolstoy, like in the movies, cross the border, and God alone knows the effect of that — a blow, an explosion, a flash of light, and I'd be in the other world, the West, which we knew as many legends about as we did about heaven and hell, but which we had no means of proving, no matter how much we wanted, in this sinful life of ours. I rather fancifully believed that with her help we could overcome all the political and bureaucratic obstacles and prohibitions — other people had, though at what price nobody knew — and since she was inclined towards matrimony, only one small detail remained — convince her I was the man she wanted for a husband.

There was only one way I could accomplish this — by convincing myself I couldn't live without her. It isn't always simple, but in this particular case, everything came together very neatly — a perfect match.

An important point here is that despite her limited means — by Western standards, of course — she felt, like any foreigner in Moscow in those years, more or less like a fairy godmother. She possessed knowledge of a higher order, which the rest of us mere mortals could never have. She could communicate with other forces and other worlds. She had the power, say, to penetrate foreign embassies, anybody else would have been struck by lightning for daring to do that, to make international telephone calls, any mere mortal rash enough for that would have incurred the wrath of unworldly powers. Finally she possessed magic in paper form, convertible Finnish Marks, too dangerous for me to touch even in the dark, and she could walk into a hard-currency shop or a hard-currency bar as casually as I could go into a chemist's. Probably at a certain stage in a relationship every woman wants to appear to her lover as an enchantress, a generous and crafty bearer of gifts, except that in an age when sex had been totally demystified the possibilities for this were diminishing, and what chances had a simple Finnish girl of playing the enchantment game, and at low cost, except as an appendix to an exit visa from the Soviet Union.

There is, of course, a nuance here. Fairy godmothers only help fairytale heroes, even foolish ones, but that question wasn't on the agenda as far as I was concerned. I was a young unpublished writer. In the Russian climate and geographical space that was a tried and tested circumlocution for heroism, as she most certainly knew, given that she was studying Russian literature. One more thing: because I frequently spent the night with her in her room after a party, something which suited her Finnish colleague, a red-haired beanpole with the face of a desiccated reptile — in comparison with her my girlfriend was a model of feminine perfection — I was taking a real risk, not only by breaking the strict rules of the residence, but also by being in contact with a foreigner. On their own, these sins could be forgiven, combined and multiplied they would lead to trouble, they might, for example, have me chucked out of the magazine where I'd found work. I used to catch myself lowering my voice and looking for microphones, and this also undoubtedly helped my romantic image, my readiness to undergo constant danger for love. It only made our nights more passionate.

On the other hand, though I found her nothing

special to begin with, I steadily became convinced that this ordinary girl, who liked a drink and a laugh for all that she was very industrious, filling up her card index with notes on the language and style of her author, deep down had something quite unusual. It was little things mostly, her accent, an unexpected naivety with regard to certain obvious Soviet realities, and little things I'd never seen before, the way she put on make-up and those bizarre Tampax things, which in case of extreme necessity you could yank out by the string. Of course, it's the little things that excite a lover, even if his chosen one is an ordinary mortal, but this one was different, she was from the other world. Every time she opened her generous bosom I quivered, out of considerations mystic rather than erotic, as if I were entering the Holy of Holies. It is an ecstatic lover who perceives a woman as if it was from her womb that he came into the world; but when I entered her, I felt only that I might by this means grope my way into the unknown and transcendent, into another world... Two months passed, not a word about marriage, but by now if I hadn't spend the night with her, she'd call me in the morning, and every third or fourth day provide some token of her affection, things which at that time could have only been produced by a fairy's wand: for example, a two-volume posthumous edition of Shukshin, which I didn't really need, but had been bought in hard currency from their magic shop, or a wonderful Miro album — I'd never even heard of Miro — bought at Stockmann's no less.

Our most touching evenings were spent in the far corner of the cafe in the Hotel National, an establishment which has at various times played an important role in the lives of Muscovites of different generations — in mine, too, at certain points. Neither she nor I were rich, but then the National wasn't expensive in those days. Ten roubles would buy dinner for two, and for twenty you could gorge yourself on caviar and champagne. But to get inside the cafe if there was a queue outside, and there always was, even on Mondays, called for special tactics: my girlfriend went to the hotel entrance, showed her Finnish passport and explained to the doorman she was a translator, this was because she didn't have a hotel guest's card; she went up to the first floor, past the restaurant with the balalaika players and the hard-currency bar, came down another staircase into the cafe entrance hall and began working on the cafe doorman from the inside; finally the door would open a crack, I would slip past the heaving crowd of prostitutes and young people, who, alas, lacked a magic helpmate, and duck behind the doorman's shoulder. Once inside, you could always find a table, the cafe had an unwritten practice of vetting its clientele, though there were always free places even on Saturdays, but an outsider who didn't know the rules could only get into the National by a miracle.

A successful joint assault brings you closer together than food, which we never had enough of in Zone B, than Armenian brandy, which we drank as we gazed into each other's eyes. And maybe it is those very moments, which remain in the memory when all the rest is just an approximate reconstruction... But then our evening idylls were always overshadowed, always felt fragile, because we never knew whether we could spend that night together. After 11 p.m. Zone B was particularly closely guarded, the doormen, strange as it may seem, were incorruptible, but the odd one would recognise us and, thinking I was a resident, not bother to ask for my pass, sometimes I managed to get into her bed by the back staircase from the basement, where quite often the door was left unlocked; it was always worse towards the end of the week when guard duty was taken over by Komsomols. They were as merciless as iron Felix Dzerzhinsky, the founder of the Soviet secret police, and though they were formally voluntary auxiliaries of the police, they actually reported to the KGB. We had to keep an eye out for them most of all, because they were young and keen and tireless enough to track us down and set a special watch on her door — and there was something sweet in this uncertainty — and it all lent our lovemaking the nagging twinge of infidelity and imminent separation.

One day we were joined at our table in the National by O.O.; a scriptwriter, a very successful one, specialising in historical dramas, he won a prize later, a strange hybrid of intellectual and crook, so he chose the right trade, bang in the middle — incidentally, he wasn't the only one of that kind in the brilliant flowering of Moscow youth that came to prominence during the now legendary Youth Festival of 1957 — a scrapper, a swashbuckling man about town and sentimental adventurer — I would have said he was a friend had he not been fifteen years older than me and referred to me in public as his student. I did, indeed, learn a few things from him. Once I bet him two bottles of brandy that in ten days I could write a 150-pages long novel, 15 pages a day, and I won the bet, you can understand what it cost me to do it, but he never produced the brandy, and merely remarked after reading the novel just to check: well, you managed to hit a few clear notes here and there, a bit like a pub tenor singing opera... In short, I was delighted to see him.

At this point I should describe O.O. His appearance, like his behaviour, was mannered: long dark hair and a tangled beard that concealed a small, quick, toothless mouth: I've no money for doctors, he used to wail as he stood in front of the mirror, though he would squander hundreds in restaurants, I think he was simply petrified of dentists; he dressed on the parrot and cabbage principle — lots of layers, vest, jersey, shirt, jacket, and all different colours, yellow-red-green, a Panama hat that looked sort of Tyrolean which he never took off in restaurants, but pulled down over his super-dark glasses — he gave the impression that what he was really frightened of was being taken for a Soviet. He certainly didn't look like he came from here, more like a half-crazed sort of Scotsman, the bosun, say, of a freighter washed up by a storm here in

Moscow, the port of the five seas. I introduced my girlfriend. He looked at her from behind his glasses, yawned rudely and pulled forward his jacket lapels, pinching them along the seams below his collarbones — a backwards version of the underworld chic of pushing the jacket back so the lapels lay on the shoulders — and intoned: Holland? Finland, I corrected him. I felt flattered, his casual boorishness was surely a front for surprise and interest. Listen, loves, he suddenly switched to a whisper, and grabbed each of us by the hand rather too familiarly, will you get me something in the shop, tea, cigarettes, vitamins for my daughter, there's a bit of cash in the old purse, that be ok? His wheedling like that was also supposed to impress — O.O. himself actually asking us to do him a favour. Not that my Finnish simpleton knew who O.O. was, but she promised politely. And we drank brandy — to international friendship, to the USSR and Finland, to our meeting, to cinema, to Shukshin whom O.O. had known personally, of course, to my girlfriend's delight, and then to everything good under the moon, including Holland. We drank till closing time, O.O. suggested we go to his place to read poetry, in those days you never just went home after a restaurant, you had to go to somebody's place, so off we set.

Once at O.O.'s we discovered we'd forgotten to bring any drink with us and he had run out. I hope you're not going to make your old host fetch it; you've got money I presume, and there's a new custom — the young treat the old... Everything, except the last proposition, which struck me as dubious, was true — according to the rules, I should go fetch; of course, I didn't want to leave my girl alone with O.O., but I went, fast, no arguments, I didn't wish to indulge the jealous stirrings of my soul.

I was back in about ten minutes. Bought half a litre from the first taxi I stopped. The door to the flat wasn't locked. O.O. and my girl were sitting opposite each other in the kitchen, he was reciting Brodsky's poetry, she'd never heard of him, it transpired. He gestured to her with a leisurely movement — as if to say, glasses are over there in the cupboard, and to my surprise, she reacted immediately, went over to the cupboard — quite at home. But what was even more surprising were the two bottles of brandy, one opened, standing on the table. But then O.O. always was a bit stingy...

I saw him three days later when we bumped into each other in the Writers' Union buffet, had a drink and then we were off, as we say. By eight that evening we were sitting in the Peking restaurant, by nine were semi-pissed, could still steer a path quite freely, had not yet switched to autopilot. Surrounded by the racket from the band and the dancing permed women, I got bored and tried to think of ways of splitting back to my girl in Zone B, but O.O. suddenly had the bright idea of nicking a big copper tray from the waiters' table. I couldn't refuse the offer to join in this prank. One of us would pick up a coat in the cloakroom, the other would grab the target, we'd slip it past the doorman under the coat, except that in the middle of all this we discovered the tray was too big in diameter, but we did just manage to get it past him and outside. Thick, refreshing snow was falling. We had to do something with the tray. Right there, at the entrance to the hotel, I used the tray as a gong and O.O. struck up an aria from Rossini. Meanwhile, the wind was chilly, the snow was coming sideways and stinging, not ideal weather for music making.

We stopped to think. O.O. said:

"Your Finn's a load of shit."

"Why?" I asked calmly.

"Doesn't wash."

"You sleep with her?"

"Had it off with her."

I put the tray down on the snow.

"When I went for the vodka?"

"When.. Ah, no. She phoned me yesterday, brought me some tea , and then down in the entrance, I told her to bend over and gave it her... funny, a foreigner and doesn't wash..."

I hit him the way he taught me — a sharp jab with the right. It was slippery and he went down on the pavement. Now I couldn't let him recover and stand up, otherwise I'd have as many teeth left as he did — he had been a good boxer in his time, and despite his louche, drunken way of life, he kept himself in shape. I threw myself on top of him just as he was getting up — after all, we hadn't agreed on boxing or wrestling. In the latter case, I had the advantage — I was bigger and heavier than him. Grappling and pummelling each other, we rolled about in the blizzard to the amusement of the pimps, prostitutes and taxi drivers hanging around the hotel. I don't know how long we carried on like this, but I came to in a police van. O.O. was swearing like a trooper and showing two pensive policemen the torn collar of his winter coat.

However, at the police station he sobered up, changed tactics, and started mumbling about it being him who started the fight — despite his obvious disinclination to any play of chivalry — pulled out his Cinema Union membership card and told the duty policeman it was he who made the great hit *White Sun of the Desert*.

They still put us in the lock-up — in separate cells, and at seven, when they changed shifts, they wrote us receipts for a fine and let us go.

As we walked down Gorky Street in silence O.O. suddenly said:

"I've been feeling something in my bones all these last few days... And now, there you are — yesterday the snow came."

He was an animal, and I was an animal as well. Probably we're all animals to a great extent. And it only remained for me to learn from a rogue male how to lie in wait for and lure the female. Actually, I always avoided using friends' women. That and pride — it's like failing to catch a fish and stealing one your friend caught. And a certain fastidiousness, too — if you're going to sleep between someone else's sheets, best not to know who slept there before you... At eight precisely we were at a little table in the Hotel Moskva, the one with the curiously asymmetrical facade, and when we had been brought beer, food and chilled vodka in a little decanter, O.O. said:

"You know, Kolya, until I was thirty, I used to be very proud that I could get any woman first time of asking. And then I began to think — Lord, who I have been living with all my life!"

We drank, without clinking glasses. His head drooped towards the table. I looked up at the mosaic on the ceiling — a good Stalinist mosaic of the kind nobody does anymore, anywhere — except maybe North Korea. O.O. was completely out for the count. At that time I could drink and carouse for days on end without sleep...

Six months later I was married. I fell in love with a sweet girl and decided that my adventures were behind me and that at twenty-five I deserved a little happiness with my own little family. She was a general's daughter — you can imagine how pleased the general was — and a novice artist, and the Miro album migrated to her shelf. A few years later, at some exhibition I met my old Finnish girlfriend. She'd gone flabby and lost her vivacity. She told me she'd also been married — to a doctoral student from Volgograd, she'd got him out to Helsinki, but he'd left her and gone to America. I didn't ask why she'd come back to Russia. To get married, no doubt.

<u>*Gulya*</u>

1.

It would have been hard to find anything grubbier than this alley cat — to say nothing of the humanoid inhabitants — in that North Caucasus town. But he was the one she chose to pick up and press against her light-coloured dress. We'd come to look for treasure. A lot of gold, diamonds, old jewellery, which her granny had stuffed into a hole in the brick flue of a stove before fleeing to Constantinople. We'd been staying three days in a motel on the road from the airport into town, sat around in dangerous, dirty bars, twice been to church, where she lit candles and prayed for someone or other and made a mess of it, because she was an atheist; now she was clutching this mangy creature with matted fur and the stink of rotten fish on its breath. In the poverty-stricken gloom of the slum I could see the tears trickling down her cheeks.

She'd cried in church, too, and when we first found the tumble-down one-storey red brick house, which the Soviets had converted to a hospital, for railway workers, I think. She even cried when I balked at waiting with swarms of grubby children for an ice-cream in an enormous queue that smelt of female sweat, and she tried to convince me she had to stand in that queue in the heat with all of the people. Later, when I got to know her better, I came to realise it was more a case of reverse snobbery than sentimental nostalgia.

To this day I cannot understand why we didn't have our throats cut. She was quite the victim and seemed to draw the sad cases — a tall, slightly round-shouldered, blonde with a model's breasts and legs, a dippy foreigner who handed out money to beggars, gave away expensive foreign cigarettes with ingratiating eagerness to swarthy young men who had menacing, pimply faces and gold teeth, doled out chewing gum to the children of the gypsy women who sold lipstick at the station; and she was a cry baby into the bargain. At the time I ascribed the latter condition not so much to sentiment at this encounter with her *lares et penates*, as to the fact that we were, of course, never entirely sober. It was unlikely that in France she would have been used to such quantities of poor quality strong liquor, but vodka was essential with the local food, especially since the wine smelt vinegary and the champagne was warm. Fortunately, she didn't have any stuff, and her more experienced companion had forced her to throw the packet of grass she'd brought with her from Paris down the toilet on the plane. I blocked all her attempts to score from the local crowd — I was frightened the local drug squad would plant something on her, and then keep her inside for a month or so before throwing her out of the country; not to speak of what would have happened to me in such a case. However, wary of certain peculiarities of her character, I didn't describe this scenario: had I tempted her with such brilliant Isadora Duncan-esque possibilities, she would have gone for her scag and nobody could have stopped her. So I merely lied that we were bound to be ripped off and sold a bum deal, but that when we got to Moscow I'd get her as much shit and gear as her heart desired.

We'd known each other a week. She was grateful to me for volunteering to go with her to the Caucasus rather than soak up the sun in Yalta, and the adventure itself brought us closer: it did because she turned out to be good and appreciative company in any adventure, and she couldn't have found a better companion than me. We met like this: my colleague Dima S. was in the midst of a long, potentially matrimonial affair with a Parisienne of Russian origin and heard she was off to the USSR on a tour from Yalta to Moscow, and that she was taking two girlfriends. Knowing her ways and the other two by reputation, my friend concluded, rightly, that the situation would be too much for him single-handed, and he suggested I help him out. I, of course, agreed readily — no question about it! — even though, if the truth be known, I had things to do in Moscow that June: I had a very interesting situation going with a ballerina — a pretty girl with unusual erotic abilities, that's why I forgot to book a ticket to the Crimea, remembered my commitment at the last minute, dashed to the airport at night, wheedled my way onto the early morning flight, got to Alushta with enough time to catch the boat, enjoyed a local Madeira in the buffet and snoozed on deck all the rest of the way to the quay at Yalta.

We'd agreed like this: Dima would meet the girls independently, and I would meet him at midday in the cafe on the veranda of the Oreanda Hotel. I got there dead on time, but there was nobody in the cafe, and the waiter gave me a note with directions to the Yalta hotel. Half an hour later I was there and trying to suss out what was going on. There was my friend — he was five years older than me, two charming Parisiennes his age — one pale and plump, with strong limbs and a decisive look, who was his putative fiancée, the other very tall, with incredibly long and beautiful legs and a low fringe, she was pale as well and had huge, unfocussed, bright blue eyes. Lastly there was their small, pregnant friend — a former Soviet, in her second marriage, this time to an American, not a Frenchman, she was only slightly pregnant, incidentally, in her fifth month. So there they were — Olga, Gulya and Ritulya. The fiancée greeted me graciously, my former compatriot was most cordial, while the third was fairly aggressive, which prompted the thought that she was probably the one for me, though there had, of course, been prior agreement on this count.

I understood. In her situation the first thing she had to do was dig into her forward positions, and then take a good look round. What if I turned out to be a stupid fart who started claiming non-existent rights and exploiting the possibilities of chance encounters, and so spoil what would otherwise have been a wonderful trip. It was her first visit to the Soviet Union; she probably imagined it as some kind of sub-polar Cuba, where her ancestors had lived, strangely enough; Lord, how many great possibilities she saw; of picking up, say, the elder of some Tartar tribe who doubled as a GPU operative, or seducing a real Orthodox priest, not one of your Parisian ones, with a beard to his girdle, or if it came to that slipping into some dimly-lit dive masquerading as a Party school, smoking weed, grooving to psychedelic balalaika sounds and chanting quotes from the Marxist-Leninist canon... She had a resonant Russo-Polish surname, bore a sweet, homely Christian name they used to give children in pre-Revolutionary Russia, but whichever way you looked at it she was a child of the May events of 1968.

We had a couple of glasses of champagne on the spot — to our acquaintance, after which they went off to see the sights, while I had to find a place to sleep, because none of them, naturally, had offered to put me up.

I managed to find only a bed, and then not indoors, it was out under an awning in a garden — not far from the hotel. I had been invited to join Dima's tour group in a restaurant that evening, but I had my grounds for believing that I was possibly *de trop*. Nothing of the sort; my insurance was superfluous, the table was booked, I couldn't get out of it. We were seated on a veranda, being regaled with a repulsive variety show and worse food. Things didn't gel at table; Dima and Olga bickered — maybe because of me; Gulya and I stared in different directions; only Ritulya felt at home. The only time I danced with Gulya I put my hand on her breast; she threw it off and snapped disgustedly: *just like a Frenchman*; she was disappointed, but I didn't know at the time whether it was to do with French techniques of coming on or the inept application of them; I found out later it was the former, but not that evening. In the end I went off to my garden bed, where I fell asleep — for the first time in many days — alone and serene. But I was made to get up early: at around six a panic-stricken herd of semi-naked residents of the house came rushing past my refuge, and I was forced to join them — the place was being raided by the police, to flush out unregistered holidaymakers.

That day everything was put to rights. Gulya must have realised where she was and reached the sad conclusion that our habits here were not much more uncivilised than, say, in Marseilles, though she was absolutely gobsmacked by the hamfisted Soviet Russian attempts at westernisation. There was nothing she could do, dissident writers hiding in her and her friend's room like Latin American guerrillas was the sexiest thing she could rely on happening here. Also, both Dima and I had beards, and his made him the spitting image of Che Guevara. We had lunch in a restaurant out of town, we took dessert in the Oreanda, we dined royally in our room, liberally supplied with a decent little wine we'd bought with some fruit at the market. Gulya and I ended up in bed, where we made seaside love — without tricks or fancy stuff — like the surf, and were pleased with each other, I think. At any rate, I liked her long body, her sweet talk, and the fact she came time after time, it only seemed to take a touch from me.

Next morning I knew I was happy. I chose to play the role of a rich currency dealer: mix with the foreigners, swim in the bar-side pool, go down in the fast lift to the beach that was hermetically sealed from the Soviet world beyond, and also play on games machines I had never seen before. The one I liked best was a shooting game. I wasted a heap of fifteen-kopeck coins before I managed to hit the target and stop knocking the hunter arse over tit.

Our girls introduced us to the other people on the tour. They were mostly old ladies who hadn't the first clue about Russia, even though the tour was organised by the Franco-Soviet Friendship Society.

Never had I felt so free and at ease as in Yalta that summer. This unprecedented sensation was based on being in possession of a certain amount of money — I'd just received the advance for my first book — and the ready availability of certain natural pleasures. Plus there were hitherto unknown pleasures like: smorgasbord breakfast, sitting with a newspaper and a cup of coffee in a clean bar that didn't stink of rancid fat, polite service, functioning sanitary facilities, being able to have a drink or a cold lemonade a second after the idea came into your head, the scent of the sea wafting on the breeze instead of the stench of sweaty fat bodies, being able to take a shower any time you wanted and ask the maid to launder your sweaty shirt. There were moments when I felt I wasn't in a

Soviet resort hotel — though there were only two like that at the time in the USSR — I was actually abroad, where people are always clean and smell good, get up in the morning and drink ice cold champagne on a balcony with a view over the sea and the mountains, take a nap in each other's arms, and then play on a games machine before going out to a show. I felt I was different, too, not a Parisian, naturally, but certainly not a product of the Soviet world, and this was all the more startling because you only find such complete lack of recall of reality in post-traumatic amnesia. Yet this state of grace was utterly ephemeral — a wink from the doorman to one of the plainclothes boys who were a permanent feature in reception, keeping a beady eye on things, and that would be the end of my brief happiness. But we thought of the threat hanging over us no more often than rock climbers or racing drivers think of death. We just took, almost by reflex, the necessary precautions to blend in with the surroundings, wearing foreign clothes, a camera around the neck, making sure we always looked the dumb hyperactive tourist, enthusiastic and interested but completely out of it. The one thing we absolutely could not do was look anybody in the eye — our eyes always stayed warily Soviet.

We entered the part. We turned ourselves into Europeans in our country, which at the time was going through the end of an era of amateurish tyranny, an epoch which ended abruptly with the invasion of Afghanistan — a time of convulsive high spirits, expectation of change and presentiment of upheaval. That year, I remember, it was the height of chic in certain circles to drink Bolls as a pick-me-up, sing the old Moscow underworld ballad Murka in English translation, wear Indian cheesecloth shirts — following last year's Paris fashion, and get ready to split: either by the fiddly method — marriage, or the less certain, but more direct route — an Israeli visa. The idea of leaving was a buzz that went to everybody's head, no exaggeration, not just the young; and the tone was set, of course, by the post-war creative intelligentsia, except the officialdom of the cultural world, but who ever regarded the officialdom as part of the intelligentsia? This universal, mass movement had its leaders, its dregs and its outsiders, but the energy of the exodus was such that even the last category found themselves, they knew not how, spat out of their homeland and carried far, far across the ocean. Today you even get ethnographers making studies of everyday rituals of the late seventies, when the rites of marriage and death were supplanted by the single ceremony of leave-taking, a festival of sobbing for those relatives left behind, of final, tremulous, adulterous encounters in bathrooms, of auctions of items not permitted by customs regulations, of joyful partings with friends for we knew not how long. We lived in one big happy gypsy encampment so refreshingly unlike the usual dreary daily grind: nobody bothered to try and make a career, nobody sucked up or was envious; people stopped worrying about children's school grades or about improving their living standards; actually even thinking about where the next meal was coming from receded into the background — after all every family had something to sell, and the act of selling things off made retreat impossible. Also nearly everybody received parcels from obscure Jewish organisations, ugly women's boots or impossible fur stoles, but you could live well for six months on the proceeds from them; life in general was ridiculously cheap then, we rolled off to the seaside three times a year, commuted between the two capitals, and out of season we would spend time with our friends, and even perfectly serious people succumbed to this disease with a flippant lack of responsibility. It may seem monstrous, but the cleverest and subtlest of minds could and did seriously claim, when explaining why you had to go, that any decent person ought to spend the second half of his life in his own villa with a veranda looking out onto either the Atlantic sunrise or the Pacific sunset. And yet most of us, regardless of intelligence or education, age and social status, remained narrow-minded, egocentric and petulant. We thought we were the centre of the world, reckoned the commies, the *kommunyaki*, had done us an injustice, though we would have found it hard to define in what way precisely, and had every hope that in the future, in the West, we would be compensated, we would get a kind of apology from destiny and a whole heap of bright new toys. We had happily swallowed the bait when Soviet newspapers had trumpeted how utterly superior we, Russians, were — hadn't Dostoyevsky told us about the loftiness of the Russian soul — we indignantly refused to believe anything that might cast a shadow on our dream, and so many Soviet émigré hearts skipped a couple of beats at the sight of the migrant hostels in Vienna, the transit camps at Ostia or the homeless sleeping on subway vents in New York.

What makes it the more surprising is that in our circles we rubbed shoulders with foreigners — exchange students, Slavists, occasionally businessmen, correspondents and cultural attachés, and none of them ever tried to dissuade anybody: like grown-ups never tell children the truth, they'll understand when they get bigger. And for our part, instead of asking questions and trying actually to understand something, we used them simply as a source of good booze, or as postal pigeons, or as agents for moving simple items of property out of the country, and felt superior in the process, after all, we Soviets — and they were happy to back us up — had a unique experience of life in a totalitarian pit and of the constant struggle to defend one's inner spiritual freedom. In fact, most Westerners in Russia indulged not just our weaknesses and complexes, but their own as well: they were not nearly as rich and important at home as they allowed their Russian friends to believe, and it would only be possible to check them out in a very dim and distant future, if at all.

But — and this is the most curious aspect of all — as soon as we got to the point where speech ended and body language came into its own, we were tentative, sometimes nearly panic-stricken, so different was our behaviour in everyday situations. This was the bridgehead where eloquence was of no use, and our sole weapon was impotent.

We did not know how to sit, walk, eat, drink, hail a taxi, use a handkerchief, carry things, answer the phone, light a cigarette and stub it out in an ashtray — we couldn't act like they did. In some situations it was so obvious it made us cringe, like the poor émigré who arrived in America and found he'd been taught the wrong language for years. And so we Russian Casanovas, after discussing life, literature and the universe with a foreign girl over vodka, would rush her into bed — they took this as the charming Rasputin temperament — when it came to the crunch, we simply didn't know what to do with our hands. Yet the meta-language of intercourse for whites is the same everywhere.

But sporadic discussions and coitus are one thing, co-existence twenty-four hours a day in close contact quite another. Dima and I could not just debate the merits of Sartre and copulate with our Parisiennes. And so it was in the intervals that were needed for eating, drinking, washing, that the differences in our habits were revealed: you can agree on your love of Tyutchev and Lautréamont, but an awful lot still comes out when cleaning your teeth or washing your dirty underwear. Nothing could have been more instructive in this sense than two Soviet men cohabitting with three Parisian beauties for a week in two twin-bedded rooms.

The first thing I noticed was that after a bath they used to leave the towel lying on the floor of the bathroom. On thinking about it, I concluded that we Russians have an instinctive dislike for one-time use; we re-use anything and everything — from plastic bags to condoms — and we know it's because we're poor; but why in a country where there is no shortage of time and fuel do we cook soup to last us four days, explaining it away again by a prejudice, that the flavour only really comes out on day three? I was just as baffled by the way they shampooed their hair every day, like we washed our hands with soap; we'd had it drummed into us that over-frequent washing damages the hair roots. Had this golden rule also arisen from a displaced consideration of economising on soap products? But what we found hardest to take, what provoked our secret and jealous admiration, was the simple freedom of doing even the most banal things, little everyday things we would never even have thought of. For example, Dima, who told me that when he was a kid he spent a lot of time trying to imitate the way Yul Brynner walked and moved his hands, was astonished when Olga walked in on him when he was in the bath and started scooping up water in a teapot to rinse it. It seems odd, but this gypsy-like behaviour struck us both as the height of elegance and emancipation. Little details like that made us feel a real sense of our own gaucheries. Of course we were such slobs that these were just pinpricks which we hid behind our usual raucous carryings-on, but they made us watch our friends very closely, if quietly — and to try and learn.

Copying them straight out was absolutely impossible, of course; we would have made fools of ourselves so easily. What I tried to do, in actual fact, was not copy, but try and work out the general line of the path and then follow them down it. In our life together two delicate moments immediately became apparent: the attitude towards money and the attitude towards the body, and you might say there was an inversely proportionate relationship between them. Our Russian lack of inhibitions when it came to money — our own and other people's — was matched by reticence in the bodily sphere, while in financial matters — particularly between each other — they were absolutely punctilious, which didn't stop them splashing out from time to time, whereas with regard to the body they were quite the contrary, generous to a fault, though they could show unexpected delicacy here, too. And so, while we were living with them we tried our hardest to hide our Russian prudishness and stop being slapdash with money, which meant we let go the reins just when we ought to be pulling them in, and put on airs at the very moment when we should have graciously accepted an offer. This is what makes cultures different — not knowing the nuances.

I remember the way all three of them sunbathed topless on the balcony in front of us, not the least embarrassed; on the beach Ritulya once asked me to rub suntan cream on her back and legs, and I was rubbing away, meanwhile Gulya chatted away to her as if it was the most natural thing in the world, though it was she I was sleeping with and not Ritulya. And yet one day after lunch Ritulya sat on my knee in just her bikini, and I couldn't help stroking her thighs, but when she got up to fetch her cigarettes, Gulya, who was sitting on her own in an armchair, reached out a long arm, picked up a massive ashtray from the table and hurled it at Ritulya with such force it went flying out the balcony door, which was fortunately open, and probably went into orbit. And not one of the three of us uttered a word.

On another occasion, at roughly the same time of day, Gulya and I settled down for a nap on the bed. Olga and Dima were out on our balcony — Ritulya's mother had flown down from Moscow, a real peroxide blonde Jewish mama, in a permanent state of tears at how foreign her daughter had become, and yet keeping a sharp eye open to make sure not a scrap of clothing or piece of French soap slipped through her fingers — Ritulya found her embarrassing and kept her locked away in another room. Gulya felt drowsy after the sun and the beach and wanted to make love. I presumed that, since they paraded naked in front of us, these emancipated flower children found it acceptable to have intercourse with their friends around as well. I overcame my shyness and set to work, trying to prove it was as natural as breathing for me, too. When she heard Gulya's moans, Olga poked her head through the balcony door — she was drying her hair out there — and asked me icily: not getting in your way, am I? Lord, how long ago it all was, how sweet and naive it all seems today, and yet it was really quite recently...

2.

We never did find the treasure trove. And Gulya had to let the cat go. Apparently, it isn't just people who become degenerates living on the street — that creature followed us for several blocks, slipping along the dark walls of houses from corner to corner, flitting like a shadow through the light of the occasional street lamp, flicking its tail and meowing viciously, probably demanding food, the way some tramps do, convinced they have a perfect right to it. Obviously that cat could read faces: Gulya would certainly have taken him back to our room at the motel and fed him on boiled sturgeon or beluga flank from the restaurant, but to the cat's misfortune we had to catch the early morning flight to Moscow.

All the same, we did manage to get inside Gulya's granny's house. I had a sudden bright idea — get Gulya, she was a doctor, to go and introduce herself to the staff and say she was interested in seeing the medical care provided for railway workers; and so the hospital people wouldn't panic at an unauthorised visit by a foreigner, I had to pretend to be an Intourist official. Actually, they reacted very calmly. They gave us white coats and took us round the wards, which were surprisingly clean. It was lunch time, the ambulant patients, dressed in grey pyjamas, were making their way to the dining room, each carrying his bowl, mug and spoon. We looked in there as well, and the food looked edible, but Gulya nearly managed to burst into tears here as well — the hospital reminded her of a prison, she told me later. Alas, it hadn't entered my mind to say we were from the fire department — I'm not sure quite how I would have presented Gulya — and there was no way we could get to the chimney in the attic. Grandmother couldn't stand this, Gulya whispered to me, though her granny had died several years back. There wasn't a single clue from the inside that this had once been a wealthy residence, and the stove had probably been rebuilt, so I explained to Gulya later that the family valuables had probably been used to help the war effort and post-war reconstruction of socialism, though I was fairly convinced they'd gone into somebody's private collection. But it was a good move — she did take some comfort from my explanation — she was, after all, on the left, an admirer of Trotsky, Mao Tse Tung and Enver Hoxha; she probably hadn't read any of their works, but she liked the idea of complete equality, permanent revolution, total freedom and social justice, which satisfied her revolutionary masochism. I was horrified by her pro-Communist sympathies, she was prepared to agree that Marchais was a butcher and an old pig, but she enthused about Emperor Bocassa who pounded the French ambassador on the head with a shoe — it hadn't come out then that Bocassa was a cannibal, but if he had just eaten French bankers, it would only have given him added weight in her eyes. In actual fact there was no point in my getting heated; I should have explained to her that for Soviet young people in the seventies any left-wing idea was the same as Le Pen's political programme to her; and anyway I didn't fully understand then that she was over there what I was here, and we were both victims of two different nonconformisms: I was incensed by the profanation of the sacred idea of Western democracy, while she said that were it not for the opportunism of the Soviet leadership, they would have built a just society long ago, as Fidel Castro had on his little island. I hated the Bolsheviks with all the passion of a person who had read *The Gulag Archipelago* the night before, she was disgusted by the rich West — with its double standards, egotism and materialism. But then on the plane, she looked at me almost plaintively with her short-sighted blue eyes. Now I understand what she was feeling. While we were staying in Yalta, she naturally felt a mixture of disappointment and pity at Intourist's pathetic efforts to reach the standard of even a provincial hotel in the West, but when we went to the little town, where her mother's family had come from, she would have had to add a feeling of disgust to the list. Of course, she had seen poverty in India and Brazil, but that was picturesque poverty, almost theatrical against a backdrop of other people's wealth, lavish natural surroundings and beautiful temples. Here she was immersed in a sea of specifically Soviet squalor, which was completely turned in on itself and therefore ineradicable. It is this immutable self-contained greyness that is so depressing in the Russian provinces, a flaccid idiocy, slovenliness and carelessness that pervade everything, and underneath it all that suppressed animal spite. How could you feel anything other than a complete fool here, how would it not make you almost ill, and I could see the symptoms of that illness on Gulya's face.

But then Moscow welcomed us with a fiesta.

I don't remember much about the four days before they left. The tour group was staying in the Central Hotel, which had a horrendously strict regime. There was no question of anybody spending a night in someone else's room. Not that there was any real need for it: there was a twenty-four-hour-a-day party going on in a huge studio belonging to a certain ageing libertine, artist, antique dealer and collector who was away at the time. His mistress Galya (nicknamed Galchonok) was charming and thirty, with laughing brown dissolute eyes and the body of a Rubens bacchante — broad thighs, ample hips and breasts, a narrow waist, little nimble hands, little legs and a rococo mouth — a raspberry-coloured little trumpet, with a perpetual smile on her plump lips. She only wore long Russian sarafans since they revealed her luxurious neck and shoulders — and was a real child of artists' studios. She'd seen a few since her seventeenth birthday, when she'd run away from home after falling head over heels in love with a mediocre sculptor twenty years her senior, who then left her when he applied to emigrate to his "historical motherland". No sooner did we all come tumbling into the studio, than my situation instantly became doubly complicated, since I immediately plunged into an affair with Galchonok.

Well after all, Gulya was leaving in three days, and we were unlikely to see each other again. I didn't feel myself bound in any way, and I also knew that being on your own after too long a party makes you feel much more lonely than you actually are. For some reason, one particular scene comes into mind: noise, hullabaloo, alcohol flowing in rivers, I'm dancing with our hostess, her fat naked hands are resting on my neck, her fingers ruffling my hair, the walls float past hung with folksy painted chopping boards, a large copper cooking pot, something resembling a minor Dutch landscape flashes past between a pair of bast shoes and a distaff, and an early Kuperman, and then I see Gulya. She's sitting on her own on the edge of a divan, showing her incredible legs, smoking and staring straight ahead with a look that cannot, because she's short-sighted, catch the little details.

Or this: on one of the days Gulya and I were on the Arbat at dusk. I felt worn out the way you do when you have spent too long hanging around with visitors from out of town; no, I wasn't bored with her, though I confess I was beginning to find our mechanical, sewing-machine-like sex a little tedious; I was just tired of having to spend all the hours of the day with her, an obligation I had undertaken of my own free will; besides, I couldn't help feeling somewhat constrained with her, her being foreign meant even our intimacy had a kind of — how to put it — official etiquette. In short, I was sick of protocol, I needed to relax, I hadn't the foggiest when she would go back to the hotel, so I could race back to the studio to Galchonok, who could anticipate male desires so well that you felt completely relaxed with her: I could have a shower, a cup of strong tea and a chance to catch up on lost sleep. I was so tired I let my irritation show a couple of times, but each time it just made Gulya be nicer. Finally she sat down on the steps of the metro and gestured for me to sit down next to her. "What do you want?" I asked her rudely, desperate to be shot of her. She stayed sitting. It was one of those idiotic scenes that sometimes happen between people who don't know each other too well when they're pushing things too fast. Maybe, she asked with a timidity which you would never have thought possible in her, maybe you'll take some money from me?

No, it wasn't the actual offer that made me feel insulted, it was her feeling sorry for me in the way she said it. At the time it seemed to me she took me — a free player, a writer with an advance — for something else: in actual fact there was a maternal instinct behind her offer, she was older than me, could see things better, and from the outside I seemed to her very different to the person I felt myself to be. This probably hurt me most. I got up and walked away, abandoned her on the steps. I hailed a cab, but when we got to the Garden Ring, I asked him to turn back, it took a while before we were at the Arbat again, and she had, of course, gone. It took me a long time finding a coin for the phone, I dialled, Olga answered: she informed me coldly that Gulya was in the shithouse: knowing her manner, I didn't take it personally. I said I'd call by for Gulya tomorrow after breakfast, doubting she'd wait for me after what happened today.

Next morning, while I was standing in the lobby, the Intourist guide herded past a clutch of our old ladies. Gulya appeared: she was fresh, bright, enchanting, and I caught myself thinking that one's perceptions radically alter just by not sleeping with a girlfriend two nights in a row. I put my arm round her shoulders, she put hers round my waist, a mutual gesture that yesterday was forgotten. I took her up to the rotunda at the top of the Peking restaurant, where there used to be a charming and usually half-empty buffet, where you could drink Georgian Kinzmarauli, nibble olives and look out over the rooftops of Moscow. She said she'd phoned Paris that morning. And that while she'd been in the Soviet Union her flat had been searched. She said it casually, with none of the romantic excitement of our local dissidents when they managed to get into a similar scrape. I asked what on earth the KGB would want from her? At this she broke into such uncontrollable fits of laughter, I thought she'd gone crazy. It was Interpol, she gasped, and seeing the stupid look on my face, explained she'd let members of the Red

Brigades spend a couple of nights at her flat, Red Brigades or Red Army Faction or whatever, the people who'd been frightening the wits out of West Berlin that year. They were just old friends from the Sorbonne, she added, probably trying to reassure me that she wasn't herself a kidnapper and didn't put bombs in cars.

It's hard to explain, but at that precise moment I understood with incredible clarity the depth of the void that divided our worlds. It was an instantaneous feeling of envy and despair, what children feel when the grown-ups go off to a party or the theatre and they're put to bed. Then the feeling changed to one of shame: for our small, glum world, for our wretched partying and dangers, for the fact that we don't know how to live.

She must have been able to read it on my face. She began to talk about herself: surprisingly I'd found out very little about her all the time we'd been together. What she told me was exactly what you might hear from millions of women anywhere — about her being married at nineteen, her talented fifteen-year-old son, her being in love for years with a man, he was married, they tried living together, the three of them, but it didn't work out, about Russian Paris, about her gambler father, who lost everything and then left her mother, who now grows a Russian variety of cucumber in a castle garden near Paris which his new wife let him have. She wasn't trying to impress me, just show me that people everywhere are just people, and then when I'd relaxed, our talk somehow turned to the Mediterranean, to Greece, to the fishermen who eat olives pips and all, whereas the French leave them, they just nibble off the flesh and suck them clean. Like you and me? Like you and me. We were coming to the end of the fourth bottle and we were happy in each other's company again. Before going to have lunch, I took her out onto Herzen Street, to show her the famous sculpture of a Red Army man gripping his banner just so that when you look at him from side on, he is in fact wanking, with a look of blissful triumph on his face.

They flew out next morning. I don't think I'd ever been to the international part of Sheremetyevo-2 before, it had only just been built. The tour group was still huddled in front of the customs desks — on this side of the border, you could still hear Ritulya's squeaky bass mama trying to suppress her sobs, Olga and Dima were still saying things to each other, Gulya and I were still in a clinch, but I already felt the sobering realisation, that they would now present their bags for inspection, then as they picked them up they would turn and give us one last look, and the curtain would fall, they would breathe with relief the air of their own world, difficult and free, while we would be left like fish out of water, flapping our gills under our Soviet bell jar. I nearly burst into tears.

3.

It was just before New Year, and here I was again at Sheremetyevo-2, hanging around the customs hall, not upstairs in departures this time, but downstairs in arrivals. The plane was delayed. Only a few people were meeting the flight, so there probably weren't many passengers. I was trying to identify which of them were KGB — at that time we used to see them everywhere, and it was a favourite pastime, even kind of bon ton in moderately respectable circles, to work out who of your acquaintances were *stukachi*, informers — when I saw what struck me as a most improbable person in these surroundings. He was a thug, about seventeen, of desperate and dissolute appearance, who looked as if he'd been sleeping rough. He was dressed with some claims to criminal fashion, flared trousers of a dirty grey colour only the Soviets managed to produce — we stopped wearing flares ten years before — but with a feature that obviously made them super-chic — one half of a metal zipper sewn onto each leg; despite the bitter cold outside, all he had on top of an improbable shirt printed with cockerels was a miserably thin jacket, albeit double-breasted and with a half-belt, that was obviously too small for his strapping shoulders; his incredibly stupid-looking face was dotted with the red splodges of recently squeezed pimples, tufts of straw stuck out of the corners of his big wet lips, and his crooked pudding basin haircut looked piebald and shiny — maybe he rubbed in sunflower oil to get it to stick down better. He was holding exactly the same bouquet of red carnations, wrapped in cellophane and spotted with drops from melted snowflakes and was peering just as timidly into the hidden depths of the border zone, and his tin-coloured eyes had the same look of alarm as mine, as if he were being sent out on his first burglary. No, he couldn't have relatives abroad, Lord above, he couldn't, and was probably meeting a girlfriend. Like I was.

I had plenty of time to savour the similarity between us at leisure. Of course, in our backyard we lived on different levels, but here, face to face with the West, so to speak, I had no real grounds for claiming I was very much different to him. I was merely curious to see the person who had spent her hard-earned pounds — the flight we were waiting for was from London — to spend New Year in chilly Russia with this particular beau. And see that person I did. Never before or since have I seen such an elegant man. He was a lord. He was a man who spread the scent of wealth, luxury and abundance far beyond his person.

Glowing, his arms spread wide, he flew across the space separating passport control from customs, leaving the other passengers behind; he said something to the customs officials in English and then he was here, his radiant smile obscured by streams of tears, a step way from the object of his affection he suddenly stopped and covered his eyes, then he bent forward and nestled his carefully groomed greying head against a stubbly cheek. The lad went crimson and tried to push his flowers at the lord, shoving the fist that clenched the bouquet into his ribs. I was so riveted by this scene that I failed to notice

Gulya, waving a rolled-up glossy magazine at me in the distance.

I had gotten a telegram from her two days before. Before then there'd been letters — tender, grateful letters. Of course, the very fact of keeping up a correspondence presupposed a meeting at some point, but that she would decide to spend Christmas with me came as a complete surprise. She was wearing an incredibly beautiful full-length fox fur coat, a light golden colour with white underfur, the tips gleaming silver in the artificial neon light. Her bare head rose graciously from out of this gleaming russet cloud, and her clear blue short-sighted eyes gleamed from afar.

She had problems with customs. I couldn't hear what she was saying to the young officer, I could see her explaining something animatedly, not looking in my direction, opening her magazines and shaking them in front of his nose. A more senior officer came over and the question was settled — not in Gulya's favour. She gestured in vexation, grabbed her two suitcases, which hadn't been examined and stepped onto the Russian shore. After we had kissed she gave me a crafty look: I had them, she said. It turned out the couple of issues of *Playboy* and *Penthouse*, which the guardians of the moral purity of Soviet territory had fought to keep out, were purely a diversion; in one of the uninspected bags she was conveying some banned books on philosophy: two fat volumes of Sergei Bulgakov, several pocket editions of Berdyaev and the latest issue of *Kontinent* — all of which she'd bought at YMCA-Press, the Russian publishers in Paris. I thanked her, of course, but she could see I was taken aback and explained that this was what Dima always asked Olga to get him and Gulya had decided I'd probably like them, too. I already had Nikolai Berdyaev, reading *Kontinent* always made me as morose as reading the Soviet literary magazines, while Sergei Bulgakov was, I must confess, way over my head. So Bulgakov and Berdyaev and *Kontinent* were all disposed of for a very decent price and secured the funds both for visits to restaurants and drink. I presume Dima did the same with Olga's books, if in fact those books, which were fairly pricey even in Paris, ever reached him: Olga preferred sending him clothes picked up from the flea market — *merde aux puces*, Gulya used to say — which he used to sell, and one of Gulya's trunks was intended for Dima.

I cadged a ride back on the Icarus bus from the airport by pretending to be a relative. We laughed about Gulya having the presence of mind of a partisan, but as we chattered I tried desperately to think of a way to tell her about my current situation. Over the past six months a lot had changed in my life: I had divorced and was free, my book had come out, I was renting a comfortable dacha in Vnukovo, and kept my champagne in the snowdrifts around the house, and everything would be great were it not for the fact that a week after Gulya left a certain person had appeared in the little room I rented as a work space in a half-burnt-out *kommunalka*, communal flat, on Novoslobodskaya with a suitcase and an ageing spaniel — Galchonok. And as always when a woman arrives with a suitcase she stays a while longer than she thought, and so she was now preparing a feast out at the dacha. What had happened was this: her artist *cohabité* had also decided to emigrate to the promised land, and he, too, decided not to take her with him, because to do that he would have had to marry her, and getting married, he told her, was the last thing he wanted to do. I didn't come out the loser at all, because Galchonok was a marvellous cook and housekeeper, was cheerful, prudent and adroit in handling money, and was very understanding about Gulya's unexpected telegram, even quite excited about it. I only had to explain the situation to Gulya, whose reaction — despite her broad views and experience of life *à trois* — I was none too sure about. Of course, it wouldn't be difficult to pretend I thought it was completely natural, but I had my doubts about whether Gulya, if she knew in advance how things lay, might not find somewhere other than Vnukovo to see in the New Year for the same money. We arrived at the hotel and I still hadn't told her.

This time she was staying at the Intourist on Gorky Street. In the lobby a delegation of Scandinavians couldn't take their eyes off her, all the men in the group turned, as if by order, and watched her walk past. Swedes, said Gulya, and explained: they're looking at my coat, not me. It did look fabulous. Do you like it? I didn't have to pretend I was deeply impressed. Great, it's for you from me, for Christmas!

This was too much; while she sorted herself out in the room, I said I was going for a drink. Of course, I couldn't accept the coat, but the coat wasn't the point. Gulya, obviously, had serious intentions. Naturally I had a reserve position: my friend Zhenya had a two-room flat and had promised me shelter. I was certain Gulya and he would get on. But I couldn't run away and hide all the time Gulya was here: guests had been invited for New Year, and anyway Galchonok was waiting for me back at the dacha — for us, as a matter of fact. But then you know very well what a pain it is to be caught between two women, neither of whom you want to lose.

Not less than an hour had passed, I had come to the end of my third glass of champagne, but Gulya still hadn't come down. I went to fetch her. As soon as the *dezhurnaya*, the floor lady, saw me come out of the lift on her floor, she came scurrying over in alarm. Your relative, she gasped, she's looking for you... She came out into the corridor... I couldn't see what was so sensational about a guest coming out to look for her cousin in the corridor. Yes, but she came out... naked, said the *dezhurnaya*, and added — and she was crying!

Gulya's door wasn't locked. She was lying in her underwear on the bed and was, indeed, sobbing. Quietly, though, whimpering, really. I asked what the matter was: you went away, you didn't even kiss me, you just ran off to your tarts... I examined her eyes, sniffed the air: no trace of grass, so she'd either been dropping tabs or, which would have been much worse, was on the needle. The last supposition, fortunately, turned out to be false. She hadn't taken any tablets, either: there was a large bottle of Beefeater with the top unscrewed behind the bedside table. And no sign of tonic. Naturally, I comforted her: and splashed myself a gin, since I was in a mild state of panic. For all her impetuosity, there still had to be a pretty good reason for such a storm of emotion. She was behaving like someone who has made a decision. Her sentiments made her want to do something grand, and ignoring my protestations, she ordered dinner from room service: caviar, champagne, sturgeon. It didn't enter her head to get dressed when the waiter wheeled a little table into the room — she just wrapped herself up in the sheet. We had a drink, fooled around a little, kissed, though I was on tenterhooks the whole time. The hotel staff knew there was a Soviet visitor on their floor; in these cases their line of action was absolutely predictable: I would be lucky if the *dezhurnaya* came to throw me out and told security afterwards. Usually they covered their backs and did it the other way round. Gulya sensed I was uneasy, but interpreted it in her own way: she poured us more champagne and ceremoniously raised her glass — I've decided to get you out of here. I didn't understand immediately what she had in mind, for a second I imagined she had worked out a plan for shipping me out in a double-bottomed suitcase or the boot of a car; and I automatically raised my eyes to the ceiling — for some reason I was firmly convinced that the microphones in hotel rooms must always be there and the smoke detectors always raised my darkest suspicions. Fuck them, said Gulya, catching my look. And she explained that I mustn't worry, she'd spoken with her son; the son understood and wasn't against it. And then she began with icy matter-of-factness to enumerate the steps that had to be taken: go to the French Embassy and have them send a declaration of the forthcoming marriage to the Paris mairie; go to a translation bureau and have them translate her divorce decree; go to a notary, then the registry office — she pulled out the paper on which she had all the necessary steps written down, and showed me some very serious-looking document with seals and heraldic stamps that certified the dissolution of her marriage. The phone rang and it was for me. I took the receiver and told the *dezhurnaya* I was on my way out. Things began to turn nasty. I had difficulty persuading Gulya to get dressed and pack what she needed in a separate bag: she resisted, she wanted to drink champagne and was going to shit and shit on the KGB. When I led her past the table at the end of the corridor, a man in plainclothes was standing next the *dezhurnaya*. He didn't try to stop us and we made it out of the hotel. We found a taxi and set off for Zhenya's in Kuntsevo; it was a long way and Gulya to my relief dozed in the car. It was silly, of course, but I wanted to go to Galchonok at the dacha, and I certainly didn't want to get married. Strange, but the thought of marrying Gulya had never entered my head. I suddenly felt good at home. This was a long-awaited opportunity, but I didn't want to take it up. I was happy with the winter, the dacha, I was writing a new book, I was living with a woman who had been born in this city, like me. I knew that in the future I would regret missing this chance more than once.

When we awoke next morning on a low uncomfortable ottoman in a room with peeling wallpaper and a battered piano into which the owner sprinkled rolling tobacco to keep away the moths, and out in the middle a single armchair in which Zhenya used to sit, his knees tucked up, and compose his virtuoso texts in tiny handwriting that criss-crossed the pages of the school exercise books, I did my best to explain. I have to hand it to Gulya — she took what she heard perfectly calmly. She only said that her offer of yesterday remained in force, and she would be very pleased to see in New Year with my friends and girlfriend. I was very grateful; I dished out champagne, I asked Zhenya — and he read his poems; it was the thirty-first and we had to go, and everything, it seems, was passing off very well.

She didn't cry until the evening. We were all sitting at the table, but the television was turned on, "Man and the Law" was on — the manager of a railway restaurant car had stolen a couple of cases of condensed milk and ditto tinned meat; Gulya burst into tears. The guests looked at her blankly, but she explained that in France they would only put a man on national television if he'd done something like *barbecue his grandmother*, but not for stealing tinned pork — and I began to have my suspicions that she was definitely becoming disillusioned with left-wing ideology.

Actually, New Year passed off well, everything was very cosy and people behaved themselves, we just couldn't go to bed. It would have been silly to put my ladies in separate beds and then for me to go and sleep somewhere else. So at about five in the morning, the three of us — Gulya, Zhenya and I — set off to Moscow by train. I can remember, there was an unreal snowfall, an intoxicating light-headedness from lack of sleep, a joyous feeling of the beginning not of a new year but of a new world, and of happiness at the fact that we were in Russia. Maybe I had a vague notion that I ought to reveal this country to Gulya — explain its frosts and snow, its power to bewitch, and so justify myself, soften the blow of my refusal, make her understand that it wasn't the other woman, it was this snowfall, the hoar crystals swirling over the deserted fields; I suggested we get off at Peredelkino and we got there in time for morning service. Dawn was already pale in the sky, but the candles inside the church blazed as if it were dark. Strangely enough there were a lot of young faces, and the priest was young, there was a week to go before Orthodox Christmas. Zhenya was concentrated in prayer, I lit a few candles — for Gulya, and also crossed myself before the icon of the Virgin.

The idea of visiting Pasternak's grave was Zhenya's, strangely enough. I had never fancied this ritual, and three pine trees on his grave "like three girlfriends" made me sick, though that wasn't the poet's fault, naturally. Anyway, we had with us some fortified Crimean sherry — that sherry, I remember its cloying taste in the cold so well. To get to the cemetery we had to wade through snow that was nearly waist deep, so we had to stop a few times, drinking wine from the bottle every time. Here I found myself thinking, how durable everything in this world is — everything except us, transient mortals — and how nothing has changed in the twenty-odd years since the poet was also walking along this path to catch a train just after first light, and shivered inwardly, exhilarated by his trackless homeland.

We spent the last days of Gulya's stay in Moscow, drunk; we hardly ever left Zhenya's flat, we talked and talked, or more precisely Gulya talked, and she sometimes struck me as being a Russian cosmopolitan and not a very happy woman, who had come to Moscow to talk. It was touching how well she got on with Zhenya and he gave Gulya his guitar as soon as she mentioned she'd always wanted to have a seven stringed one. Poor Zhenya, he mourned the loss of that guitar long afterwards. He didn't play it himself, but he needed that instrument: at that time all the kids, almost literally, could strum something, and it was actually quite a handy way to get things going, ask somebody to play something, pretend you liked it and say how good it was.

As her departure drew closer, Gulya began to slide. She would grab for a glass, she was drinking much more than usual, then she would suddenly fall back and go to sleep in mid-sentence, but no sooner had Zhenya and I tiptoed out and pulled the door to, than she'd call us back and demand another drink. She was tired, of course, who wouldn't be, but at the same time there was something feverish about her. She would start telling us how she dreamed of selling her apartment in *Quartier latin* — sell her practice, her patient list, and go and work in Cambodia or Africa. She told us how she spent last Christmas in a flashy mountain resort in Switzerland, and once the people in a restaurant made her so angry she went up on the stage, grabbed the microphone from the singer, swore at all the diners in Russian and sang the Internationale. Those arseholes joined in, she recalled with understandable irritation.

At some point Zhenya asked her cautiously to take some of his work and send it on to a publisher, she agreed with much enthusiasm. It's only now that Zhenya's texts are printed on both sides of the border, but at the time there was no point in him trying to publish even a line of his gay confessions here, and during his lifetime — he died three years later — he wouldn't have seen himself in print. Gulya apparently decided that the texts were undoubtedly subversive, hence extremely dangerous, and approached the business with the seriousness of a seasoned conspirator — her tactic was simple, she chose the most effective weapon against the customs and the easiest for her to carry off — she got dead drunk.

Before we got on the bus she looked decidedly squiffy: dressed in her expensive fur, blurry eyed, with her seven-string guitar and swaying. Dima came as well, looking very Brynner-ish in a leather jacket and boots, but still Che Guevara-ish. He brought a five-kilo tin of black caviar for Gulya to give to Olga — Olga sold the caviar to a restaurant and Dima received yet another parcel of *merde aux puces* — and tried to explain that you had to put the tin on its edge in the bag so that it was at the right angle to the movement of the baggage through the X-ray machine, but Gulya's answer was concise — don't give a shit — and left Dima to ask me, if anything untoward happened, and if it should be possible, could I bring the tin back and return it to him, Dima. I promised.

Zhenya and I put Gulya on the bus, sat behind her, and we were barely on our way when she demanded a sip of brandy. Things weren't going too badly until a little way beyond the Ring Road, when we were out in the open fields and Gulya wanted the toilet. Despite our protestations that she didn't have long to wait, Gulya would have none of it and began pressing the stop button to tell the driver. He eventually got fed up and stopped. Swaying dreadfully, Gulya got down onto the road — not a bush in sight. She fell in the ditch, swam the crawl about three metres over the soft snow, got to her feet, hitched up her fox coat, dropped her trousers, flashed her white bum, but then she tried to squat, and her bum plunged into the snow. *Bidet à la russe*, somebody joked, the bus laughed, the tension eased.

Her fellow travellers supported her past customs. She wasn't in a state to kiss us good-bye, although when she was propped up against the passport control booth, she suddenly roused herself and started waving frantically, though not at us, at somewhere else. She dropped the guitar with a terrible crash to the stone floor, but it didn't seem to be broken. But her ruse was absolutely spot on: it never entered anybody's head to examine her bags, so that both Dima's caviar and Zhenya's works got safely over the border...

I didn't hear a cheep from her for a long time. It wasn't until the spring that Zhenya, not I, received a glossy postcard. It didn't come from either Cambodia or Africa, but from Majorca: it vaguely resembled Yalta, only the sea was bluer, the light was brighter, and the hotel in the foreground was more luxurious. On the other side she had written:

LIFE GOES IN COMPLETLY OTHER DIRECTION

in capital letters.

I never heard from her again.

Round Dance

I think of my life as going in seven-year cycles — like Tolstoy, who pinched the idea from Buddhism, and they apparently worked it out by observing cycles of solar activity — be that as it may, one particular spring I felt mighty nervous as the end of my fourth cycle approached. There were some statistical grounds for worrying about the changes I knew would happen — every fateful seventh year something happened; at seven I had ringworm, ended up in hospital, missed starting school and my copybook handwriting was never as good as my classmates'; at fourteen I first had sex — also something of an event; at twenty-one, when I was in my fourth year at University, the faculty *partkom*, Party Committee, had me expelled under dubious circumstances, I nearly had to go into the Army and even — just for a few days — ended up in Butyrki prison; this time I had finished a novel, the editor had written his report, which concluded that unless the author changed his ideological-artistic stance the book was unpublishable, I had been awarded official status as a writer, which simplified relations with the police, and had finally made up my mind to leave the country but was lazy about doing it, I kept putting it off — finish one more story, stay one more spring... Pushing fate, however, I kept trying, of course, to get as close as I could to the West, and at the end of March I broke loose from my moorings — heading for Lithuania and ending up in Palanga, where I settled into a small but perfectly decent room — sit-up bath, cable radio and a view over the tops of pine trees — to write my next book — it was to be taken from me in due course. The new work didn't go well from the start: I began writing without a plan, to a great extent at random, letting my fingers walk across the keys, couldn't catch the tone, but kept on moving forward regardless, I still hadn't twigged that application and diligence are not the best allies when writing, took Hemingway at his word, and gave myself an honourable discharge for work completed in terms of quantity, if not of quality. Actually, something of what I wrote did end up in the final text, but later all my drafts, plans, notes and the almost finished manuscript, plus a whole heap of papers accumulated during fifteen years of writing, were seized in a search, so that today all that remains are the book's two epigraphs, which is all I can quote from memory, but which give a pretty clear indication that one of the principle forces behind my pen was claustrophobia. The first was from Montaigne, something along the lines of: I love freedom so much that I cannot imagine the existence of people who are denied access to big towns, and were I forbidden entry into some remote corner of the Indies, I would even then feel myself in some part slighted. And a note: a tribute to our national self-abasement. The second one — prophetic — was from

Dostoyevsky, a remark of Epanchina: Stop getting carried away, it's high time you saw reason; all this abroad business, all this Europe of yours is a fantasy, and us going abroad is a fantasy, you mark my words, you'll see!

It all happened eighteen months before the Moscow Olympics, and young artist-craftsmen were summoned from all corners of the empire to this *Dom tvorchestva*, Artists Resort. Young meant under thirty-five, the age limit set by the art mafia for membership in the so-called youth section, a kind of cesspool of excessively keen young talent, desperate to get its snout into the trough of the *goszakazy*, state commissions, which were the only way to make a decent living in the visual arts — only the most experienced had the courage to sell their work independently to foreigners, while local buyers paid peanuts, if they bought at all. Officials from the Art Fund and Ministry of Culture brought them together in Palanga, banking on youthful inventiveness and reduced circumstances, so that they would invent Olympic souvenirs, which could be flogged off to Olympic visitors for hard currency, and ambitious crafty types, hoping to snatch an intangible prize, came for the freebie. The craftspeople were almost all if not exactly youthful, then at least, let us say, relatively young women — of a great diversity of eye colour, shape and size: two Leningrad ladies, who worked in textiles; a Kirghiz girl who embroidered felt; an Uzbek who made ornaments for carpets; a Tadzhik who did linocuts; a Kazakh who worked in metal; a Georgian who painted frescoes; an

Armenian engraver; an Azerbaidjani designer; a Ukrainian tapestry weaver; a Belorussian lace maker; a Moldavian towel embroiderer; a Latvian jeweller; no less than three Estonian potters; a patriotic Russian lady from Vologda who made bast shoes and did poker work; a shy Selkup girl who made some kind of national instrument with ornamental encrustation — whistles, I think they were; and a Turkmen smith from Ashkhabad. The only nationality not on the team were Lithuanians, but we were in Lithuania, so they might have had their own separate gathering. Besides them, the Resort had also acquired a number of mining folk from the Donbass — they never left the building, spent the day playing billiards and the night on the bottle — plus a ridiculously minute ballerina from Kiev with a sad leather-clad husband — her choreographer and, from certain indications, an unsuccessful homosexual. So, not counting the Turkmen smith, I was the sole male representative of the intelligentsia with heterosexual tendencies and at the centre of an international gathering of women.

Sometimes I'd invite two or three of them for a walk when I'd finished work, taking care, when I was out of bed, not to stay too long alone with any one of them, but more often wandering off on my own through the empty streets. The weather was sunny, the little town was clean, the air was filled with that special seaside light. In the cool basement bar they served black salty nibbles with the beer; in a little cafe they served thick Turkish coffee;

in a glass pavilion on the sea front they provided the local curative water; out on the T-shaped pier, which pointed towards Sweden, they sold crude beads of rough, dark amber. The gulls watched over a strip of dark water left by the ice as it retreated from the shore. It was a corner of the empire that had not been despoiled by deliberate neglect, by Russian backhandedness and socialist inefficiency, it was still cared for, and to so many Russian kids this little strip of Baltic soil had seemed to be the West, after all the West was just a stone's throw away. Even after being Sovietised, this land breathed the memory of its European years: churches here showed the influence of Gothic; the streets had been touched by Art Nouveau; the private cottages and villas had retained an honest face, their interiors proudly displaying a familiarity with Biedermeier. Even the peasant faces of this little country expressed, somewhat to their own surprise, something distantly reminiscent of solid Hanseatic values. It seemed that the atmosphere itself, the national spirit of tidiness compelled us mid-continental multi-tribal heathens to throw our cigarette ends into the pottery urns on the street, to drink Balsam, the local herbal infusion, with our coffee and not on its own, by the glass, to sip Bocha like schoolgirls out of ridiculously tiny glasses and to come down to the night restaurant in jacket and tie — if only to catch the unprecedentedly erotic show put on every Friday night. The secret thrill was spoiled by a certain amount of irritation: why couldn't they do everything any old how in this place, why couldn't everything be done off the cuff, instead of trying to ensure that every day, day in day out, you could breathe easily, respect yourself — why not, why couldn't they? They were part of us...

We settled down quickly together in the Resort. Everyone was affected by the spirit of Western moderation and tolerance, there was almost no room for crude Asiatic passions. One of the Estonians — she painted on ceramics — a thin girl with a very full lower lip called Eve, went on and on about how she had been married in Finland, and when she was asked why she'd come back, replied that all was not lost, she was now going to marry his friend. The Kazakh — the metal worker — had small, strong hands and a dry, flat pelvis, her name was Anna, not at all Kazakh, which is why I remember it. One of the Petersburg textile designers, the younger of the two, liked to remind everybody what a good wife she was; the Uzbek — she of the carpet ornaments — avoided traditional methods, fooling herself that she was still a virgin, but was considerate, and often asked whether I minded her smell — when she sweated, she did, indeed, smell a little too spicy for my taste, rather cloves-like; the big-bosomed Armenian engraver really was a virgin at twenty eight; the linocut maker from the mountains of Tadzhikistan was forever writing letters to her fiancé, an Aeroflot pilot, also Tadzhik; the Belorussian was trapped in a loveless marriage, I was her second, and after intercourse she often wept quietly and gratefully; the Azeri designer turned out to be a cheat, several times she was caught using other people's brushes; the Georgian fresco painter was a real artiste, she laughed whenever I kissed her, and then would suddenly back away and frown in a fine theatrical demonstration of surprise; the sliest of all turned out to be the Moldavian, with her skinny legs and mean disposition, she intrigued against the Latvian girl, who had big feet and very long ears, distended, probably, from wearing the horrible earrings she made, she was also not averse to a bit on the side; the crafstwoman of patriotic bent liked to recite lyric poetry, but that wasn't all — every time I was about to come she would break into a throaty, cloying warble — uuu-tyu-tyu-tyu-tyu, as if she was calling in the geese, and the sperm would stop dead in the middle, like something stuck in your throat. The Turkmen smith spent his evenings in his room playing Selkup whistles — very dolefully. We didn't include the ballet people in our family though the diminutive dancerette, fifty years old, but not looking a day of it, tried her best to attach herself to us, while her leather husband disappeared off to the billiards room, though she warned him aloud, publicly, that sooner or later he'd get hit there. In short, we enjoyed a decent, well-ordered lifestyle that was ennobled by the Baltic air, even if it was a little patriarchal and monotonous. To keep myself amused, I would suggest ideas for souvenirs to one or another of my craftsladies, but it seemed there was an unwritten canon law in these matters, at any rate they all took their Olympic projects very seriously, and maybe not just in the hope of making the break and earning serious money. I think all of us, half-consciously, had our private hopes in connection with the Olympics, after all it was going to be a world event, which could not in itself be anything but a boost for us provincials. We felt the Olympics would make Moscow the capital of the world — if only for a short time, the Iron Curtain would be left in tatters, nine months later the Moscow Region would be full of different coloured babies, and our geriatric rulers, weeping tender tears, would say to us, their loyal subjects: go out and make love with all the different kinds of people there are on our little planet, go on, all of you. Distances would shrink, and all of us would hear the song of a friend from far away, it had already sort of happened once, though it hadn't quite come off. Who could have known then that our leaders' paranoia was so grim that the KGB would make sure that the millions of Muscovites never met the thousands of foreigners, and the Intourist buses would speed down deserted streets, watched on every corner by groups of policemen with Asiatic faces. In short, I was not admitted to the mysteries of Olympic applied arts, and all I could do was return to my typewriter and the pages of my forthcoming ill-fated, freedom-loving novel.

Actually, I do recall a nagging dissatisfaction at the incompleteness of my international, even within the restricted framework of the then Soviet Union, harem. A yearning for perfection and a naive fondness for simple symmetry compelled me in the end to seek out Lithuanian girls — and if craftswomen were not available, then what was wrong with the numerous retainers of our Resort, first and foremost the girl from the library, who shared the closest kinship, it seemed to me, with Russian letters — a tall, spotty female of about nineteen, a bit sabre-toothed and the legs ditto, long and curved like a blade. I abandoned this tack when I went into the library after breakfast one day and spotted a bright red motorcycle helmet on the low periodicals table. The helmet's owner was not, it transpired, a reader, because in the gap between the shelves I saw the librarian pressed back against the classics, her skirt hitched up and her face as puce as her admirer's helmet. My gaze turned to the dining room, especially since I was in there more often than the library, and where every second shift was taken by a very pretty blonde waitress, strong-looking, with powerful, thick, quick legs in dark nylons, a short skirt hitched up on her bum and flashing thighs; but then, as is so often the case, the lower half of her body, tailor-made for child-bearing, failed to find the requisite matching characteristics in the upper half — she was completely flat-chested, yet her lips were voluptuous and the skin under her chin was a tender bluish shade, she had a winning smile and mischievous eyes. I have to admit that my flirting and making passes made little impression on her; she had no connection with culture as the craftswomen, her sturdy legs were planted firmly on her own soil, and to her we were just visitors, temporary residents, perhaps we all — the Turkmen, the miners and I — all looked the same to her. We were many and she was one, and for the unsophisticated mind that is a very seductive state of affairs, it breeds self-assurance, and this is something that service workers, taxi dispatchers and clerks at the *voenkomat*, the army draft board, often suffer from, a conviction that their uniqueness is not the product of circumstance, but goes with the job, and so often these girls turn out to be disappointed and unhappy. In short, all I could do was reflect vindictively on the situation, since it seemed the miners were much more likely to score with her, and the more sober specimens among them possibly did. It was annoying, but not the first time. I was chronically out of luck with the service sector — stewardesses and hairdressers, and with other trades, and sometimes I reflected bitterly that I was doomed to dragging out my days in the company of female members of the various creative unions. On only one occasion did a compliment of mine if not strike, then at least graze its target: she confessed her name was Grazhina, smiled languidly and for some reason added that her sister was called Myaile.

Curiously, I then started bumping into Grazhina in various places nearly every day, even when she wasn't on duty. I encountered her one afternoon in a cafe, looking a bit tousled, her lips feverish, shadows under her eyes; she was sitting at the next table, heavily made up and wearing cheap costume jewellery, she didn't seem in any obvious hurry, though in an hour's time she was supposed to be serving us dinner; the man she was sitting with had his back to me. He had on a long brown leather overcoat and was bent over the table, his right elbow stretched out, his head low, and he was looking out from underneath his brows. I could see his slender fingers, his nails clean and even, playing with the hair on his right temple. She was upset, looked through me, occasionally our eyes did meet, and then her heavily mascara'ed eyelashes immediately dropped — with weary coquetry. Who knows, maybe she just didn't feel like flirting with me at work; or she wanted to get back at her partner. Whatever — I winked at her.

The next bit was strange: her partner gave a sudden start — when I'm sober my reflexes are equally speedy — moved his head as though to identify the source of the intercepted signal; then without turning shouted hoarsely in Lithuanian. The barmaid immediately came out from behind the counter and brought him a glass of brandy, even though the place was self-service. Grazhina — for a moment she seemed to me to be full of deceit and danger — became even more languid, though it was a poor disguise for the obvious fact that she was scared. Where did she get it from, that strange glow of hers, that mysterious way of smiling without parting her lips? He caught her look and turned round clumsily: a red face, bags under his eyes, and yet he was undoubtedly good-looking, too good-looking for a thug like him. He threw his arm heavily over the back of the next chair, poking the woman who was sitting in it under the shoulder blades. He studied me closely for a moment, then said: *"Ei, truputja konjako? Kodel tu toks lyudnas shiandien?"*

I thought he was asking me to treat him, but the waitress was already hurrying over with a glass of brandy for me. Take it easy, when in Rome... just go with the flow. I thanked him, pressed my hand to my heart and, making a bow, picked up my glass. He raised his. His hand was steady. "How come you know her?" He pointed with his glass at the girl.

She turned away. It felt like the beginning of one of those dumb situations you should never get involved in in strange places. I put the glass back down on the table.

"Doesn't want to drink", he said to his companion. "Wonder why that could be? Who is he, anyway?"

She replied in Lithuanian, though he spoke in Russian specially so I would understand. She was obviously denying all knowledge of me, which was strange. I decided that Grazhina must be terrified of her boyfriend, though what there could possibly be between us seeing as all she'd done was serve me breakfast... I hadn't managed to come to any conclusions, when up popped a country bumpkin with a flat pockmarked face — in police uniform. He made a lazy pretence of saluting before barking something that sounded like *serjantauskas*, and then more comprehensibly — *vashi dokumenty*: your papers...

Really and truly, who was I? An alien, a foreigner, who was not protected by the unwritten male laws. The laws of the Lithuanian police weren't for me at all, a Russian. I gave my writer's ID to the *serjantauskas*. The lad turned it over with indifference and handed it to his leather boss.

"You have your passport?" the boss asked in Russian.

"Your passport?" the policeman translated with an accent.

I explained I was staying at the Artists Resort and that my passport was with the concierge. With reception, I hastily translated.

At this Grazhina's beau leant over the table and laughed theatrically. She burst into giggles, too, her fingers, with their fake gemstone rings, flying to cover her laughing mouth, though there had been nothing wrong with her teeth earlier that morning.

"You hear that, the Artists Resort", he chortled, poking her in the chest with my ID. "Grazhina..." He turned to me, looking remarkably sober: "They're twins. Everybody mixes them up. They like it. Take it in turns to date the same guy. But I can tell the difference. I can tell the difference, right, Myaile?" Mechanically clicking the two halves of my ID together, he played with it a moment before dropping it into his leather pocket.

This revelation I did not find in the least titillating; so what if they were twins? I was interested in something quite different — my ID. In those years, it was to me like a licence is to a driver. Without it I wasn't a writer. Not as far as the authorities or anybody else was concerned. Or even myself, perhaps. Without it I was unemployed, a bum and a *tuneyadets*, a work-shy element. The *serjantauskas* was leaving the cafe, and I went after him. A police jeep was parked in front. "Hey," I called to the sergeant, "what about my documents?"

He looked at me in surprise. "Nothing to do with me. He's not my boss. He's KGB. Ask him."

He got into the jeep and sped off. No, I didn't want to ask him. Quite the opposite, I quickly strode away from the cafe, wondering whether it wasn't high time I packed my bags and split for Mother Russia. The little town, meanwhile, kept making out it was Western Europe as if nothing had happened. Why the hell did I have to go flirting with this Myaile and this Grazhina? They were probably Polish anyway. But residents of Lithuania for all that, and so entitled to fill the vacant fifteenth place in our merry round dance... The next morning I was finishing off the interrupted chapter when a billiards-playing miner came charging into my room, out of breath: hey, writer, the manager wants to see you, you've got orders to come down. And added: there's somebody come.

Got orders, it sounded right. Asking would have been Jesuitical, hypocritical. I was spinning out time, walking slowly down the stairs, when it suddenly came into my head that the manageress, a plump peasant-looking woman who had ended up doing Party business purely by chance, could also figure in the charge sheet. I had no connection with the Artists Resort in her charge, according to the rules

I had to have given her some kind of letter of authorisation from the Writers' Union, not the full tariff for the room in cash. Ah well, in any case, with or without the manageress, I felt I'd landed myself in it and rightly so, even though strictly speaking I'd broken no law and wasn't guilty of anything in the narrow legal sense. But I was guilty in a higher sense, like any citizen of the empire, for the fact that I had fallen awkwardly under the screw of the mighty ship of state. Justice — according to the psychology of people at the fringes — is not from the Latin *justus*, but is a kind of vaguely existential category; innocence a rare stroke of luck, a gift of Fate, all the rest an ill-starred mouldering in a state of sin and godforsakenness, how on earth else did you come to have been born in this bitch of a country? Outwardly all meek and mild, but inwardly steeled to dissemble and dodge, I entered the manager's office. She was sitting at her desk, my red ID nestling in her hands like a baby bird, while my friend from yesterday sprawled in an armchair against the wall. When he saw me, he stood up, relaxed and smiling; today he was fresh; he didn't try to shake hands, but said affably:

"Come, come. How can you stay here without letting people know who you are? Kazimira Vitautasovna didn't know she had a guest from Moscow, a writer. We had to tell her."

The manageress gave me a mournful, bovine look.

"How do you like it here? How's the work going?" He was staring at me hard.

That was the magic power of an official paper. You could see that this KGB man, after he'd got hold of my ID and checked it wasn't a forgery, had absolutely no doubt — that ID would not have been issued in Moscow to just anybody.

"Terrific", I replied.

"By the way, Kazimira Vitautasovna, when do you have the event planned for?"

"Traditionally we round off the programme with it," she leafed through a flip-over calendar. "The twenty-sixth."

"And today is — the twenty-fourth. Excellent. Top level treatment, the full works. We'll do our bit..."

I remembered my craftsladies had told me that some kind of excursion was, indeed, planned to a fishing kolkhoz — rumour had it the day included a visit to a sauna and free booze. But the manageress was gabbling, and I knew what was on her mind: they'd always managed quite nicely in the past, thank God, without their help.

He was dark auburn, like me. Five years older, perhaps. My height, but narrower in the shoulders and bones. He had a short nose and dark eyes with a shifty, sort of sentimental, criminal expression. He smelt strongly of a disgusting Polish floral after-shave, which came in little straw-wrapped bottles and was on sale everywhere in those days.

"It's out that way," he said, flapping his hand westwards, towards Klaipeda.

"A tradition," said Kazimira Vitautasovna.

No, I really could not understand the delight, the suspicious euphoria of these on the whole not-so-young women, who didn't know each other terribly well, many of whom were wives and mothers, guardians, so to speak, of home and hearth, when given news of the programme and the date of the visit. Their readiness to take part in so dubious an enterprise as a communal sauna in a completely unknown place, probably in conjunction with God knows what else besides, I found distasteful... What do you expect? With what else other than hypocrisy could I conceal from myself the basic fact that I was jealous about my harem? While we were assembling at the bus, and then when we were on it, there was that special excitement in the air that always accompanies the anticipation of sin and the breaking of taboos — the way we had looked forward to a *bardak* at fifteen — and always creates a false sense of brotherhood among those present. The bus bowled along between two rows of poplars, pedantically whitewashed to the knee, the Moldavian girl was sharing a seat with the Latvian, the stingy Azerbaijani was offering the meek Belorussian the use of her shampoo, while the patriot was trying to persuade the Selkup and the smith to sing a folk song in chorus. After ten kilometres we turned towards the sea, dived into a pine wood, a sign stating that we had entered the closed border zone flashed by, and we were now as close to the West as we could be.

We stopped between two wooden buildings with fretwork ornamentation resembling Olympic souvenirs. We clambered out. A tall Lithuanian in suit and tie was waiting for us. He was the director of this progressive fishing enterprise, but he said not a word about inspecting the impressive production facilities. The director explained that the lower building was the sauna and the upper building was the guesthouse. Everything became horribly clear: we'd landed up in a reserve for entertaining the local *nomenklatura*, party and government bigwigs, maintained in herds under the communists — chief of police, head of the local KGB, postmaster, director of the food outlets, public prosecutor. The kolkhoz did, actually, net other fish, because when we were taken into the vast salon, which in more modest saunas would be called the dressing room, a milk churn was brought in, on which drops of condensation immediately formed, and a big dish of smoked eel. There was also an enormous electric samovar and a juke box with a light show, very popular in those days, was playing. Rainbow coloured specks of light danced on a collection of bottles at a bar that was as ethnically diverse as our little group. The next room contained heaps of fluffy towels and sheets. The director briefed us in broken Russian — basically he told us to make ourselves at home and enjoy our sauna the traditional way, boys and girls together. The door shut behind him. Great, my God, how wonderful, thank you everybody, this is great, trilled the lyrical patriot and did a pirouette. This was a summons to the rest, it stirred them to action. Oh, come on now, girls, the patriot exhorted, quick or the steam will go. But the steam was right there, and the girls needed no urging, they rushed to undress, paying the smith and myself not the slightest heed, and the keenest of all to strip naked, I observed, were the Muslim girls. Soon there was an abundance of naked flesh, breasts and shoulders, buttocks and pubes, and in such quantities women were not really stimulating, though there were a few, I must confess, with whom I hadn't made it. What struck the eye were birthmarks, pimples on backs and buttocks, lumpy skin, ugly, twisted toes and red crotches. They crowded, chattering, into the steam room, and the Turkmen and I followed them. In fact, the poor smith didn't share my rather negative reaction. His eyes shone, they sparkled, his manhood rose and seemed disproportionately large for his size, for his skinny, stumpy, bandy legs.

It would have been all right had it been a Russian bath house where you could make yourself busy, have a drink, lash someone with birch twigs, wheeze away; here it was like sitting in a hen house, looking at the legs opposite, classifying breasts by shape and dimension, by the direction of nipple thrust, classifying nipples by shade ranging from the almost black ones, with big pores, that stuck out like mushrooms of the sort you're never quite sure are edible, to tender pink ones, almost invisible, that just seemed to merge into the redness around them. Differences in the thickness of haunches, variations in the form of thighs, whether shoulders are rounded or angular, the number of folds in the stomach, the positioning of birthmarks, even differences in breasts are all secondary in the end, you quickly become inured to them and almost stop noticing. The real differences, the ones you don't forget, were, alas, hidden under identical little triangular black, auburn or ginger wigs. The Turkmen was fidgeting next to me, but my penis was as impeccably behaved as before, so that I undertook on our joint behalf to divert the ladies with amusing conversation. I must confess, though, that I was watching one of them very carefully — one of the Estonian team, very exotic-looking, half Estonian, half Buryat, I'd got her marked down for later because I hadn't reached the autonomous administrative units yet and she was laughing louder than anyone, though a sauna, to my mind, should incline one more to languor and contemplation.

Then the first ones in, all steamed up and raring to go, started dashing out and leaping with a squeal into the cold dip. I pushed the smith in there with them. He needed it. I wrapped myself in a sheet and went to check out the beer in the milk churn. A hurricane of hoppy fumes swirled up as I lifted the tight-fitting lid, fat dripped from the smoked eel, I dipped in a beer mug, drank deeply and felt that blissful rush, which may be no substitute for love, but for the sake of which our ancestors invented the steam bath. My nymphs emerged one by one while I was their cupbearer, serving each a mug of the ice-cold beverage that was halfway between country *kvass* and country beer, and a most deceptive drink it was, too. At first taste, it seemed harmless, but then you discovered its stunning ability to knock you off your feet. On top of all this the smith, feeling refreshed and wrapped to the throat in a peacock pattern sheet, thrust a glass of his own Turkmen brandy at everybody, and the unsuspecting ladies supped their beer, ate eel, and washed it all down with brandy from the desert sands of Turkmenia, where, if my knowledge of geo-botany tells me right, even the *saksaul* doesn't come into bloom every year. Whatever order might have still remained now disintegrated: some girl lingered in the sauna, some were taking showers, others couldn't tear themselves away from the churn; somebody was splashing in the cold pool, somebody else had gone in search of wine at the bar — I decided to follow the smith, wrapped myself more tightly in my sheet and went out onto the balcony for a cigarette. I inhaled, but when I looked down from the sky to earth, I saw, thirty metres away, my friend from the local KGB. My God, how could I have forgotten about him? He was fussing around a fire, tossing neatly trimmed logs onto it. I could see two women busy doing something a little way off, and though it was dusk by now, I recognised the twins, Myaile and Grazhina. He straightened up and waved to me lazily. In the remains of the daylight and the flaring fire I could see him well enough: he was in hunting costume as they would have said in another age, a fringed suede jacket, matching short boots and tight leather trousers — I'd dressed that way in my student days, thanks to the fact that Poland lived off

Western credits, things like that flowed to Moscow in an endless stream. But he was handsome, you couldn't deny it, the bastard. The sea, the sea, I heard behind me. The patriot pushed me aside and flitted out into the yard, a white sheet twined around her long naked body. She was obviously far from sober; she wove her way towards the bonfire, exclaiming with an enraptured smile — where is the sea?

The sea was where it had been all along, the other side of the nearest sand dune, and you could hear the sound of the waves distinctly in the silence. But I wasn't interested in the sea, I was overwhelmed with depression. As my tipsy naked lady friends drifted hypnotically past me to the fire, I felt a tide of compassion swell within me. Suddenly a shadow lifted from my inner vision and I saw all of them individually in amazing relief. I penetrated the soul and fate of each as if by magic. I saw the Vologda bast shoes maker suffering with her failure of a husband — a deputy director of a railway goods yard where there was a young nihilist train controller who was in love with her and wrote poetry, he had him fired and thrown out of the workers' hostel; I caught my quiet little Belorussian pulling her officer husband's boots off when he came home drunk, and then lying in bed pressing her hot breasts against his unresponsive back and whispering — hateful man, hateful; the Georgian had acquired a reputation as a *kikelka*, a tart — just because she'd been to art school and travelled to do her training, lived with a whole bunch of other artists in Prince Mochabeli's old palace, and how was she going to find a husband now; the Armenian's blood ran cold at the thought her brothers would find out and her thirty-year-old virgin girlfriends would understand everything; the Tadzhik girl cried a lot, flying Aeroflot Dushanbe-Moscow, Dushanbe-Leningrad, Dushanbe-Kiev, because the only place she could have her lover to herself was in aircrew hotels — back home he had two wives and a good few children; there was no such thing as *his friend* for the little Estonian, Eva, in a little town near Helsinki, from where she'd fled, homesick for her home town, for the view onto the cathedral square and the town hall from her window, even if her flat had no hot water or toilet. "Poor girls", I said to myself, "my poor, poor girls", because what else except sympathy and compassion are of any assistance when we know we are about to be made to suffer.

Because that was what was about to happen. The KGB man was going to start on my harem. Cut a swath through my defenceless herd: because I really could not declare here, a stone's throw from the civilised West, that all these fifteen women belonged to me alone. Even if we'd been in the Middle East, how could I, without eunuchs and devoted servants, have kept these poor creatures safe from the depredations of this greasy monster with the eyes of a crook and the authority of the Lubyanka.

I also came up to the fire. To one side all the gear for a barbecue had been set out. The charcoal was heating up, meat was marinating in two big enamelled dishes, and rows of thin skewers filed to deadly sharp points were stuck in rows into the frosty ground. It was all in the charge of the twin sisters, who looked very stylish: each in jeans, identical black woollen tops, snow white aprons, and a deep claret-coloured somewhat wilting rose pinned in her blonde hair. The KGB man was, indeed, an artist in his own line.

"Algis," he introduced himself as I approached, but, as before, did not offer me his hand. He knew my name well enough without having to be reminded, so I said nothing. He gave me a long treacherous look, full of menace. Then he threw up his hand. A light came on in the guesthouse — followed by a deafening blast of music. The ever-present driver emerged from the doors dragging a case of champagne. One of the sisters handed out glasses, while the other dispensed astringent bubbly, corks popped, the fire blazed, everyone clinked glasses with as much excitement as on New Year's Eve, and someone was already dancing, holding another of the girls round the waist, fooling around and laughing.

Algis gave me a glass. Raised his to mine. Our glasses touched for an instant, and looking each other in the eye, we drained them. There was something depraved and criminal in his manner and gesture, something cracked, displaced from its axis. It seemed as though he was silently proposing something in the nature of a duel. At this point one of the sisters appeared by his side, he slapped her heartily on the backside: Nice, aren't they, my girls? Bet you wouldn't mind mixing up these two!

He knew where to strike. It was most gentlemanly of him, offering me that kind of compensation. "Nice girls," I agreed, feeling not quite sober.

"Let's dance, dance, girls," the Vologda patriot called huskily, "drink and dance."

Our putative MC was as tight as a lord while the music thundered over the deserted dunes and the champagne flowed. The Turkmen was dancing, trying to keep his sheet around him, and the peacocks danced with him, the Selkup was clinging to him, she kept looking around and every so often let out a little squeal. "Bohemians," I said to Algis, as if in apology for the carryings on. "Yes. Artists," he nodded and put his right arm around my shoulder — in his left he was holding his glass. His thigh pressed against mine for a moment, and I could distinctly feel the hard leather holster hanging under his armpit.

This made me see red. I looked with contempt at the identical twin sisters, and then switched my gaze to my blossoming international round dance. No, you bastard, keep your hands off art, waitresses and tarts, that's your line of country, you KGB arsehole, us artists... He interrupted my inner monologue, beckoning me to follow him.

We walked side by side, to the sea, I in bath slippers and wrapped in a sheet, he all in suede and leather, with a pistol under his armpit. We crossed the dune, the horizon opened up before us. It was nearly dark, a wind was blowing from Europe, emptiness all around and the sea seemed naked; only a little light glinted somewhere to the left. See that? He pointed in its direction. See the light? That's already abroad.

"So close," the thought flashed through my mind, "Lord, so close!"

"Want to go there?" he asked. And then supplied the answer himself. "All you artists want to."

That's probably why they fenced off the border with these impenetrable kilometres-deep zones so we couldn't even see it... My companion reached under his armpit, I stiffened instinctively, but he pulled out a bottle of brandy. "Drink."

"You first."

He took two greedy pulls, screwed on the top and stuffed the bottle back in his pocket — his left one, I now realised. His hand slipped under my sheet and squeezed my naked shoulder: he suddenly leant over and started nibbling my ear passionately. God, what a cretin I was not to have seen it right from the start. Well, at least there was a certain logic: I had had the whole of the Soviet Union, with the exception of one republic, and the KGB, who kept its borders under lock and key, was going to fuck me. I pushed him hard — no, pushed not hit, I always considered answering a kiss with your fist to be in very poor taste, only women in male professions did that sort of thing — but he flew back about three metres and nearly fell. A second later I saw the muzzle of a pistol pointing at me.

The muzzle was small, a tiny hole that was almost

invisible in the gloom. Until this moment I'd only ever seen toy pistols pointed at my stomach, and maybe for that reason didn't really feel frightened.

"You're in a border zone," he said, quite without accent.

"He's not really going to shoot me, is he?' I thought. For attempting, in KGB-speak, to violate the state border. And to a degree this would be justice — by their laws. I might not have made the attempt, but the desire, the desire to break out of this country — cannot desire be equated with the attempt?

"Coward," he said.

I didn't consider myself a coward, though he said it with such hatred, that I felt the dark and cold come on me, what the hell had Montaigne to do with this. And suddenly he laughed. The same pseudo-Mephistophelian laugh I'd heard once before.

"I could shoot you like a dog," he shouted and reached in his pocket for the bottle and took a swig. "Or arrest you. But I don't need you. In five years you'll have lost your figure. Your arse'll be all flabby. An old arse that's no use to anyone," he shouted. "You'll have lost your hair, you'll have a pot belly. You'll just be another stinking Russian. You'll stink of shit. You already do smell of shit..."

Well, it didn't seem to me he'd be capable of soldiering on for the Party for too much longer. I wasn't going to listen to that hysterical homosexual crap. He waved his gun and kept shouting at my back as I climbed the dune. At the top I stopped and turned to look, no, not at him, at the feeble, glinting light, which was already abroad, the West. I could hardly make it out in the deepening gloom.

There was a round dance at the fire. Squeals and groans could be heard through the darkened window of the guesthouse. Judging by the fact that the Selkup was sitting on the porch and weeping inconsolably, I gathered that the smith was striking while the iron was hot. I grabbed one of the sisters and also went to use the facility. I did mix them up — in the light I think I would have been able to tell them apart by their smiles, but we didn't turn on the light. She was trying to tell me something in Lithuanian, but I had other things on my mind. I got on top, took aim — and the round dance was complete.

Anna and the Fountain

***W**e are all of us superstitious, even if only a little, cabalists of a kind: we see the text of our lives as a cryptograph, which we hope to be able to decode, harkening to our premonitions, trusting in omens, collecting coincidences, parallels, signs and portents. But the cipher is secure, and our efforts are useless. Does anybody really hope, even if he should manage to penetrate the scheme of fate, to alter it in the slightest? And so our curiosity is akin to Odysseus' courage in sailing from Ithaca and setting course for the pillars of Hercules, knowing full well that beyond them was the Ocean and water, water without end or limit... So, while we're on the subject of coincidences, they're how this story begins, and the sheer number of them, as any initiate in cabalistic ontology knows, is the surest sign of authenticity — so let's describe them in chronological order.

In the autumn of the pre-Olympic year described in the previous chapter, I had a fleeting affair with a Polish girl from the U.S. She was called Lola, she was beautiful and adventurous, though of a somewhat melancholy cast of mind. We met at my friend Osya's farewell party — he was leaving for America on an Israeli visa. We travelled together to Leningrad and watched *Bakhchisarayski Fontan* at the Kirov, then fucked in her room at the Moskovskaya

Hotel; we returned to Moscow and slept at Duda's place in Peredelkino, and it was only on the last night before her departure, when I came with a big bunch of roses and she murmured "not so gentle," that I knew I would never see her again. I was sad, I was rather smitten, by her full plebeian lips, the Slavic mould of her eyes and cheekbones, her breasts out of a *Playboy* centrefold — she had actually once worked for Hugh Heffner, as a secretary — the beauty of her arms and legs, and was quite prepared for a sequel. But — and I might as well admit it — I behaved like a besotted lover, I was attentive and tender, but even without all that crap, an impoverished Moscow author was the last thing she needed in a life in the fast lane.

Fast forward a couple of years. One hungover autumn morning I was breakfasting with a girlfriend in the National when I noticed a woman sitting a couple of tables away, close enough to catch odd snatches of conversation: hourglass figure, dark curly hair, international look in her eyes, fairly strong Russian accent — and for all my undiminishing interest in pretty women, I still can't explain why I couldn't take my eyes off her. I'm not going to start the premonition bullshit, I really don't believe in it — and this despite the fact that premonitions have saved me from serious danger a few times, so my lack of faith is a bit reckless — but I kind of recognised her. No, this wasn't your everyday boring déjà vu, but recognition of a kind that slows the speed of time, of something distant, remembrance of something that had happened either to you or someone else. Naturally, my companion was curious to know what I'd seen, I had to explain I was busting my head trying to work out who that woman was over there, on her own at mid-day in the National talking in bad Russian to two provincial ladies up in Moscow on business who she obviously didn't know and happened to be sharing her table with.

A week later I was invited — to mark, I think, the regular anniversary of the October Bolshevik coup, as we always said in our circle — to have dinner at Vika's, the selfsame Vika, art collector, one time redhead spitfire, now already ageing dame, lesbian in theory and nymphomaniac by conviction, who spent lavishly on lovers and young independent artists, who kept a salon on the top floor of a block for generals on the Garden Ring, a salon frequented by important foreigners and Moscow bohemia, amongst the former were several ambassadors, amongst the latter hardened informers, a salon which had the reputation — as did Vika herself — of being financed by the KGB, which certainly contained a grain of truth, but more of that anon. I was a little late and found a mixed crowd at the table: there was a priest from the Orthodox church in Antioch, in a black cassock, long tarry beard, hair tied back in a ponytail, who was part Lebanese diplomat and part Syrian spy; Fima D., a Gypsy Jew, a very colourful personality who specialised in little girls and gypsy folklore; the Mexican cultural attaché who was suspiciously adept at telling Soviet jokes with a Georgian, Jewish or Chukchi flavour and was later shot in some kind of spy case; some artists and her — Anna.

I recognised her right away, but, naturally, she did not recognise me. We had been given seats opposite each other, so I could now get a good look at her face. She had slightly watery greenish eyes, which would darken with emotion and sudden rage, which I would experience for myself a little later, a straight, slightly aquiline nose, a pronounced outline to her lips and a regal way of holding her head. She was beautiful with that special aristocratic ugliness, such a long way from the mass image of prettiness thrust at us by the glossy magazines, her breeding was conspicuous: she was a model of her type. And she happened to be American. I had a completely different image of the female denizens of that continent, even of the ones who demonstrated the results of two hundred years' selective breeding — sturdy blondes with aggressive mouths and freckled noses, with their farm girl origins written all over their faces. Anyway, it turned out she was Italian, though she'd been living in the States for fifteen years. What brought her to Russia? The early 20th century writer Shershenevich. Jesus Maria! But soon our talk turned from the more obscure representatives of early twentieth century Russian Futurist poetry to the latest scandals in the émigré literary world and Limonov's *Diary of a Failure*, and I remarked that émigré and failure were almost synonymous. "I'm also an émigré but I am not a failure." My dear Anna, you should have touched wood, especially since Vika's flat was full of the stuff, the carved mock English style sideboard was right by you, or spat three times over your shoulder. Naturally, after a few glasses of champagne and some sturgeon, we both rose spontaneously from the table to wander round the huge flat and look at the paintings, and round the first corner, in front of the first painting we fell into each other's arms. Later she let slip that with her it happened either straightaway or not at all — just like with me. I always liked the aphorism Zhenya, dead by that time, came up with about courtship not being fit for the blue blood, and you shouldn't take any notice of the rather boorish way it takes place, because the most important factor in love was the instant short circuit.

But this is all by the by. Then — we slipped away from the salon, ran out into the street, grabbed a taxi and leapt straight into bed as soon as we got out to my place, which was miles from anywhere, in Bibirevo, ghastly just thinking about it. As dusk fell she said she had to go, but I didn't want her to. The evening was just beginning, I had plans for other forms of entertainment, but I really kept her back because I wanted the reward of hearing her whisper in the morning: thank you for talking me into staying last night.

No, I had absolutely no thought of artificially prolonging our affair. What was the use when I knew that nothing would come of it anyway — our continents were too far apart, the Iron Curtain was too strong, even simple wishes were totally unfulfillable, which meant that international love was superficial and fragile. And the simplicity of our coming together was a kind of answer to this sad state of affairs. Seen like that, it couldn't be simpler to step outside convention, throw off the differences in status and education, habits and language, it couldn't be easier to kiss and fondle each other, or more wonderful to whisper English-Russian sweet nothings, or more bitter-sweet to breathe the scent of that mutual finding of each other, snatched from chance, its end predetermined by the date typed into her exit visa. Maybe such circumstances are ideal for lovers; at any rate nothing would have distracted my attention from her delightful femininity — neither the transparency of mutual hopes and calculations, nor silly, tiresome thoughts about a common future.

Let other people call it a play of chance. But only I — and she, too, I think — knew what such an accumulation of coincidences means. In this instance, one of two things: either you are a metaphysicist, whom Jung described as being no more than psychology's charlatan, or an artist, and in this second case you immediately spot the most transparent artistic scheme — of the clarity of the landscape outside the window. Of course, the thought of premeditation made us sick, it only harms the poetry, and so we began instinctively, little by little, to row in the same direction. Of the many definitions of love, this is one I like: the breaching of discreteness. You might say we saw to it day in, day out, breaking down discreteness in every possible way, flouting it, trying to live, figuratively speaking, without ever letting go of each other. Naturally, everyday life impinged on our idyll, taking the form either of the security guard at the Pushkin Institute, where Anna was in charge of a bunch of American adolescents — her students — or some other administrative tomfoolery, but having unconsciously adopted our general plan, which our strange acquaintance was just the start of, we successfully steered past all these snags and said to hell with the KGB, the management of her institute, the American cultural attaché and certain of my — I have to say, not very burdensome — living conditions.

She was, in fact, an Italian countess, though she hated talking about it. America, like the Soviet Union, teaches you to forget titles and blue blood. She was born on the family estate near Turin, was a Catholic, and in her teens had been sent to an exclusive girls' finishing school — her family name contained both a *de* and a *la* — from which she emerged at eighteen still a virgin, which is probably why she immediately fled to California. She grooved around Frisco a while before taking up with a boy from the American wilds who became her husband. They settled out in the sticks and she went to university to study — Russian, he was already teaching, she went to the pool three times a week, became a moderate feminist, jogged, fought her cholesterol level, espoused a relaxed radical liberalism, partied with neighbours on Saturdays, dieted, Let's go and fuck? — OK, yeah, let's go — they were a nice American university couple, and lived peacefully together until they divorced, which was right after her first trip to Russia at the beginning of the seventies. What happened was that in Moscow she had an affair — no, not with a member of the Soviet Writers' Union, but with an American diplomat, and this affair, I suspect, left its mark on our fate together. As you would expect, the diplomat worked for the CIA and invited her to social occasions with the CIA officers present as well as to a couple of receptions with Soviet counterparts where protocol demanded each side bring their partner. But to go back to her divorce: she got a neat little house in a small university town. I saw plenty of photos of that house — Americans adore taking photos of their property and showing the pictures to people they meet, as if they had just put it on the market — Anna in the garden, Anna by the garage and Anna on the porch, Anna on the neatly mown lawn, but the one I liked best was one where she was standing on the veranda, in the cold, dreamily inhaling the scent of the trees, her shoulders wrapped in a delicate Orenburg shawl I had given her. But all that came later, meanwhile we spent evening after evening sitting in my kitchen in Bibirevo, drinking old vodka, Starka — for some reason it became our drink — and talking. I filled in a lot of the gaps in her eighteenth-century Russian literature course: for example, did she know that the poet Fonvizin at the age of eighteen married a rich woman of eighty to pay off his brother's gambling debts? She knew a bit about totalitarian art and architecture, but had never heard of Frezer. However, neither Starka, nor the full biography of the poet Fonvizin, nor my love — nothing could explain her ever growing craving to drink the dark poison of Russian woes, slovenliness and greatness, of the monotony of its vast expanses, of the slow pace of time, of the discomfort of its cities, of its primitive animal warmth. Undoubtedly, Russia does have the capacity to distract a Westerner for a time from the Heideggerian discomfort of existence-in-the-world, and what's more Anna lived between two continents, she was herself a tramp and a wanderer and was, no doubt, trying to ease her rootlessness with a Russian narcotic. Whichever way it was, when we were thrown out of her room at the Hotel Astoria in Leningrad onto the street in the middle of the night — it involved doormen and a *dezhurnaya* and all the washed-out faces indistinguishable from each other — and I wasn't sober, of course, as I burst into tears at my impotence and shame for my country, she proposed to me...

We were carefree, stupidly, enamouredly and drunkenly carefree, but even in this relaxed state of ours, there was, if you looked closely, both haste and desperation — and understandably so, danger was palpable in the damp air and we swallowed it like Starka, and hurried, hurried, hurried as if we could run away from the danger — run away in this place, in the heart of one of the two great powers to which we belonged and which for several decades had been hell bent on finding a way to wipe out the other side first. Her proposal sounded even more natural as we sheltered from the wind under the looming bulk of St Isaac's Cathedral: a proposal of her hand and freedom. I could have taken it as no more than a feminine gesture, a maternal desire to comfort the hurt, a Christian gesture to shelter the persecuted, but no matter how drunk or confused I was, I understood instantly she really was asking me to be her husband and for us to fight the world together.

It's even easier for me to remember the silly little details of our Christmas journey to Petersburg, which ended up in our engagement even though we'd known each other less than two months, because later I had many opportunities to wander with her as much as I pleased in my thoughts, criss-crossing the dank city in the dripping winter gloom both during the six months that intervened before she next came back to Russia, and later when she disappeared from Russia for good — though not out of my life — since that July was the last time they gave her a visa. Of course, we should have gone underground, nurturing our daring plan: I should have vanished, instead of spending every night in her bed in her room after bribing the *dezhurnaya*; and she should have taken herself in hand instead of kissing me in front of her students at the Christmas Eve party — under the effect of champagne, under the shocked stare of the informer/translators attached to the group, under the fizzing and sparkling glare of the roman candles. But had we not been so intoxicated by each other, had we not celebrated our union so noisily, had we not been able to relish our freedom under such seemingly unfavourable circumstances, it would not have been us, two dilettantes, as she wrote to me later, but a pair of grim conspirators, secretly hatching their own particular version of détente. We felt that we were without sin before God.

Anna, looked a real countess in her fur coat against the background of the dirty, visibly disintegrating city with its former pomp. We walked along canals filled with rusty, rippling water, we wandered through stinking markets, we looked into rich churches, that gleamed with gold and candlelight, examined what had once been grand entrance halls with miraculously preserved Art Nouveau décor, passed stores and warehouses — God knows why, but we found it all amazing — until we came to the unforgettable station which had been the terminus of the first railway in Russia — the Tsarskoe Selo line. We sat down in the restaurant under a stained-glass window and opposite an incredible, carved oak buffet of huge proportions — they say it was ripped out a while back — drank foul vodka, ate sausages with hot mustard and desiccated sandwiches with a thin smear of red caviar and were happy. Remember that day, Anna? Towards evening, when they turned on the huge chandelier, we decided to go and dance in the hard-currency bar of the Leningrad Hotel. On the station square we discovered a photo booth — in America they're called photomats; we both squeezed in, you and I, put a coin in the slot, and who knows, perhaps they were lying around in your Washington flat, in the building round the corner from Adams Morgan, those photos that made us laugh till we cried when we got them; two people squeezing against each other, two faces all awry, drunken, happy faces, yours and mine...

I took Anna to the Exhibition of National Economic Achievements (VDNKh) on a bright July day three days after she arrived. This time she was booked into the Cosmos Hotel, and her window looked right onto the main entrance of the exhibition complex, onto the giant sculpture of the mighty toiling couple, he with hammer, she with sickle, mounted on top of the heavy arch and raising high on uplifted hands a golden sheaf of ripe corn that she had reaped. We passed under the archway and entered an area full of light and warmth from the bright summer sunshine that was completely sealed off from the outside world by a massive cast iron fence. And right at the entrance our early days came back to us. The previous three days we hadn't really been together, driven demented by the innumerable fantasies, bureaucratic hurdles and formalities that the state erected in the path of one of its citizens intending marriage to a foreigner. All three days we were trying to find the right note, lost during our time apart, and I felt I was at that place in the story where you suddenly lose the flow. I was assailed by gloomy thoughts, and with good reason. When I met Anna at the airport, she was held up for nearly two hours, they hadn't even asked her to open her bags, just kept talking on the phone with somebody higher up: the bouquet had wilted in my sweaty hands when she finally appeared from out of the deep recesses of the border zone, which had lost its mystique, like a too often-repeated fairy tale, but become no more accessible for all that. She was little, pushing two big bags across the empty customs hall. It was a bad sign. So bad that I mistook the rudeness of the doorman who blocked my way into her hotel, which was no more than the usual attempt to extract money, for a conspiracy of the state against us.

I became a little calmer when our documents were accepted, and they were even obliging, they gave us something that was a cross between a note of congratulations and a money-off coupon on bed linen, and the wedding was booked for the end of November. And now, as I showed Anna the Friendship of the Peoples fountain, I told her that it was not an allegory of the love the fifteen multi-national Soviet republics felt for each other, it was our nuptial round dance.

We walked hand in hand around the exhibition that demonstrated the permanent triumph of an eternally hungry nation. I showed her the huge bull looming high overhead — its mighty body casting a shade over the exhibition, in silhouette against a background of the blazing sun — Apis the bull, the god of fecundity, into which the soul of our pharaonic country had been turned, perhaps. We walked past eastern summer-houses and

Moorish palaces, past a steel hangar for airships, Doric columns yielded to Ionic and Corinthian — in the same order as in the Coliseum — leafy palms were enclosed in light arcades, aeroplanes hung motionless over flower beds, wild vines sprawled over an endless relief showing happy peasants interspersed with vegetables — root crops, cucumbers and tomatoes. We walked through a Pompeiian peristyle into an apple orchard. We walked across a clover lawn studded with beehives to two statues of huge stallions, Square and Symbol, the tablet nearby explained, and then a little further away we discovered another sculptural ensemble: a kolkhoz girl was pointing out a distant object to a border guard. She was obviously alert to the signs of enemy danger, and he was down on one knee beside his border guard dog; the dog also had its sensitive, intelligent nose pointed into the distance. What is all this? Anna whispered, scared and enchanted. Well, to her, a Westerner, all this pool of kitsch could only be the fantasy of some drunken confectioner, but I knew that this honeyed Slavic paradise was my Utopia, and the faithful border guard with his loyal mutt was safeguarding its boundaries. Why? I hurried her across the large empty square — she could hardly keep up — and we reached the heart of this enchanted land. "Look," I said.

In an enormous pool lined with coloured polished marble some bronze fish and bronze birds swam; they were all pointing their heads in the same direction and spitting endless, sparkling streams of water from bronze beaks and mouths. "Look over there." I pointed to the very centre. There, gleaming under the splashing water, frozen in inhuman, eternal tension, was a stone flower in the act of opening.

"What?" Anna whispered. She had not understood that from this place, lovingly embellished with coloured alloys of rare metals and a thousand different semi-precious stones, from this holy place sprang all the monstrous, unbearable plenty that surrounded us. "It's a vagina," I said. "Vulva. *Pizda*. Cunt."

Alas, she hadn't understood a thing. "*Pizda*? she echoed. "What's that?"

I had to take her by the hand again and drag her away. The branches parted. In the middle of a large pond, water splashing in every direction — the seed of the earth — rose a gleaming, gilt, triumphant wheat ear, every plump grain bursting with goodness and oozing moisture that glittered in the sun. Little coloured boats drifted peacefully round its base, rowed by boys and girls, girls and boys.

"*Khui!* A prick," gasped Anna, "it's a prick!"

She looked at everything around her with new eyes now. Out there in the real world there was class war, the Cold War, the streets smelt of dust and exhaust fumes, but this land of marvels was sanctified by the light and seed of an inexhaustible phallus, and all around it was eternal summer, the stone flower drank in the juice, fifteen maidens in national costume danced a never-ending nuptial round dance, the bull towered overhead, a happy pair of toilers showed the whole world the fruit of their kolkhoz soil, and the vigilant border guard vigilantly watched over the borders of our happiness.

They sold beer here. I bought us a glass each. Women in summer dresses with sunburnt necks and backs shielded their eyes from the sun with their hands and their kids were moderately boisterous. It was difficult to talk in view of all this well-being, but if we did discuss anything at that moment, she who combined the status of Italian countess and American professor of Slavic studies and I the Russian writer, it was of course Russia, and Anna admitted that, yes, she supposed you couldn't fathom this country with the mind, but with love, and with love alone.

Hungry now, we went to eat in the restaurant, called, of course, Zolotoi Kolos, the Golden Ear. That was the year they banned the consumption of alcoholic beverages in places of workers' recreation, so I had to obtain a bottle of vodka and a bottle of champagne from the doorman, who sold them quite happily from under the counter.

Apart from us, the restaurant was empty. The waiter readily transferred the vodka to a decanter, opened our champagne for us and filled our glasses. We touched glasses, not caring about touching wood, which was foolhardy, of course. We drank silently to everything passing off alright, we'd get married, and after that — *che sera*: somehow the certainty came back to us that we were living in a free world and were at liberty to do as we saw fit.

We had caviar and salted sturgeon and a pinkish coloured juice that smelt fetid but had a few cubes of ice floating in it. Towards evening a band appeared and without warning started to play an Italian tune that was very popular in Moscow at the time — Felicita. And since we were drunk by now, we found everything hopelessly funny and we started kissing, whispering about love and I think, reciting Russian poetry. We decided to win come what may.

We left the restaurant long after sunset. The lush vegetation was fragrant, a pure moon shone in the clear sky. I reckoned that rather than go through the whole exhibition back to the main entrance, we could climb the fence into the Botanical Garden, and from there come out on the road on the other side, which would be much closer to my bed in Bibirevo.

The fence was a hundred metres behind the restaurant building. It loomed forbiddingly in the darkness, and had we been less drunk, the task would have seemed impossible. But we were drunk, happy and in love, a rebellious spirit lifted us, tore us away from the ground, left us scrabbling a minute or two on the railings, slippery with dew, and then we were over. We had abandoned one paradise, but immediately found that we were now in a second.

Here and there we could see Brazilian palms entwined with African lianas, or Mexican cacti, or Central Asian saksaul. A nameplate gleamed white beside each plant, and if you bent low you could make out the Latin inscriptions. We walked on into what seemed impenetrable woodland, but suddenly we saw before us a glade all lit up in the moonlight with a comfy heap of very Russian hay in the middle. We fell into the haystack, throwing ourselves at each other as if we'd only just met. We unbuttoned each other's clothes, French-kissed, pressed breast to chest as fervently as if we'd only reunited that evening. We were ready to fuse in that heat of rare happiness, when how doesn't matter, just to take and accept complete dissolution, when we both sensed some kind of movement of the ground, a thickening of the air and anxiety, as when a thunderstorm threatens.

I raised myself and could distinctly hear barking dogs, they were coming closer. The sound approached very quickly, and you could make out the individual barks, hungry snarling, yelping, howling, the frantic yapping of a bitch in heat — even the foaming saliva falling in great gobbets from their jaws. What quarry were they after?

It felt as though the pack was coming straight for us, it was frightening, we clutched each other involuntarily. Several long seconds passed as we watched the silhouettes of big Alsatians — just like in the monument to the border guard — skitter growling past — on the other side of the fence.

Everything suddenly went quiet, and all you could hear was the insects that filled the air. "What if we'd been there?" asked Anna. I'd been thinking that, too. "Nobody warned us," she exclaimed with that characteristic American way of lifting her voice at the end of the sentence. "How do you say it in Russian? They could eat us!"

That was true. If we hadn't climbed the fence, the Alsatians would have got us. Well, such are the laws of this paradise, I should have known, but this time we got away with it.

Fucking shit, Anna swore, and her light-coloured eyes had gone quite black. In the darkness her naked figure looked just like a white chess queen. She tossed her curly head: Fucking shit! To drive her point home, she punched the haystack. A small woman with no clothes on, she was trying to ride roughshod across a world that was alien to her. And now I saw for the first time — for the first time and the last — tears appear in her eyes and roll down her cheeks.

Girls on the Way Back

I was still dreaming foreign dreams. I dreamt of the approaches to Warsaw, long high rise suburbs dirtied with black dust, a dreary leaden colour under overcast skies; I dreamt of New York, a district of low-rise buildings — how did I know then I'd see ones just like them in Queens — a decrepit landing stage, decorated with cheapskate strings of lights, two burnt-out bulbs for every one that glowed dimly, a rickety gangplank leading to a bar with a bamboo curtain that rattled in the breeze across the door, and the shoulders of the drinkers, slouched low, not one of whom turned when I walked in. I also dreamt of Paris, and this was the only sunny dream — a bright city space, brilliantly lit — but the feeling of recognition and freedom was clouded by disappointment; an unshaven old man was tailing me and muttering Russian obscenities under his breath. Finally one night I saw Rome in a dream, pathetic ruins covered in mould and the patina of age.

At the time I couldn't fathom the meaning of these strange dreams, I merely recognised the astringent taste of melancholy and rootlessness, and kept waking up with this depressing feeling. The dreams were suggesting that as far as I was concerned the whole world was essentially one big Russia, a vale of sorrowing for things that could never come true, and there was nowhere to run to. But I never did believe in dreams.

Actually, times were bad in my day life, too. One of my writer friends was in the Lefortovo jail — he'd written something cheeky about the sacred tenets of Bolshevism and published it abroad. Now his actress wife and I took him smoked sausage and cigarettes once a week, and on the way home we invariably got drunk in a revolting *shashlyk* establishment at Taganka. As part of the investigation my place was searched, every last scrap of paper was scooped into plastic bags and taken away, they even took my two typewriters; what's more the KGB didn't just drag me in for interrogation as a witness, but decided to work on me, to *profilaktirovat'* me, pulling me in for interviews that ostensibly sought to save my soul, but were in fact outright blackmail, at which they reminded me of Zone B, of Anna, of course, and many other details going back to when I was eighteen, and when I refused to answer, they would say in that smoothly sarcastic way: well, you just think about it, just think about it, you've got to live here, anyway. Worst of all was what I heard from one drunkard of a poet whom I hadn't seen for ages. Some plainclothes had called round and in the middle of the conversation asked, casually like, whether my friend, the one in jail, and I had ever offered to sell him icons. This was complete garbage, of course, I'd never handled an icon in my life, and the poet wouldn't have needed one except for saying his prayers, but their trying to float that idea was a signal that they were playing around with various ideas: in those days trumped up charges were not uncommon.

And then in some strange way a new character appeared in my life, a Georgian from Simferopol who for our purposes I'll call Misha. He was a colourful character, and for that reason I went drinking with him a few times — later I learned from other sources that, yes, he had done time — eight years. He was full of schemes; he took on contracts for seaside restaurant interiors, produced coloured tiles with pictures of naked women, once he asked me whether any of my ecclesiastical contacts might want a batch of cassocks making up. One day he appeared at my door without phoning and started laying all sorts of jewellery out on my kitchen table, each item carefully wrapped in a piece of cloth. He kept asking me to take one or another and have a closer look — diamond rings, antique earrings, enamelling — but I kept my hands behind my back, putting him off, saying I didn't know anything about that kind of thing, all the time expecting the doorbell to ring and men from the uniformed branch to appear on the scene. Nobody came. The Georgian did, though, call me a couple of hours later and say he'd forgotten a gold ring, but I answered that after he left I opened all the windows and swept the floors. He disappeared for good... It was that winter I met her, and by a slightly ridiculous coincidence her name was also Anna.

I first saw her at Laima's place. She was a Moscow beauty, a former model with a face too smooth and pink for her years, married to a foreign trade official and mentor to young models, something half way between a gangster's moll and hostess of a social salon. Her crowd, naturally, wasn't the bohemians and disaffected intelligentsia, like at Vika's, nor diplomats, but people with money, people who had made it in one way or another serving the regime, pop singers, successful members of the Artists' Union, foreign trade people, even famous sportsmen, musicians allowed to perform abroad, tried and trusted people, though that, incidentally, did not stop some of this pretty cynical bunch defecting to the West — whether the son of a famous Soviet composer, or a set designer, or a KGB colonel. This salon had absolutely no hint of bohemian easy come, easy go, it was stuffy and circumspect, conversation never touched on anything remotely controversial and as a rule was completely frivolous, and there was no reason for people to gather to do this, except to be able to change partners. They hardly even drank, for fear of saying too much. There were foreigners there too, of course, mostly businessmen, at least that was what they called themselves, but they were really just international hucksters who were of use to the regime in one way or another and who knew how to cosy up to it. In short, it was a rotten milieu in all respects, a kind of informal brothel, because men bought here, and women were sold, but the inexplicable laws of Russian life applied here, too, and purity of the genre wasn't maintained, otherwise what was I doing there? I had no money.

That evening was designated a pyjama party, and Laima greeted her guests in a see-through neglige, some of the girls were in bikinis, but mostly the women were in evening dresses and the men in suits and ties, so this was a mixed bag as well. The only people dressed casually were me and a rock singer, about to get famous, a hysterical nerd accompanied by his pretty pregnant wife.

I didn't notice this Anna straightaway in the crowd of guests, but I do remember she caught my attention at one point, perhaps only because, though she had that slightly underworld and totally Slavic look about her, she was talking in French for some reason. She was absolutely not my type — very tall, blonde, with a thin, unattractive, asymmetrical face, with little, colourless, nervous eyes, sunken cheeks, elongated yet puffy lips that looked like two worms, with sharp, expansive gestures, and — I spotted that, too — very big feet, my size, very likely. She didn't even notice me. And I didn't give her a second glance. I was flirting with Lyuska Dashkova, a former model and outrageous wild child, who set Moscow abuzz — until her lover married her off to an Englishman — with reports of her sexual escapades.

Laima called me a day later and asked me to come round. We'll be in a foursome, she said, and it wasn't how she said it that was strange — she was Latvian, after all — but the actual invitation: we weren't that close. My first thought was that it was a summons from Lyuska. But instead of Lyuska I found this Anna, whom I'd never said a word to before, and what's more, Laima and her husband were in a hurry to get off to some party, and Laima made it plain without saying anything that all this was nothing to do with her. Dinner was over in record time, and by nine we were in a taxi heading back to the hotel where Anna was staying with her husband, a Frenchman.

Preoccupied with my own current difficulties, I didn't see anything strange in Anna's behaviour: a lady who had made it out to Paris, had had to come back and do time at home, because her husband had been sent to Moscow on business; at the party she'd been on the look-out for a boyfriend to keep herself amused. I couldn't give a toss, basically; drinking her husband's whisky beat sitting in a bar.

The hotel was institutional and belonged to Aeroflot. Anna and her husband had possibly the only two-room suite. Her husband, an electronics engineer, was installing some kind of equipment and staying at the hotel at the expense of the purchaser. This was convenient for me: the hotel regime was a far cry from Intourist establishments. I was surprised by the amount of gear in the room — including a stereo system and VCR, and Anna explained as she poured me a Teacher's that her husband would be here for a while. She put all her charm into play, and it was really most effective, and my initial reaction gave way to a most pleasing impression. There was especial piquancy in her position as a Frenchwoman combined with her accented Russian — from the provincial south; to cap it all, she lisped, so that when she talked it was like barbaric, vile music.

To raise the temperature, she put on a video of *Emmanuelle*. Curiously enough, in those days this unsophisticated piece of soft porn was a real discovery in the Soviet Union, not to speak of the fact that the vast majority had never even seen a video. The local porno product consisted of xeroxed Scandinavian magazines at best, and at worst home-made playing cards, which deaf and dumb men used to sell in suburban trains, it was their traditional area of business. Anna was watching me, teasingly, searchingly. How immoral, she remarked, and I caught no trace of irony in her words, I really did find the movie in some way shocking: we are all such terrible prudes here in Russia, after all. Actually, I think that was the first time I saw an erotic movie...

She turned out to be thoroughly depraved. She was, most certainly, one of the Moscow whores, but she possessed a strength of will, a superb figure and that amazing provincial adaptability. Later she told me that even she found it hard to come to terms with her circumstances in Paris — doing nothing, living in isolation and relative wealth, not to speak of suffering from what is called with extreme approximation — émigré culture shock. She didn't drink, wasn't on the needle, didn't smoke, didn't read books, so the only thing that had really ever kept her occupied was sex.

She was in a way a sex performance artist. Moscow

provided wonderful opportunities for giving a show. Here she was almost a foreigner, her husband spoke not a word of Russian, and she kept the money she made on the black market in a suitcase — she literally had a suitcase full of money, a little brown leather case, the kind old ladies have for letters and other keepsakes of their youth.

She had the arrogance of the provincial turned foreigner and was uncommonly — from a cultivated point of view, of course — uncouth, but she did also have her particular good points: she was perceptive, energetic, had taste in everything that concerned her looks and a rare appreciation of human weaknesses, which only comes with long experience in service. As was expected of someone in the semi-criminal milieu she came from, her inner strength took on an aggressive form, and she loved humiliating people. She had a childhood friend she grew up with, either in Taganrog or Krasnodar, who turned up in Moscow, and the girl became Anna's maid, of course. Actually, and in this she was no different to genuine foreign women, Anna liked to play fairy godmother to us denizens of the Soviet world, so that the victims of her inclinations were generously rewarded... Incidentally, it was a photograph, one allegedly supplied to her husband that started my suspicions, suspicions that came to gnaw at me inside. And this was despite the fact that I was scared stiff of discovering in myself the paranoid symptoms the whole country was suffering from.

One day Anna showed me a photograph in which we

were kissing without a care in the world outside the Composers' Union, I think. It was taken at night with a flash. She said it had been sent anonymously to her husband. See, they're following us, she said, which was indeed very probable. I was immediately concerned, but there was something in her voice that made me wary. Something like mockery. At any rate, she was not in the least worried.

Her husband would disappear to Paris on business, then reappear for short periods. I met him one day — a strong guy, balding, with a fine forehead behind which lurked, you could tell, complex electronic networks. We drank beer together in silence, watching a recording of Wimbledon. Anna said he only liked sports, jazz and marijuana, and had no interest in women. He'd been a hippy, though he came from a good family, and was now getting socialised, if you can say that about a Frenchman married to a Soviet whore. She first began to have some respect for him when he came home from work one day and found her drunk and giggling. He didn't say a word, went out into the kitchen, and tipped a bucket of cold water over her head. He passed the second test when she was in a car crash with her lover: he opened his wallet to make sure the hospital fixed up her face properly. The third and last occasion was when the Dee-es-tee got onto her and started pulling her in for questioning and shining lights into her eyes, her husband phoned his parents whom he hadn't spoken to for months, they pulled strings, and

Anna was left alone. I love him, she used to say pensively, but I don't want his child. I want my children to be Russian.

From the time we first met and our first evening in the company of *Emmanuelle* my time was fully occupied: between interrogations at the hands of the KGB and diligent assimilation of the sexual experience of my Parisienne, which she had acquired in Moscow bedrooms, the shady squares of her native southern city and the backyards of the capital of the world. One day Vika called me. To my surprise there was just the two of us. She offered me wine, put on a record, laughed happily: it was peculiar, the flirtatious stage was long gone as our relationship smoothly progressed to platonic friendship. Looking at her closely, I noticed her eyes were concentrated and sober. She stopped laughing and suddenly leant over and whispered into my ear very distinctly: be very careful. And laughed out loud — for them. What can I say, other than thank you, Vika, and not so much for the warning — it couldn't change anything, but the trust you showed in me — how were you to know that for all the playing silly buggers, which we were all doing then — and you couldn't afford to take a risk, you had to be absolutely certain — that unlike you, I was able to avoid getting caught in their net...

In the spring Anna suggested slipping off to Yalta for a week. Her husband wasn't really a problem. He was indifferent to her Moscow escapades, or at least was very tolerant. However, it was now Anna who was visibly on edge, worrying about where we'd stay, counting her *days* aloud, which was very weird, and even ringing her mother — to warn her of our amour in case her husband phoned her, though what they were going to say to each other when the only known language her mother spoke was straight from the gutter. Anyway, all this fuss struck me as bluff. After Vika's warning, after the business with the photograph, I didn't trust Anna. And I grew even more suspicious when in bed once she suddenly embraced me tightly and whispered: I'm frightened for you. Well, if my suspicions were justified and were not the fruit of persecution mania, then you had to agree; like everything else in this country, the secret service, too, were grossly inefficient, you weren't going to go very far with *seksoty*, secret agents, of Anna's or Vika's quality. What Anna blurted out in bed was obviously not simply an outburst of passion, but also a warning of its kind.

Anyway, whichever way I looked at it, I couldn't see the snag in Anna's suggestion. We decided to go. It was the end of May and we had no difficulty finding a room in the same hotel where I'd had such fun with those other Parisiennes. True, according to the rules, we weren't allowed to share a room, but Anna had money, and a bribe soon settled it. She was away half an hour before coming back with the key and said she'd registered us as a married couple under a false name. This put me on my guard: for money it would have been easier to take two single rooms next to each other, but under our own names. Anyway, she probably chose this manoeuvre, I told myself, because she didn't want to reveal her French surname at the hotel.

Lord, how dismal and lousy that hotel was now, five years later. And the weather was no good, either. And the champagne tasted more sour than before. And the sweet aftertaste of youthful freedom had evaporated without trace. And I wasn't in love. Anna, on the contrary, was romance itself. At night she never let me be, and abandoned all her usual variety of turn-ons for one simple position. When, finally, she'd had enough, I lay on my back, hating this hotel and this room, strewn with her clothes, her Gulliver-sized shoes and her wads of money. During the day there was absolutely nothing for us to do together. It pissed with rain from morning till night; I wasn't allowed to drink before one p.m.; after dinner we went to a dreary show here in the hotel and a couple of times we were invited out by a Ukrainian Academician who was living in a suite with a pretty, narrow-shouldered, drop-bottomed lad. Unlike me, this couple were enthralled with their honeymoon, during the day they played like dolphins in the hotel pool, in the evening they danced in the empty restaurant, and the bald, fifty-something member of the Academy of Sciences tangoed with his moustachioed young lover, all languor and limp wrists, in contrast with the crisp, sporty demeanour of his *papa*... I was irritated by Anna's suddenly awakened insatiability. And by her asymmetrical face and by her successful black market trader's stupid vanity, and I used to reflect vengefully as

I tried to release my shoulder, which she liked to sleep on, that in Paris, that magical city beyond my reach, she was just a housewife, and once a week her niggardly husband would count out the centimes for the ingredients of onion soup and tacky ready-to-wear clothes. I was irritated by the sea, always rough and a dirty colour. And by the Swallow's Nest Castle, which we went to by boat in the rain. Standing on the veranda of the castle I listened to her voice with repulsion as she was telling me about her lovers. I felt sick. I was angry with myself. I was a hostage, living here on her money — by some intuition, I had avoided spending the little money I'd brought with me.

On the fourth day she started misbehaving.

At lunch she started making eyes at the waiter in the restaurant, then disappeared from the room for two hours, and when she came back said we were going to a restaurant in town that evening. She'd chosen the most dubious one, next to the dock where the big passenger ships tied up. You could cut the smoke in the bar with a knife. The clientele consisted of sailors and local prostitutes getting ready for the summer season. One chick at the next table kept trying to catch my eye, and when she succeeded, put her finger in her mouth, nodding in the direction of a dark veranda: a crude old trick, they'd have picked me clean out there in the dark. Anna was drinking heavily, which was unlike her. How do you want to love me tonight, she came on to me, reaching for my fly under the table, from behind? To cap it all, a young man with a strangely clean-cut Komsomol look for this establishment asked her for a dance a couple of times. My paranoia bubbled to the surface; sober, clean, tidy, you could tell the KGB a mile off — that's what they'd looked like at the university. The more she drank, the more I tried to limit my intake.

When we got into a taxi outside the restaurant, a guy, the spitting image of Anna's fancy man in the bar, asked if he could share the ride. As we drew up to the hotel entrance I felt a sharp sense of danger. It's only happened to me a few times in my life, and it's never let me down. Long ago I'd made a vow to obey this instinct without question, never mind whether it made me look stupid in front of other people or hurt anybody. Anna could barely stand up — it was pretence, I thought — and was dawdling in the lobby, I said I'd wait for her in the room. I got up there, packed my bag in a flash, looked out into the corridor — it was empty. I ran, past the lift, to the fire stairs, sped down and left the hotel by the back entrance. I took a taxi, not from the square, which was all lit up, but from two kilometres away. I told the driver to go out of town to Gurzuf, and it was from there I got a bus to the airport in Simferopol. There were plenty of seats on the Moscow flight. At the check-in I acted like a spy waiting to be arrested. But no one was after me. And once we were in the air I had the feeling I had avoided an unknown, but deadly danger.

I was home by morning and immediately phoned

her in Yalta. Judging by her voice, she hadn't slept, she spoke rapidly — things were bad, she was flying back that afternoon. It seemed to me she wasn't alone in the room, but I was unlikely to have interrupted an erotic encounter, in that case her voice would have had that special vibrancy.

I got myself together and met her at the airport. The way she looked shook me; her face was even more pinched, there were shadows under her eyes, her skin was an unhealthy grey colour as if she hadn't slept for days. And yet she seemed happy to see me. She looked at me with radiant eyes, put her arms around my waist, and we went off straightaway to the airport restaurant. We drank brandy, nibbled at caviar and expensive fish, she talked in spasms, laughing every now and then. In the night the local KGB had come. She'd got out of it somehow, she winked. Besides, three days was plenty long enough for us, eh? Of course, I thought, so it was me they were after, and she knew it was coming; and in fact she'd done everything to let me get away without saying a word. That's why she'd drunk so much — the KGB had only themselves to blame for letting me escape... It never entered my head that to get me in Yalta for breaking hotel rules was too elaborate a scheme for the Lubyanka.

After our Yalta trip we didn't see each other very often. One day when I called her number, a drunken male voice answered. When I asked about Anna the man told me I was a dirty bugger. Why, when I didn't trust her, had I phoned? Because evil binds us to others much more closely than good? Besides, without her, there was one puzzle I couldn't work out — had the secret service really wanted me to go to Yalta, and was Anna just carrying out a mission? Subconsciously, I suppose, that was the way I wanted it to be. As if it hadn't been a case of me going off with a common tart on a romantic tour at her expense, but of the all-powerful secret service entrusting one of its secret agents with a mission. Whichever, except the second version might just raise my self-esteem a little, while the first didn't do much for it at all...

In fact, soon afterwards the KGB declared its hand. When next I was summoned for my regular dose of *profilaktika*, they put in front of me a really stupid piece of paper called a protocol of warning. There were several points, but it all basically boiled down to a warning that if I continued publishing abroad and distributing knowingly false and slanderous information — their elegant way of describing my prose — then they would place the case before the Public Prosecutor for his decision. This was their usual legalistic crap, the Prosecutor's Office was, naturally, completely in their pocket. I scribbled in the margin that I rejected the document's accusations, but had been familiarised with them. And signed. They took away this worthless scrap of paper with relief; they were also sick to death of me. As I stood up to leave, the one who'd played the nasty interrogator, the other had always played nice, advised me in silky tones to stop mixing with foreigners. A timely warning, since I had a meeting with a reporter from one of the foreign agencies planned for later that day.

I did see Anna once more — six years later. By that time my life had changed completely, and when she called me, I couldn't think at first who I was talking to. She asked if she could come round and I told her the address — I'd long since moved from Bibirevo. To my surprise she wasn't alone. She brought with her a sweet little girl who looked about six. It was her daughter. Anna and I chatted and drank Akhasheni, and then she asked: Do you like my daughter? Who do you think she looks like? The girl was like her mother: the same narrow face, same small eyes and full lips. "Like you," I replied. Anna laughed: Not you? Remember Yalta? I looked at the child. I hastily calculated dates. And I suddenly saw the whole story in a completely different light.

Navigating a Fjord

*T*hey were a model couple in every respect. He was a naval officer from one of the NATO countries, a powerfully built Viking of about fifty, with a masculine face that was tanned, glowed with health and always wore a good-natured smile. She was a striking woman, the wrong side of forty, moderately extravagant, outgoing personality and with strong white teeth. His smile and her extrovert manner were, in fact, part of the job for them, since the husband was a military attaché and his wife had to do the obligatory entertaining on a grand scale at their place in Sad Sam, the name the western diplomats and correspondents gave the block on Sadovo-Samotechnaya where the high class foreign diplomats and correspondents lived.

They did their job well, he had learnt quite good Russian, in the evenings they used to party at the American ambassador's or at Kremlin receptions. She was also learning Russian, and the flute. They used to jog every morning to keep in shape, but for preference they liked their company more bohemian than the enclosed, protocol-bound, rather gloomy world of the Moscow diplomatic corps — it couldn't have been any other way but that at the heart of the Evil Empire — and so they wanted to make Russian friends, and why not, even during Stalin's time foreign naval personnel, given the slightest chance, would chase gypsy girls and marry actresses.

I fell into their net just as they were first launching out — at Vika's salon, at one of her opening nights. We happened to be looking at the same painting, when the wife switched on the finely-tuned socialising mechanism and asked me if I was an artist. To be honest, at that moment I really wasn't interested. And this mechanical courtesy of Western socialites to whom I had absolutely nothing to say and who looked at you as one of the curious, colourful natives, drove me mad, and I snapped that no, I was actually a writer, and an unpublished writer at that. I turned to walk away. What is your name? she asked regardless. I told her. And I am Ulrika, she said as she held out her hand and bared her white teeth. She found it hard to pronounce my name and went over it syllable by syllable. I was puzzled by her persistence; she told me later she was surprised by my reluctance to make her acquaintance — all the Russians she'd ever encountered, whether at the salon or elsewhere, dreamt of nothing else but making friends with rich foreigners. What's more, she recalled later, I made it clear I thought she was a Western fool, her expression, and didn't understand a thing. More than anything, though, I feel that she was not used, as no outstanding woman — and she was beautiful — to men being indifferent to her beauty, but alas she was not to my taste, her figure was too sporty and muscular, whereas what I liked in matrons of that age was a certain spreading softness and the thrilling charm of slightly over-ripe vice. Her open face had honesty and provincial impulsiveness written all over it, while her eyes had a girlish glint. It was as if everything she had was already there on display, and this sinewy certainty and quivering keenness — without any trace of hysteria — I know are often the mark of well-bred, good and profound women, but if I had been inclined to flirting at that particular moment, I would have wanted someone simpler and tougher, and less fizzy... I was very surprised when a couple of weeks later I got an invitation to dine with her.

She invited me herself. Not in writing, either. She called me — Vika gave her my number, I found out later. She called — I could tell immediately — from a public phone, and at the time I didn't know whether this was simply a coincidence or sober precaution on her part. She was obviously reading from a prepared text, not trusting her command of spoken Russian: later I learned she always thought out and prepared what she wanted to say in advance. From her recital I managed to unscramble that I should wait on such-and-such a day at such-and-such a time at the Hall of Columns. "OK," I said and we hung up. If she was flirting, then I'd never experienced it done this way before — none of the local ladies I knew would have made her first assignation with her target at home, dining en famille. Anyway, I thought, it's probably not dinner, but a big buffet supper.

I remember that when I came out of the KGB building

on Dzerzhinsky I strolled to Pushkinskaya, since I had forty minutes to spare. I didn't have to wait long: a correspondent I knew called Wilhelm, or simply Willi as everybody called him, waved to me as he drew up in his BMW, an incredible luxury by the Moscow standards of the time, and I slipped like greased lightning into the back seat — the front seat was occupied by his wife, a colourless sort of creature she seemed to me at first sight. Soon we were speeding past the guard post and inside the yard of Sad Sam, and a distant memory with a Caribbean flavour stirred in my soul.

We were met at the door by the husband and wife, dressed for a picnic; on the whole the ambience in the flat, as Gogol would have said, suggested take us as you find us, and it showed how sensitive they were — our hosts knew that their Soviet guests could not come in black tie, so they had abandoned formality. While our hostess showed us photos of their three children — how had she kept that figure? — gave a tour of the flat and served aperitifs, our host dashed outside to the street and brought back yet another Russian lady, a naive painter, who they'd also dredged up at Vika's, with a figure like a log, a face like a shovel and wearing some kind of folk costume, Karelian I would have guessed, but ethnography never was my strong point. The tour of the apartment was repeated hastily, but expanded this time round to include the hosts' bedroom where the guests were shown a vast bed with a weird mattress full of water, and it never entered my head to ask — was it sea water? Maybe there was a motor somewhere which the husband used to reproduce the briny and supply the requisite gale force effect; but more likely the mattress was mechanical and the mirror calm had to be broken by the rowers' own efforts. One way or another, our hosts used the mattress and the demonstration of its properties as an excuse for some good natured chaffing at their expense, and it broke down protocol to create a cordial atmosphere and set the tone for the coming evening as one of pleasant familiarity.

Supper was laid in the kitchen — en famille. There were four couples, including a Norwegian couple, who lived in the same building, he was a strapping sailor, she an equally strapping sculptor, I think, who I'd also seen at Vika's. Every place setting had a card with a guest's name, and according to my card I was on the right of my hostess, who was at the head of the table. Our host was at the foot, and on his right was the Karelian lady painter, so that she and I formed a sort of social diagonal. The Norwegian — he was called Hugo — and Willi, exchanged wives and sat on opposite shores. I was enchanted by the simplicity of it all: besides *zakuski* of black caviar and Norwegian salt herring to go with the Absolut vodka, there was only one main dish — baked fish with mashed potatoes and French beans, with red wine to drink; there was no cheese, no champagne, while coffee and fruit were served later, after going into the drawing room and with a long drink. My naivete was such that I decided that this was a simple family menu devised specially for us Soviets so as not to insult our proud Russian poverty by flaunting their accustomed luxuries. It never entered my head that this dinner was fairly flashy even by the standards of rich Westerners.

Absolutely nothing happened at table, not counting a momentary episode under it — right at the end when the fish was almost eaten. Willi turned out to be a firebrand, never stopped talking, cursed the KGB which kept on slashing his car tyres and damned the Soviet regime as well, later he got what he wanted and was expelled right on the eve of perestroika, which did his career a power of good. He spoke Russian absolutely fluently, the others had to tag along behind as best they could. The Viking nobly looked after the primitivist, she clucked gratefully, and interjected leading remarks into Willi's monologue. Ulrika played the sly coquette with me, occasionally grabbing a piece of English flotsam in the tempestuous sea of Russian. I behaved impeccably, dredging up the rules of etiquette my late grandmother had managed to teach me, but then I felt I had to respond to an eloquent glance from my hostess, so I slipped my left hand under the table and squeezed her knee. To my surprise, she jerked her leg away as if I'd bitten her, as though she'd expected nothing of the sort; but her smile never flickered, she just gently touched my forearm with the tips of her fingers and shook her head imperceptibly.

Really, that little touch should have been the end of it. They went away on holiday to the south of France —

they discussed their plans that evening, I bought for peanuts a semi-derelict wooden hut on the upper reaches of the Volga and sat there like a recluse until late September, fishing in the lake, picking mushrooms, drinking *samogon*, moonshine vodka, with the men and trying to write. I only managed a few pages. It wasn't supposed to be a new book, but a reconstruction of the one, nearly completed, that I'd lost, and for a very long time I could not reconcile myself to the idea that it is impossible to resurrect a lost text, that it is a chapter in the past and the last page has been turned. I recalled Hemingway's stolen suitcase, the burning of Gogol's *Dead Souls*, the shopping bag with a new manuscript lost by Venedikt Yerofeev when he was drunk, and then all the writers' lives that had been annihilated, and the tons of their archives burnt and destroyed in the Lubyanka, the crumbled magnificence of Rome — none of it was any comfort; my unfinished novel and half a shitty play were dearer to me than the entire library of Alexandria.

This was the emptiest period in my life: I would go back to an empty Moscow and an empty flat; my writing desk was empty and my pockets were empty, too; and conversations on the phone with the numbers I had left were empty as well. The cage door had slammed shut for good, it seemed. Could it have ever entered my mind that Ulrika's call at the beginning of October was not just the beginning of a new relationship, but news, perhaps, of release.

She was nervous. She couldn't find the words in Russian. Like the first time, she was reading from a text. I tried to make out her impossible Russian, which nervousness rendered almost completely incomprehensible. It seemed she wanted to say she had to see me. She repeated it several times — syllable by syllable. I said I was at her disposal. She dictated time and place letter by letter. I must confess, I was surprised; I could not think of any more or less plausible reason why she had to see me. Trying desperately to guess, I could only suppose that she shared some of her husband's workload. Husband was a spy, of course, but what earthly use would I have been to NATO. I didn't have access to a single strategic secret. I suppose I could have shared my observations on the mood of the creative intelligentsia. My report would have been extremely concise — fucking awful. It did cross my mind that the KGB would not like my conspiratorial meetings with the wife of a western intelligence agent, but then just imagine how my reputation as a writer would rocket if the secret service made me out to be a spy.

We arranged to meet on a bench in the Akvarium Gardens. Leaves fluttered down and there was a smell of decay. Ulrika apologised for her Russian and asked me to give her time to speak without interrupting. Holding a Russian phrase book and dictionary on her knee, she proceeded to talk the biggest codswallop I have ever heard, either before or since, from any woman in her right mind. But she didn't look crazy, even though what she said was utterly fantastic. It boiled down to the following: she and Otto had been in love for twenty five years now, and a result of that was their three children, two boys and a girl, she was careful to add, though this I already knew. Neither of them had ever been unfaithful, which was as true as the fact that we were sitting in Moscow during a late Indian summer. They were deeply attached to each other and each respected the other — this point was checked twice in the dictionary. But now the children were growing up, their youngest, the girl, was almost an adult, and Moscow was for her, Ulrika, like the start of a new life; and in this second birth she was starting all over again, and it had been decided that you — in other words, me — will be my second man. I didn't have time to find such frank Protestant rationalism repellent, had no time to resist with all the fibres of my Russian soul, because what came next was spellbinding. It seemed the decision wasn't that earth-shattering, it had all been settled long ago, but as for the choice being me, well, that had not been easy. On the one hand, I had passed the test that evening at dinner, on the other, nobody ever gropes the hostess's knee under the table. Also, I drank too much for an intellectual, which I was, in her opinion. But then again, Otto liked me, which meant she could often invite me to parties... She kept looking things up in the dictionary and leafing the phrase book, she didn't make me mad — she intrigued me. She was so genuinely nervous, you could never suspect her of playacting. She was trying as sincerely as possible to tell me what a difficult decision it had been, and it never crossed her mind that I might refuse the honourable and responsible role she was offering me in her utterly decent lady's life. Apparently, by squeezing her knee I had already said, from her point of view, my last word. Naturally, the cynical thought struck me that all this was being done with the knowledge and approval of her husband, and all this crap was just to keep me in line and stop me compromising the family by impetuous action. But there were no grounds for that either, her story about them not breaking their marriage vows would have been quite superfluous in that case, and her going all red and then all pale were quite unlike the usual marks of coquetry... And as it happened, later on I often had occasion to be ashamed of my own suspiciousness, so concentrated and self-sacrificing was she towards her second love.

Of course, I was frivolous. At first her seriousness seemed to me to be piquant, no more, and the situation itself enjoyably risky. To be a western military attaché's wife's lover in those days was both dangerous and bold. The western secret services would believe I'd been put in their agent's bed by the KGB; the KGB itself would find itself on the horns of a dilemma — to try and recruit me, whom they'd searched, made into a literary outcast, forced to remain a bachelor, a man with a grudge against society to use KGB-speak, would be pretty stupid; they would have to let me in on at least some of the techniques of spying — we weren't catching idiot writers, which was, as my friend Evgeny Popov used to say, like teasing cats — real spying, and what's more with a one-hundred-percent guarantee I'd write up the whole story somewhere like *The New York Times*: but nor was it in their interests to cut short this liaison, in fact they ought to encourage it, gradually collecting compromising materials, *kompromat*, on her, and on me, and on her husband and NATO in general. Whatever, we sealed our agreement there and then on the bench as the leaves fell with a long kiss on the lips that was another way of putting our signatures to Ulrika's love plan and a mark of my consent.

But — things didn't happen that fast, not that fast. There was a multitude of circumstances — which I knew of only from century-old French novels of adultery — preventing instant ratification. Ulrika led a very busy diplomatic life, and though I was now *persona grata* at receptions at their home, the most we could achieve was a furtive holding of hands in the hallway. Her husband, quite properly, didn't work weekends, and so the weekends were out, too. During the week a maid from the Diplomatic Services Bureau, a hypocritical proletarian slut who managed to maintain a pose of meekness, kept the flat tidy daily from ten to four. For her to come to my place in Bibirevo was out of the question: Ulrika only left the flat to go shopping and she was always driven by another KGB man, Kolya, a cheerful bloke of forty or so who was, curiously, a fan of *Mashina Vremeni*, a semi-underground band. She could get away unescorted only on the odd occasion, by saying she wanted a walk, and when she did she always took the same route — to the Central Market and back. At the market she always bought — obviously as a camouflage — a huge quantity of flowers and exotic fruits from the Caucasus, which were not on sale for coupons at the special diplomatic department store on Krasnopresnenskaya. For a whole month the Central Market and the immediate area around it were the scene of our meetings tête-à-tête, and — naturally — I was soon sick to death of this marketplace platonic relationship. Imagine: a crowd of shady characters hanging around on the filthy steps, crooks selling stolen black caviar, moth-eaten Russian fur caps, threadbare Georgian flat caps, grubby Central Asian scull caps, a great many gold-teethed faces and a lot of out-of-season sunburn, and then her — chestnut hair flowing loose, a head taller than the biggest local specimen, either in a bright flowing skirt or florid ankle-length trousers, always in trainers that were beyond the wildest dreams of even the most spoilt Moscow brats, carrying a bright yellow leather rucksack stuffed with persimmons, quinces, mirabelles, pomegranates and a huge bouquet of deep red roses, walking with a brilliant smile all over her wonderful face towards me over the trampled, slushy snow that was sprinkled with cigarette ends and sunflower husks, and the crowd parts, and I — I feel shivery in my jacket under the mercenary gaze of my compatriots...

The situation was resolved in grotesque fashion — the first suitable day for consummating our union turned out to be the seventh of November, the Revolution Anniversary Day. Otto was on the tribune of the Mausoleum watching the military parade, the maid and Kolya the driver had been given the day off. After the overture on a divan in the drawing room — with a glass of Remy Martin, when we'd watched the infantry march off and the tank columns come on, we finally made it to the bed. The elements in the mattress were, it seems, already stirring. I felt a pleasant rocking as soon as I lay down. We both came while the tanks were still crossing Red Square. Ulrika had been trained for uncomplicated field sex, I would say, despite the fact we were afloat. After orgasm she needed a break, like a man. It was quite handy, at any rate, before carrying on I was able to down another couple of glasses of cognac and smoke a Camel, which was a stroke of luck for me, as it would have been for any Soviet aborigine at the time. As we launched into round two, the rocket carriers were driving past. I was distracted by the military brass band and the uplifted, sugary voice of the announcer, but Ulrika apparently was oblivious and this time came with quite a storm, gritting her teeth and squeezing her vagina, and her face contorted, as if she were about to burst into tears; I managed to hold my fire, otherwise I don't think I could have made it a third time. As the biggest rocket with a rounded head moved into shot, we came together and a mighty "Hurrah!" broke above the square and rolled over us like a wave. She opened her eyes and looked at me, her gaze clouded, as if half asleep. Then she whispered something in her own language, I complained about not understanding, though I did perfectly well: she was surprised at herself, that she could be satisfied with somebody other than Otto. I tried to make a joke along the lines of today being a day for demonstrating Soviet power, but it seemed to me she missed the point. The physical culture enthusiasts began their march past, high time for me to clear off. She walked me out onto the street, fearlessly presenting the guard in his glass booth a flower and a smile. The guard bowed — just like a Japanese; I was amazed by her self-possession, all I could think of was getting out of his sight. She wouldn't let go of my hand and was looking into my eyes, but I was in a hurry to get away — only now did I feel how tense I had been in her diplomatic flat with the inevitable microphones, under the watchful eye of my own KGB.

What I had expected least of all was a summons to Sad Sam the following morning. It turned out that Otto had gone off to a business lunch and Ulrika had the day to herself. We met at Trubnaya, and settled for a cosy little basement pizzeria, I was offered Chianti — yes, yes, you could get Chianti in pizzerias even then — and I downed two glasses straight off, since I'd managed to celebrate with my friends the previous night. Why you so yesterday say — Sov-i-et poo-wer? She read from a scrap of paper in Russian, and a fanatical light gleamed in the depths of her wide-open eyes. I gulped Italian wine and stared at her. Then I couldn't stop myself and burst out laughing.

She said quietly, hurt: It was funny for you? To my horror, her eyes began to fill with tears. I love you, she said sadly, her eyelids dropped and she wiped a tear from the corner of an eye. You not to understand.

She was right — I didn't quite understand. Of course, she was in love first and foremost with that twist in the pattern of her life, which she had planned down to the most trivial detail. She might also have been in love with me, that I can see. But what I couldn't get my head round was the combination in a woman of such cold calculation in everything that concerned cheating on her husband, and such total innocence in everything concerning her lover. The receptions became more frequent. There were always a number of Russians at them — obviously Ulrika was taking care to make me less visible in this Soviet mush. I knew nothing about whisky and tossed back scotch, bourbon anything that came to hand — chatted up women which made Ulrika suffer quietly and flash me secret, tearful looks, in the depths of which glowed that flame I had come to know.

She adopted many and varied stratagems to dispense with the maid and send off the driver, so she could sail away on her water mattress with me for crew. I was rubbing shoulders more and more often with guests in evening dress at their home — I was now invited to all their parties — whatever the occasion. Sometimes the interval between her bed and the beginning of a reception was so brief, I would leap up from the bed, dash out into the cold and just hang around Sad Sam, anticipating the drinks and waiting until Otto came out to meet his guests at the security booth and shake my hand with the utmost cordiality.

Our rendezvous in the pizzeria also became regular. We became valued customers. Sometimes the summons was urgent, and then Ulrika would pay for my taxi. Usually the urgency was connected with my behaviour at the previous evening's reception. Either I chummed up too quickly with a red-head Englishwoman, the wife of a British Airways pilot — we started off by clinking classes, then we drank bruderschaft, then we had our photo taken with our arms around each other, then her husband took her arm and dragged her home; or out of boredom I slapped some lady's backside, and when she turned round, pointed at our hosts' poodle — the lady just happened to be the wife of the embassy first secretary; finally I turned up at one particularly solemn reception with a Jewish émigré girl who'd come back to Moscow to see her mother; she was dressed absolutely stunningly — in a red mini-skirt suit, fishnet stockings and a red wide-brimmed hat, the latest Brighton Beach fashion, and the diplomats couldn't take their eyes off her... Sitting at our usual corner table in the pizzeria, Ulrika would be waiting for me, dictionary, phrase book, pad and a selection of felt-tips at the ready. Chianti would also be waiting for me. As soon as I appeared, the waiter, as if on cue, would bring a mushroom pizza. She would wait until I had fortified myself, and then with an expression of deep seriousness and concentration open her jotter. The pages were already drawn over with big printed Russian letters. These drawings represented questions that were rhetorical, but were furnished with question marks. Each was done in a different colour. For example, the following was drawn in red: you much to drink? Without waiting for my reaction, Ulrika wrote in black: yes — I suppose that, given her zeal in all matters, she was using the opportunity to master Russian grammar at the same time. Further down, in green: your prick not to stand? That was a surprise: really? She paid no heed to my protests and wrote down tidily in black: will. Another time the question might be a bit different, say, in blue: you completely without control? "Oh, come on, now," I said with all the weight of my authority and sipped my Chianti to keep the game going. Ulrika tossed aside her felt-tip and told me, verbally, gesticulating, that if I was with control, then what was I doing flirting with a married Englishwoman. I remember once she tired of writing things out, and did a picture for me — something garish and caricatured in the Kukryniksy style. The slogan in red underneath ran: Nikolai likes girls red light... Lord, if only I was as zealous and painstaking as that!

I entered the part and felt myself to be a complete gigolo. I don't know whether the pros would agree, but as a dilettante I can say — in some ways it's not a bad feeling. I didn't love her. No, it wasn't the ten-year age gap that bothered me. I just couldn't relax: because of her husband's position, because of my own position. Because to play *va banc* is not at all the same as saying to hell with everything. But I really liked her very much. She was a character and she hadn't a clue what was happening around her. She was a western fool, of a Protestant cast of mind. She was convinced that it only needed hard work and persistence for things to come right. But not in Russia, oh no, not in Russia...

Otto was in the habit of going away on business. Even she would sometimes fly home for two or three days, as a courier, I presume, taking her husband's dispatches. During his absences I was sometimes able to float on the mattress overnight, sometimes I even spent two whole days, if it was over a weekend or she managed, on a weekday, to get rid of maid, driver and flute teacher. I would wander about the gleaming parquet in thick knitted socks and bathrobe, smoke several packets of Camel, go to the drinks cupboard, where alcohol of every sort was ranged from floor to ceiling on wide shelves, and choose whatever caught my eye, discovered that Black and White Scotch went well with jasmine tea, and for desert had a Chartreuse, but it wasn't the same *shartrez* we'd drunk with the girls all those years ago — two roubles a bottle, no, this came in an expensive bottle, the colour was gentle not poisonous, and the taste was gentle, too. I spent hours and hours like that and it all blurred, naturally, into a kind of haze and the buzz was deeper, tastier than from anything you've ever smoked; my brain went fuzzy, my body started to tingle, and when I lay back down on the floating bed, her wide open cunt, also trembling and moist, seemed like a sea grotto, which I swam into, rocking in that incredible boat. It seemed this really was the enchanted entrance to that other world I longed for, and as I penetrated deeper and deeper I shook off the evil spells that had been placed on me...

Naturally, she had to meet and accompany me to get me past the security booth. She was always giving the guards little presents, but even without them it would never have crossed their servile minds to have reported me to her husband rather than their bosses. From her own trips home she brought presents back for me, by the suitcase-full. Imperceptibly my wardrobe had become considerably renewed, everything — from undies and socks to trousers, vests and shirts — I wore was a present from her, and I was packaged, as it were, in her gift-wrap, which meant, by the elementary laws of magic, I too belonged to her. Furthermore, she began rolling up by taxi at my lair on the fringes of Moscow, and I started to find things I had never seen before, all sorts of tins and tubes, containing products for washing and scouring, air fresheners, serviettes, table mats, coloured candles in wooden candlesticks, a bed cover, and even matching sets of bedlinen in various colours, and my frowzy living quarters no longer resembled the bachelor pad of an unpublishable Russian author who drank, but were more like the love nest of a gay gigolo. She brought food along, of course, good drink was not on the list, and sometimes we even spent cosy family evenings together, when I would be tapping away a reader's report on a piece submitted to one of the literary journals on my typewriter, and she would have her specs on, sewing or darning something — for all her glamour she was essentially very domesticated and a good housekeeper. How she squared it with Otto, I had stopped asking, she could be relied upon entirely in this, but she grew so bold as to start going to restaurants with me, a couple of times we even went to the races, and she won and I didn't, and then she came with me to my friends, some of whom became her friends, too, and began to appear at her parties. Gradually we settled into a natural *ménage à trois* — except that one of the parties was in the dark or pretended to be in the dark. One day when I went to their place for lunch, at Otto's invitation, because he had nobody to drink beer and watch the latest James Bond movie with — his taste was a bit crude and basic — I found my host wearing exactly the same kind of shirt she'd given me recently. I asked her later what would have happened if I'd come in mine, but she didn't bat an eyelid: the shirt was made in Finland and I could well have bought it in a shop here. Naturally, she knew Otto would never have set foot in a Soviet shop.

It was as if the KGB had vanished from my life. It sent my letters to the West, it delivered big parcels of banned books — two or three of them, if found during a search, would have brought three years' tree felling, so I read them hastily, dashed about the streets in a muck sweat in true conspiratorial fashion, but nobody followed me — it seemed our liaison was providing some kind of immunity. The seasons were changing. The Party general secretaries took their cue from them and tried to change, too. We'd grown accustomed to each other. Alas, Otto's tour of duty was coming to an end, and curled up on my knee, Ulrika kept saying the Soviet Union would change, and that we'd meet again, we would. But we both understood that to hope for this was starry-eyed idealism and she was just saying it to comfort herself and me.

One day there was a stupid incident. Otto was away again, Ulrika was busy in the afternoon, I was busy in the evening, it looked we wouldn't see each other that day. I went off to spend the evening with some western correspondents, where for a bet I polished off a bottle of Jack Daniels and started chatting up some girl — another Englishwoman, as it happened, getting her rocks off on Russia. Meanwhile, she starts explaining that there'll be a revolution any day now in England, she didn't like revolutions, we'd already had one in Russia — western innocence — and she loved Russia. In short, like all Russists she was full of shit. I volunteered to see her home. She was rather horrific to look at, stumpy, bespectacled, everything one would expect. One other thing she explained while we were finding a taxi was that she loved Russia so much she had had to get herself a job baby-sitting for an English diplomatic family. So she was living in Sad Sam, did I know Sad Sam? "Oh, yes," I assured her and told her I would take her right to her door. But I can't invite you to my place, she wailed, instantly forgetting all her Russian. I reassured her that her place interested me not in the least. The taxi drove us into the yard, and I waved cheerily to the guard from the back seat.

It was after midnight. Ulrika's entrance hall was dead still. I was very drunk, but stood listening by her door a long time. A sweet little green wreath hung under the number — similar ones must have guarded the homes of her ancestors from the intrusion of unclean spirits. All was quiet. I rang the bell. She opened very quickly, as though she'd been standing the other side and listening as well. For a moment she stared at me full in the face with a strange look. Then stepped back without a word. I crossed the threshold, she quickly shut the door and spent a long time locking it — first the locks, then the chain. And turned to me again, looking gloomy and strange. Why you here? I felt like a naughty schoolboy. I replied something along the lines of the KGB having written a permanent authorisation to visit her. She looked at me kind of helplessly, dropped her hands and wept. She wept as tired grown-up women weep.

And suddenly I realised, it came in a flash, that my joke had been terribly cruel, because never, never in the course of our love affair could she have been completely certain about me. It literally shook me, I started to ramble on about the English girl, said: no, Ulya, no, look at me, would I... would I — and then burst into tears myself, crying like a baby.

When I'd been given a cup of English tea and half a flask of Jack Daniels, I calmed down a bit. She sat quietly next to me in the drawing room, on the divan where she'd first met me alone, and cried quietly. She never took her eyes off me, tears in her eyes, not smiling, the way women look when they've lost and re-found. Sometimes she lifted her hand to my cheek. Her eyes were still wet when we floated out into the darkness on our mattress. My face was caressed by a Baltic breeze. I sank deeper and deeper into her. The fjord was narrow at the neck, but gradually widened. It was dark, the shore invisible. Towards morning I went out on deck. It was not the first time I had sailed the sea, but these were quite different waters; the wind smelt different, and the sky overhead was new.

Towards eight in the morning the first lights appeared. I couldn't believe this was happening to me. And I had no means of checking that it was me, in the flesh, and not just my shadow, sailing away to a world that was forever forbidden me, and they couldn't get me. My face was streaming, and the drops were almost fresh. I could feel no rocking, though the sea was not calm. It was getting light and the contours of other shores showed ever more clearly. Native other shores, it seemed to me then.

Ksenia

Now imagine this: a sparkling clean staircase at the University of Stockholm. We're standing looking at each other and I'm struck dumb with surprise. But she doesn't seem to find it so amazing. She's looking at me a touch suspiciously: how did he get here? "How did you get here?" I said. Truly, what business did she have being here? There was a good reason for me...

I'd lost sight of her long ago, though at one time we'd seen each other often. At Vika's, where Ksenia flirted with foreigners, which was, actually, why all the young ladies went there. Once I was at her place: we drank jasmine tea in an impeccably antique ambience. The word in Moscow society was that she was a distant descendant of Pushkin's wife Natalia Goncharova. Ksenia was a little woman with a disproportionately developed Jewish bosom, a mouth in a permanent pout and green eyes. Anyway, I reflected, everybody's started travelling so furiously now, not emigrating like before, but going on pilgrimage. Almost apologetically I explained I'd just given a lecture on the state of what was still Soviet — anti-Soviet contemporary literature to a dozen Slavists, not one of whom, it seemed, understood Russian. I automatically patted the pocket where I'd stuffed the envelope with two hundred crowns — it was stupid, I knew, but it was the first money I'd earned in the West and I kept making sure it hadn't been stolen. Ksenia nodded and said she was sorry she missed it: she'd seen the notice about my lecture, but she'd been held up at the Swedish-for-foreigners class held at the University. My husband's paying for them, she added for some reason. It was a timely remark: I hadn't a clue that her cherished dream had come true and she had eventually married a foreigner.

We went out onto the University square, and Ksenia turned out to have a car. We'd hardly got in when I detected a distinct smell of alcohol. I presumed it was coming from me: I'd spent the previous evening in the company of my translator friend, in whose bijou flat I was staying. He worked for a publisher subsidised by the Soviet Communist Party, translating Soviet classics, and it was Ulrika who shipped him to Moscow — she wasn't to know that the CPSU didn't encourage Swedish translations of young Soviet dissenting authors, but we'd become friends and it was at his invitation that I was travelling. I explained all this to Ksenia as we sped towards the centre of the city. I heard you were having an affair with someone in high places, she remarked at last: I realised the smell of whisky was coming from her.

She always was a resolute lady with a romantic past, but she didn't drink in her old life. Way back, after she got a geography degree, she went away with her student husband to a weather station in the Caucasus Mountains. Up there, on the mountain, she had two sons, but when the time came to come back down into the valley, they got divorced. When I met her she was a single and independent woman with almost grown children, a Ph.D., the latest model Zhiguli, expensive taste in flashy clothes, and yet every summer she would lead a field expedition to the White Sea. In short, a woman of intriguing contrasts. She drew up at a cafe and looked at her watch. These bastards only serve beer after twelve, she said, removing the keys from the ignition. It was just after one. It was lager beer they brought us in a big wooden jug, plus some fishy nibbles. It was just what we needed; we both drained our glasses with relish and in silence. Ksenia had changed. She was thinner, her face was darker, her eyes had lost their sparkle, and there was no hint of coquettishness in her smile. She looked like an ageing childless middle-class housewife from a prosperous European country.

Which is what she was, it emerged, even though she was reluctant to talk about herself. I discovered only that her husband was a pharmacist, not here in Stockholm, but in some little town. Down in the south, Ksenia said, waving vaguely in the direction of Denmark. Another glass later and it turned out he was an émigré, too, a Jew from Hungary. Where are you staying? she asked, even though I'd just told her. Right, yes. But you're not busy this evening? I was free. Let's book a room in a hotel, she said, right out of the blue — there hadn't been the faintest shadow of flirtation between us. I've got the money, she added hastily. My husband gives me money. I also had money. I'd left the Soviet Union with seven one hundred dollar bills, which I had bought in a Soviet bank at a ridiculous, artificially low rate something like eighty kopecks to the dollar. Plus my lecture fee.

"Of course," I said. "Why not?" I'd never stayed in a foreign hotel.

She chirped up a bit. You know, she said, I don't want to go back there today. I didn't ask where there was. We left the cafe — I paid for the beer — and got in the car. She drove round the ring road to the Stockholm Sheraton. For one night only, she clarified as we parked. I always dreamed of spending a night at the Sheraton.

She went over to reception and it was fixed in a couple of seconds. Our room was on the twelfth floor. Something went wrong, but I couldn't for the life of me figure out what. Take the car keys, said Ksenia — no doubt that was how she issued instructions to her geophysical expeditions, go and fetch my bag from the back seat. Will you find the room again?

I went outside — and once again the sweet foreign air of the West flowed over me — it only smelt of air freshener in the hotel lobby. I wasn't used yet to the special clarity of the air, to the Baltic light, to the tidiness of the streets, buildings and people. Most of all to the fact that I was here. I had to learn everything from scratch: change foreign money I'd never handled before, use the public phone and even cross the street. As a further step in my self-education, I decided to find out where I could get booze. A charming Swedish girl pointed round the corner. I chose a big bottle of Scotch, one of the cheaper brands, it was true. And returned to the hotel.

The room door was locked. I knocked. It's you? I heard from inside. The door opened. She was standing barefoot on the carpet, she looked scared. I gave her her bag and put the Scotch on the table. Oh, that's wonderful, you guessed. We drank. Her hand was shaking slightly as she drank. In the room there was just one queen-size bed plus two stools, a bar, a small table, two armchairs. Modest and very clean. I walked over to the window. From here you could clearly see the cliffs and waters of the fjord that had brought me here. Even the dark stick of the lighthouse.

It was about four. Let's go down to the bar, she suggested. Presumably she felt uncomfortable in the room. We went down to the ground floor and found a place in the bar, divided off from the lobby by a glass wall.

I began talking, Who else but her, the first fellow-countryman I had met in ten days on foreign soil, could I have talked to about this. All the Swedes I met were only interested in perestroika, drank to Gorbachev and asked whether there were any topics left that were forbidden by the censor in the USSR. I reassured them there were. Listed them. Some people noted them down. But all I wanted to talk about was this miracle of being able to move from one world to another, though I couldn't find suitable words. I remembered how when the train stopped at Brest Litovsk I was certain until the very last they would take me off. We stood there for more than two hours in the dark and the wait was unbearable. It seemed as though my fate was being decided, I couldn't believe the border would open to me. But everything was normal and the train moved on — somewhere into the night. When I woke early in the morning the train was standing in Warsaw station. It was just as I'd seen it in that dream long ago — melancholy and grey. How we crossed the border into East Germany, I don't remember — I was drinking vodka with some of the other passengers. Finally the East-West express pulled into the station in Berlin. I had learnt the instructions of people who'd done it before off by heart; I found the S-bahn to Alexanderplatz; I showed my passport to the East German border guards, smiling anxiously. They turned it this way and that, leafed through it, discussed it. I couldn't understand what they were saying. I imagined they didn't want to let me through and could hardly believe it when they handed me back my passport, and one said in Russian — go. It was already dusk. Unconsciously, as if it was something I did every morning, I got onto the S-bahn that would take me through to Zoo station in West Berlin. It hadn't really sunk in that I was in the West, I was just looking around when I saw a guy with a long scarf wrapped round his neck and a crumpled overcoat. He had that stubborn persistence of a drunk, and he was forcing his dog to balance a coin on its nose. The coin fell off and rolled off somewhere. The guy swore and fished in his pocket for another. "What kind of coin was that," I thought, "a pfennig, surely?" Just as automatically I picked up my suitcase and left the train right behind the guy and his dog. I walked along the platform with all the cool and casualness that mask delight and confusion. This was a feeling of triumph, and it was worth living just to experience the intensity of that feeling. West Berlin glowed like a rainbow in the darkness — just as my dream about it had shone all those long years. It shone in inverse proportion to the feeble lights of Soviet cities at night. On the station square I found everything I knew about the West: porno cinemas, foreign cars, huge neon billboards reaching up into the sky. Another thing I knew about Germany was that they had great sausages to be washed down with great beer. I was incredibly hungry. I wanted a Camel. I wanted a schnapps. I wanted to celebrate my triumph right now.

I didn't want to miss my train to Kiel, which was due to leave in two hours, so I decided to hold my little celebration in the station restaurant. Strangely enough, I did have the presence of mind to ask the waiter whether they took dollars. He looked at me a bit strangely when, after he said no, I asked him to take them anyway. I thought that if this was the West, then the nationality of a hard currency was of no great significance. He told me where to find the bureau de change. But that was closed: it closed at nine, now it was ten. I felt unbelievably hurt.

Here was beer, here were sausages, here were dollars in my pocket, but I was powerless to turn one into the other, as though I were in the Soviet Union. This was, perhaps, the first crack in my idolisation of the West.

However, I made a mental note of the rate on display at the bureau de change — 1.72. So as not to miss my train, I went to find the platform. I was worried by a strange number on my ticket: 235, indicating the number of the carriage. I knew for a fact no Soviet train was that long. The platform was crowded with students, hippies, workers of southern origin, looking like the people from the North Caucasus. Must be Turks, I thought. In the middle was a kiosk — exactly like the ones on the platforms of the Kazan Station in Moscow. The guy was an Arab of some sort — a Syrian or Lebanese. Or Palestinian, maybe. He had beer, he had sausages, and he had Camels. He even had schnapps, though it was in tiny bottles — enough for one gulp. I stood in the queue behind some excited American students in lumberjack tops, deliberately torn jeans and trainers. When I was in front of the window, I showed the Arab my hundred-dollar bill. "Change," I said in English, knowing that all the peoples of the East are small businessmen at heart. "Ai vont one hundred fifty marks only." He knew the rate. He quickly calculated he was coming out of it twenty two marks instantly ahead. He ran his eyes quickly over the people standing behind me, shrugged his shoulders and spread his hands theatrically: was it his fault if this crazy wanted to throw money away? In short, he agreed. He handed me four cans of beer, four sausages and a handful of miniatures of schnapps. And a packet of Camels, of course, and I asked him for the longs, because I'd never seen that kind before. And a lot of change in marks. I found a bench, tucked into the sausages and washed them down with the beer — neither one nor the other seemed to me terribly tasty. Then I asked somebody how to find the Kiel train. I was astonished to hear there wasn't one. The mystery was soon cleared up: there was just one carriage for Kiel. Eventually I found it. I had a third class ticket. There were no free seats in the compartment. I settled on my case in the gangway and unscrewed my first baby schnapps. When the train set off, I felt I'd lived in the West all my life. I'd found a neat way of changing money, found food and drink, I'd worked it all out, I'd even found myself in the right carriage at the right time. This was something to be proud of. Yes, I was at home, in my real and final home...

I opened another schnapps and a can of beer as a chaser. I smoked a Camel. I recalled my student days: we used to travel just like this, all squeezed together, all noise and laughter. The train braked. Then stopped. Soviet border troops in their grey fur caps and with Kalashnikovs slung over their shoulders were in the carriage. They shouted *schnell* and shoved the people near the door back down the gangway into the carriage. A dark horror overwhelmed me: I mean this could not possibly be the drink. Several moments, long enough to prove to me that my soul was poisoned by fear for good, were sufficient to realise we were going back through the GDR...

Ksenia was listening to me, not interrupting, just nodding sympathetically. Suddenly there was a flash behind my back that reflected in the glass, and Ksenia grabbed my hand. We both turned around: two men were walking quickly away across the lobby. Lord, said Ksenia, it was us they took a picture of. I felt sick to my stomach. We finished our drinks and hurried to the lifts. We checked carefully. The thickly carpeted corridor was absolutely empty. Only the long rows of brass door handles gleamed in the artificial light. We ran to our room, locked the door and breathed again. I'm frightened, said Ksenia. You won't go?

I remembered I had to ring my friend — to tell him I hadn't got lost, and I'd be there next day. He was very excited. By the way, he said, I nearly forgot, there was a message for you, the Soviet consulate phoned, asked you to go and see them. "Fuck them," I thought, "that's the last thing I'll do."

Ksenia was sitting on the bed, leaning back against the pillows and drinking whisky. "What's up?" I asked. "Nothing," she shook her head. "What are you afraid of?" Everything. I poured myself a whisky. I felt very uncomfortable. I was watching her face. The powder had come off her cheeks. Her eyelids were puffy and red. Her lips were dry. How old is she, I thought, and made a quick calculation; she must be about fifty, even if on the right side. Why the hell did she marry that pharmacist and saddle herself with learning a new language at her age? As if she had read my thoughts, she said dully, without expression: I stay in a student hostel here. Then she undid her blouse and pulled a thick wad of cash wrapped in cellophane and held with an elastic band out of her bra. She put the money on a stool with a sigh. It was done the way businessmen loosen their ties at the end of a hard day. I have to help my children, she said in explanation. And live. I came across from Norway today. That's where my husband... Apparently she was into petty smuggling, but then in Moscow, too, as I remembered, she'd dabbled on the black market. Everyone who went to Vika's dabbled. Even the wife of B.G., who's now made a reputation for himself in the West as a philosopher. And when I used to sell the banned books people used to bring me as a dissident writer, I was working the black market, too, even though I had never had any aptitude for business. And everything was connected with smuggling, with the illegal import whether of a few pairs of second-hand jeans or the works of Pavel Florensky.

We had another drink. "Do you think..." I wanted to ask, but stopped myself. Until that moment I was absolutely convinced that it had been KGB agents taking my picture through the glass wall of the bar.

My older boy's studying Chinese, Ksenia said, and the younger one's reading economics. She held out her glass for me to pour in some more. She had left her blouse unbuttoned; not to look sexy, she was plain tired. The skin between her collar bones was flabby. Also her neck was blotchy and red, from drink, probably. Though they've got their own flat... I left them mine... Sit closer...

I sat next to her on the bed, and she flopped onto my shoulder. She was shaking. Shaking with fear. I embraced her and, it seems, started trembling myself. It was strange that here, where everything we were afraid of was so far away, we were both even more scared. And incredibly lonely. Lonely to the point that I had difficulty suppressing the urge to phone Moscow — my mother, even. The hotel corridor was scary and ominously empty. The reflections on the glass wall were scary. The room felt empty and the unnecessarily huge, pristine bed uncomfortable.

I reached for the whisky, trying to slip from under her, but she was lying on my shoulder like a sack, awkwardly bent, her nose pressing against my neck. I rolled her away carefully, and she slumped face down into the pillow, without even a sigh. She was in a deep sleep, her bare legs drawn up defencelessly, sleeping the way an old man, all knocked up with a weariness accumulated over a lifetime, sleeps before death. I pulled back a corner of the blanket and covered her.

After some hesitation, I decided it would be bad for her to drink whisky in the morning, so I put the cap back on and put the bottle in my coat pocket. I switched off the light and went into the corridor. I wanted to run, but I made myself walk slowly. Only when I was out on the street did I feel a certain relief. All I had to do now was find my friend's place and not do anything stupid. The thing I wanted most in the world right now was to be back home on Tverskaya. I took a swig of whisky and hailed a taxi.

Two days later I flew direct from Stockholm to America, where I'd been given a grant for a few months at the Institute of Russian Studies — not without Anna's help, of course. And a few years later I heard indirectly that Ksenia was fine — she travelled back and forth to Moscow as an interpreter and consultant for a Swedish impresario who was planning a project with Russia. As for the reflection of the flash in the glass wall, I think we probably both just imagined it.

The Mystery of the
New York Ichthyology

***W**e* hadn't seen each other in over ten years, yet here we were sitting in a pub on Queens Boulevard, and even we had thought we were saying farewell to each other forever back then. I didn't detect any noticeable changes in him — his temples were greyer, but he was still trim — and, as of old, he still had plenty to say and on the same old topic: on Kretschmer's typology of emigrants, on the metaphysical guilt of Americans, whose ancestors had betrayed the girl they loved and abandoned their old mother for the sake of ephemeral success in the New World. Swarthy, half Jewish, with a simple, folksy Southern Russian surname and a thick black moustache, he might have been a Turk, and this was perhaps why he felt flattered when Americans took him for a German, a Swabian or a Bavarian. The conversation strayed hither and yon, touched on mutual acquaintances, and it turned out that almost everyone we mentioned, in Moscow and Koktebel, in Paris and Los Angeles, was alive and up to the same old tricks: drinking alcohol or smoking grass, sleeping with boys, living off women, writing prose or painting, broadcasting on foreign radios, changing lovers and wives, playing the piano, dropping out and going off with the gypsies. Mutual bewilderment, reciprocal dissatisfaction at this violation of the accustomed dual flow of time: our time — melancholic and resistant to sudden shifts and even rapid change, and the other — irreversible and devastating. To state it at its absolute baldest: each, at bottom, felt slightly miffed that the other was alive and apparently flourishing, because, it's true, meeting a friend after a gap of many years in the opposite world is something that throws you off track.

To shake off the awkwardness, we settled on Guinness. And after a couple of glasses we were off back to the Crimean spring of nearly twenty years before when we first met. He remembered Dima, he remembered Galya, was surprised I'd forgotten the name of his landlady, who had been in charge of the showers at the Writers Resort, something not to be sniffed at. I was amazed in my turn by the way he recalled incidents so very far from Queens. Incidentally, he even asked after my wife, we split up around that time, though we still kept up a nostalgic relationship. He sipped his beer and remarked that he was surprised when I got divorced, could she really not stand it, couldn't she just close her eyes, and I decided he must have fancied her himself: a tender young butt, sweet freckled face — deceptively innocent-looking, the fresh smell of young armpits and also, persistently, of fermenting sperm, which I was pumping into her all that spring without a break from morning till evening and from evening till morning. Of course he liked her and now he was looking back with regret. I remarked he was supposed to take me to the Samovar.

In the cab — the tariff is still daytime, but the traffic's already eased off — my friend waxed lyrical about the Russian roots of German fascism and, having saddled one of his favourite hobby horses, sprinkled his thesis with Baltic names — Vinberg, Shebner-Richter — I observed for the second time the strange properties of New York's perspective, as if the local air created the effect of bringing distant objects right up close. I caught sight of a brightly lit section of the waterfront, the black lopsided silhouettes of the cliffs above an overgrown garden on the slope, a garden either of peach trees or almonds, wild pear, thick waxy shoots of spurge; I imagined I saw the yellow in the empty branches of flowering cornel, the stones and dust of a basilica by a dried-up Tartar spring.

From here, from the pitch blackness of the Irish section we were driving through toward the East River, the blocks below seemed enveloped in blue air, the coal smoke just flowed, not wanting to melt away, you could see red strips in places where it was torn, vertical ones of factory chimneys, horizontal ones of tiled roofs, washing lines hemmed with laundry hung out to dry; she would be standing in front of an easel that made her look tiny, frowning and clenching her fists: in her left fist a paint-stained rag, in her right an inept brush, the last strokes, wait, not now, stop, and the brittle, chocolate laughter, and her cool, moist crotch, and very hot cunt, unexpectedly deep and unfathomable for such a frail girl. My friend was going on about how naked Aryan youths and girls would ride on Indian elephants across the Scythian steppes past the ruins of Soviet cities, but we still got stuck in traffic on Manhattan Bridge. I was now forced to listen to a fifteen-minute lecture, quite elegantly put together, on Jewish-American synarthrosis and the selfless presentiment of future catastrophes, and also on the mental Russian chemical apocalypse. Yes he was just the same, a cynical windbag, a man of straw, a charmer with a voice pitched too high for his massive body, especially when he was under the influence — he spoke in a falsetto exactly when he wanted to be baritone — a fisher of souls and an insatiable collector of other people's weaknesses and misfortunes.

I first saw him in the drawing room of a Koktebel house, where at the centre of the table he was retailing Soviet anecdotes — God strike me dead, as the saying goes, he would add deftly side-stepping the too obviously obscene bits — to the delight of his hostess, a hennaed lady of nearly seventy, a former singer at the Philharmonic, who complained to me and my wife, almost as soon as we'd been introduced, that her friend here, a princess, was a dreadful gossip who would go telling everybody that she, our hostess, had a sex life with her dog: why should she say that, I don't live with him at all. Meanwhile the dog, such a mongrel it looked almost pedigree, yellow and white and with a broken back leg that it held up to its belly, was looking hungrily, but timidly into the drawing room from behind the piano, and the singer screeched: Get-out-ta-he-re!

Just a day after we met, Osya — he was Osya then, not yet Joseph — and I were as thick as thieves. He used to mimic the way I looked voraciously at other women at the table, without letting go my wife for a second and kissing her every now and then on the top of her head with the earnestness of a dog hunting fleas. It was funny and we laughed, though anybody else would have thrown him out. Really and truly, playacting was his proper, that is, disinterested, though egocentric, calling, and in his own way he did respect the characters — they were as a rule his audience as well — he played as the necessary condition for revealing his art, which — and I was to observe this many times later — drove some people, who realised what was going on, crazy and they hated him with a passionate, impotent and suffocating rage. He was undoubtedly charming, but completely incapable of any extra-aesthetic relationships, whether of love and tender friendship, or of warm pragmatic exploitation. I suspect that this unadulterated and merciless purity of his genre, which sooner or later always finished up in betrayal, was the real reason for his emigration, an attempt to find a place in the world where naked aestheticism wasn't going to be the apple that spoiled the whole ethical barrel of decent behaviour, but alas — it looked like he missed out, and there was no such place. At that time, in the Crimea, he came to see us nearly every day — our little room, or more precisely our bed on the first floor of a miniature and narrow little tower, erected by our greedy landlady in the cramped yard of her whitewashed house, was always in the orbit of his round of social calls, in the course of which he would carry round his poisonous pollen of merry and cynical apercus from house to house. And meanwhile he drew us mercilessly into the hidden life of this little place that on the surface seemed to be almost uninhabited, while we had chronically little time for each other, even though we were never apart for a moment, flowing together like two drops, and nobody told us that intercourse was just a hopeless metaphor for the impossibility of total fusion...

We finally reached the right exit, the taxi went down Seventh Avenue and turned left at 56-th. Since my companion fell unexpectedly silent at the end of the ride, I paid the fare. We climbed out of the car, and I exclaimed: "Hey, Osya, this is my first time in New York, the Statue of Liberty, where is she?" "There she is," He pointed to a huge fat black woman crossing the street, shuffling her flat shoes, wrapped in something palmy and carrying a big black shiny bag. We went into the restaurant.

Our coats were taken by an unbelievably thin girl with shining eyes — her jeans looked as though they were grafted onto her. I winked at her, she whispered quickly: don't believe it, I'm going home, I won't stay here more than a month. The owner came over. He was wearing a good tweed, most likely a David Hunter. He and Osya kissed.

We sat at a table between the bar and the grand piano: we won't eat, my friend announced, but I managed to wheedle some *zakuski* and a plate of borshch out of him. Osya had brought his own Absolut. The waitresses were Irish, and I asked the owner, who took our order personally, why the service at the Samovar wasn't Russian. He explained that Russian girls drank a lot at work, fucked with clients right there in the kitchens and were shameless about overcharging, and the worst of the lot had been a Soviet movie star, who got the job on a very high recommendation. He'd had to hire new staff. The owner gave us an enchanting smile and moved off to other clients. We drank a glass of Swedish vodka, which lay very uneasily on Irish beer. "Who's the girl on the door?" I asked. "One of yours," said Osya, enjoying some ham, "and never known to say no." How long does it take for one of ours to become one of theirs in this Babylon? As though sensing we were talking about her, the girl looked at us. Our eyes met, she shook her head — there was a gleam of desperation in her eyes: don't believe it, I'm going home...

The house musician turned up. He began by placing a bouquet of lilac on the piano, then he sat down, tossed his long straight hair away from his face and flexed his wrists. I had a terrible sense of déjà vu. He was going to strike the keys and out would come some lousy Scriabin and the half-opened blossoms would tremble and judder. But it was an etiolated Chopin that emerged, not that it made any difference. I could only see the back of the musician's head, his thin legs under his stool, his long feet flitting from the gas to the clutch pedals. His elbows worked furiously, as if he was kneading clay. I remembered that on the piano next the flowers there was a lamp with an orange shade, its fringe jiggled and danced. Against the piano was a set of shelves stuffed with sheet music, rocking to and fro. The mistress of the house was sitting on the divan and mending a piece of tapestry, her glasses pushed up onto her forehead, her maimed pooch lying at her feet, shuddering in time to the Chopin. Osya poured more into my glass, then more again, I was in no way surprised when not far away, at a table by the bar that was not covered with a cloth, a woman of a certain age with red hair and glasses on her forehead appeared. A lone glass of white wine stood in front of her, she was laying out a game of patience. That's our singer, said my friend, with a broad sweep of his arm, she is yours to love and pity. The singer smiled and asked loudly across the space between our tables: could she read them for me? Everything was proceeding as normal: the flight from Europe in pursuit of the sun, whisky on the plane, landing at the bar in that Newfoundland airport, take off again and landing, this time in an Irish pub, then an unexpected conversation about things I'd almost forgotten — all this in conjunction with a third bottle of Absolut made hallucinations come easy. Besides, with the exception of the Irish service, everything was so familiar, so cosy: the bunch of Jewish girls at the bar, so affectedly independent in that titillating Moscow way, and the well known Moscow theatre star at the next table, as drunk as if it was all happening back at the All-Union Theatre Society; and the motley assortment of graffiti on the walls, like the motley buffet of the Writers' Union, and the group of either gangsters or auto repairmen looking as if they had walked straight out of the restaurant of Dom Kino into the jungles of the Big Apple. Yes, the lilac was in bloom then, and at night in bed you could hear the endless racket from the various frogs that lived in the pool right below the tower. Some produced soaring, intermittent trills, others croaked deeply, others squealed like hungry babies, and we took what part we could in this feast of the renewal of life, tirelessly crumpling sheets that were by now quite damp... Osya was talking, pouring again, though his face had gone red and his jowls sagged: about Russian cosmism and the revelations of Daniil Andreev, of European dandyism as a refined form of the Russian holy fool, *yurodivy* — I was letting it all wash over me, when I spotted a woman with warts, looking like toad jelly. She was the spitting image of a Crimean poetess who wrote poetry for kids and was a lesbian. The pianist was supposed to fluff his note, the mistress shuffle her patience cards and put her finger to her lips, jerk her head so the glasses fell back down onto her nose, then look down, pretend she'd only just noticed the three-legged dog at her feet and shout: Get-out-ta-he-re! I noticed there were now more people round our table. The bottle of Absolut was full again.

Osya made the introductions: a Moscow black market trader, now working as a correspondent for a Russian-language newspaper here in New York and speaking impeccable English; Mr and Mrs Kabachnik, she was a gypsy, his line of business was described to me later, something along the lines of fiddling insurance payments for furniture supposedly stolen in break-ins at his friends' apartments, both were from Odessa and now lived in Brooklyn; finally, and here my hand hung in the air, because the gentleman's name was as outlandish as the gentleman himself — Gidemin Kozlov.

They talked about Goetz. Laughed about the weaknesses of the Jewish-Russian community. Goetz was an American Jew from Brooklyn, a peaceable book-keeper of twenty eight, who recently shot a black youth in Lower Manhattan. Goetz was riding in the subway when three black kids came up to him and put a knife to his side. Instead of pulling out his wallet and giving them twenty bucks, Goetz pulled a gun. He killed one, winged the second, and the third managed to get away. It was a story that warmed the hearts of Soviet immigrants. They were more deeply and physiologically racist than the Grand Wizard of the Ku Klux Klan. Goetz is now the fourth *bogatyr*, Russian warrior chief, Osya declared as he poured more drink, the fourth *bogatyr* of New York Russian Jewish mythology! I couldn't take my eyes off Gidemin and his thin ginger moustache — he was grinning quietly. My God, he must be over eighty by now, but he looked exactly the same as he did then. He wouldn't have recognised me, of course — I was no longer the young curly-headed jealous husband of a sweet pisshead, I was a forty-year-old gentleman, going grey and bald. His dacha, which he bought off a famous aircraft designer who had made a career of longevity and philandering, was full of ghosts. It stood on a cliff overlooking the sea, and the ghosts lived mostly in the garden. Gidemin used to say they were all naked girls and very, very pretty, and he used to invite all members of the female sex, as long as they were under twenty, to come and see for themselves, they only needed to spend one night at the dacha. Looking at him now, I was astonished not so much by the fact that he hadn't altered, but by the absence of the nervous tick that used to affect the lower part of his left eye. The tick had completely vanished. Just like him, isn't he? said Osya, poking me in the side when he caught me looking at him. He burst out laughing, his jowls vibrating like the lilac on the piano. I bridled, what did he mean like, when it was him, Gidemin? Let's drink, gentlemen!

I downed another glass. I even recognised his wrists now with the creamy blotches on the skin. Of course I recognised them after the time I caught him on the edge of the frog pond which my little idiot of a wife was trying to capture in oils. He was standing behind her, watching closely over her shoulder as she painted. I called out to her, half leaning out of the window in our little tower, kneeling on our bed, and she turned, but wasn't alarmed.

Gidemin clasped her innocent little fist, the brush clutched tight, in his mottled paw and turned towards me, his eye twitching: my congratulations, young man, your pretty friend here has a character of iron, so you look after her...

"No, you tell him, tell him, Gidemin," shouted Osya, and without letting him say a word, proceeded to tell it himself. I knew about this incident: Gidemin rushed over one morning at dawn to an artist who was living nearby, shouting: get up, Lyudka's hanged herself. Lyudka was his latest flame, from somewhere near Lugansk. The artist leapt out of bed in his underpants. They were met by Lyudka — stark naked — on the porch. She gave the artist a flower with the words: I am so sorry — April Fool's Day!

The Kabachniks laughed. The black market dealer shook with silent laughter, but his expression remained hard behind his gold-rimmed spectacles. Osya was happy and having a good time; I even remembered that I heard that story in that selfsame house over evening drinks and the mistress kept repeating: what a charming monster Gidemin is, isn't he? And when I asked — who is he? — replied impatiently: akh, drop it, nobody knows, maybe he writes children's music, but anyway he's more likely a retired submarine commander...

M'sieu' Kabachnik informed the assembled company he couldn't stand Soviets. They smelt so bad if ever you met them in New York. La Kabachnika said yes, and they also threw cigarette ends into the john. And someone she knew, just fancy, checked the quality of fabric in a shop with a lit match, she didn't trust the Made in Taiwan label. Osya winked at me, the black market man frowned and drank. Have a go with this, Osya said and pushed a monocle into my hand. I tried putting it in my right eye, but try as I might I couldn't get it to stick there — it kept popping out and Osya and I had to catch it in mid air. Kabachnik thought it most amusing, and his gypsy wife was taking a closer and closer interest in me. What tunafish?! There was a loud shout. What tunafish, I'm asking you?! This is a Greek shipment! I looked in the direction of the powerful voice with a heavy Jewish accent. I recognised the man talking on the phone at the bar as the sculptor Misha Blyakhov, who had died on the rock faces of Kara-Dag that spring. Blyakhov would stride about the village with a rucksack containing his latest compact model of a human-powered flying machine. His long grey hair flew in the sea breeze. Or the mountain breeze. He made an attempt to fly every day, regardless of the weather or the direction of the wind. He smashed up one day when the weather was bad, though there was very little of it that spring. I saw his body, what was left of it, covered in a sheet, when they'd scraped it up and brought it in to the village. At first he was lonesome, Osya said, then he started visiting the ichthyological museum. And look at him now, in the fish trade. Still, he did fly, said the children's poetess. No way, no way, the former sculptor yelled with his catastrophic accent into the telephone, I don't want nothing more to do with shrimp! The black market man — quick as a flash —

had the owner by the tweed flap of his jacket and pretended to bugger him. The owner went pink, pulled himself free, he looked upset. Heil Hitler, shouted Osya, his arm going up in salute. The monocle was set in his eye, and on his head was a green and red cap in the shape of a crocodile with open jaws: a childish joke. It came back to me what he'd said back there about emigration rupturing a person's character and the inescapable sense of guilt towards the ones left behind. The singer wrapped a gaudy shawl around her shoulders, bent over the pianist, he nodded, swished his hair back, and the singer's voice came like that of our old Koktebel hostess, unhurried, peasant-like:

> *Ah, daddy, my dear daddy,*
> *It's not a father you are to me,*
> *Why did you sew me a dress of white,*
> *Give me away for a bride to be...*

The pianist tinkled, the lilac swayed, I noticed the coat-check girl making signs to me. I could tell she was begging me to keep my mouth shut. I'm going home. A bouquet of lilac just like that was ready at the head of the bed for a still life. I was inside her, making it from behind, my wife lying on her right side, her right hand under her cheek. I tried to rouse her, she was sleepy, and with every push I made the bouquet judder — right above her face. When I had come, she reached out with her left hand, raising herself on her elbow, adroitly plucked some blossoms and put them in her mouth. I remember thinking with disappointment that instead of sharing my passion, she was probably looking for five-pointed lilac flowers all the time. She spotted some, waited for me to come, then pulled them off and ate them "for luck". And now, as I recalled all this in detail, I decided she was right to do as she did. Because we really did become happy. Both there and here.

Full Moon at Halloween

*I*t was Halloween, and a Friday to boot. We were drinking in Jim's studio. Jim was Anna's current boyfriend. Anna, in an elegant designer coat, was sitting at Jim's work table which was littered with phials, jars and retorts. She told me about Jim the minute after she met me at Washington Station off the night Amtrak from New York. We hadn't seen each other for years and had stopped writing a couple of years back. She hadn't changed much. Her face was a little sharper, her shapely legs a little more muscular and tanned. Only her eyes told you she had aged. We hugged a moment, like very distant relatives who've almost forgotten each other. She told me about Jim because she couldn't invite me to her place, and had booked me into a hotel. Inexpensive. Close to downtown. After that we only saw each other a couple of times over the next ten days. Today, obviously, it would have been on her conscience to abandon me over the holiday. Or maybe Jim wanted to see what I was like.

At one time he'd been in intelligence, had worked in Munich — probably something to do with monitoring, because he spoke Russian almost without an accent. When he was completely pissed off, *ostochertelo* — and he pronounced this difficult word quite casually — he resigned and took up picture restoration. He was nearly sixty and looked nothing like James Bond. He was wearing a baggy sweater and loose fitting jeans, and had an earring in his left ear. I was surprised by the almost Russian simplicity of the studio. Anna was, after all, a bit of a snob, and, as I found out later, had lost her university job, moved to Washington and ought by rights to have found herself a more prestigious boyfriend. Maybe it was Russia that brought her and Jim together...

Then the prince arrived. Strangely enough, I'd read about him already in *The Washingtonian*. He took up a page together with his American wife, a white-toothed brunette who looked ready to repel boarders, and their dark-complexioned son, who was freckled in the American manner. The headline "Your Highness?" had a question mark after it. But the irony, as I quickly found out, was misplaced: he was genuine, with a red nose, brown eyes and a receding chin. Naturally he was a Russian prince.

I had, of course, brought along a bottle of Russian vodka, which was pretty dumb of me: Absolut is, we all know, better, but quality is always the price we pay for patriotism. Jim had absolutely no *zakuski*, unless you counted a sealed packet of thin cut bacon. There was no bread, either. We sipped the Russian vodka, exchanging exaggeratedly polite remarks with the prince. Everyone was ultra-cautious. Actually, it was an incredible collection of company: Anna the Italian, Jim the ex-spook, and her current lover, the prince who was a child of the first emigration, and me, the ex-lover and current envoy of the distant Soviet world. A certain unease hung over the table, but in the middle of the bottle, just underneath the red star on the Kremlin, we were joined by an absolute sweetie of a bimbo aged about thirty — she had an unbelievable waist, flowing dark hair and cow-like eyes. There was something Malaysian about her, but she said she was French. I wasn't surprised, I'd already learnt that if you want to be something in America, just say that's what you are. In Russia calling yourself a writer, let's say, is pretentious, here it doesn't matter, you can even call yourself an astronaut and it'll only arouse polite surprise. Everyone turned their attention to the French girl with relief, and she said she was shooting a commercial and this was almost probably the truth. The prince added in Russian that, apparently, she was trawling the singles bars — he'd met her in one yesterday — for a millionaire husband, and with her tiny waist that probably wasn't so dumb. She was very sexy and you couldn't take your eyes off her.

The bottle came to an end and the four of us — the two ladies, the prince and I — decided to go off to a restaurant the prince promised to show us; a delightful place. Jim turned us down with a smile, saying he had too much work, shook my hand and patted Anna on the shoulder: everything's fine, honey. Well, Halloween seemed to have got off to a good start: the aged prince was good company and obviously a rake: we were going to a restaurant with two very pretty women. The prince took us to a tacky

Greek taverna where we had to go to the bar ourselves to get wine. When the prince went away his friend asked was it true he was a Russian prince. She got a positive reply, but she could see what was coming and had worked out for herself that prince he might be, millionaire he wasn't. And split.

The three of us were sitting at a cramped table. I felt good because I could see Anna's face up close. I had wanted to ask whether she remembered Bibirevo, and Petersburg, and the Astoria and VDNKh, and had she drunk Starka even once since that crazy summer, but I wasn't so drunk as not to understand that to talk about it in front of Comrade Jim would have been tactless. When the prince and I had taken in turns twice more to go and fetch a carafe of astringent Greek red wine, Anna evidently felt sufficiently secure that I was in safe hands and said: You must excuse me, but Jim's expecting me. And left as well. Once again I envied her preciseness. Had this been Moscow, I could never have left her just like that...

There were now two of us at the cramped table on the sidewalk not far from Dupont, in a district of singles bars, gays and oriental eateries. It was around ten, the moon was shining like crazy, the red wine was thick and dark. I was forever anxious whether I had lost the keys to the street door and my room in the hotel that resembled a hunting lodge in Woolly, right opposite a hotel that looked like that Sheraton. I was checking my pockets yet again, when the prince said: "I'd like you to read my mother's memoirs." He added: "Perhaps they would be of interest in Moscow."

We finished the wine and moved on to the Rondo.

I'd been here before, drunk a beer during the daytime, got talking to the Indonesian girl behind the bar. She was called Yeti and had small legs and big breasts, she was a browny yellow colour, very Gauguin-ish. I was pleasantly surprised when her flat little face screwed up in a smile as soon as she saw me and she sang out: Hi-i-i Kolya! The owner came out to greet the prince. He was a Serb with a flowing moustache and wearing a good suit, like a Washington clerk. They kissed, Slav-style. I owe a hundred and fifty dollars here, whispered the prince, and I ordered wine at the bar. In fact, the prince immediately disappeared somewhere, while the moon gazed serenely through the crystal clear thin glasses. The prince reappeared, with an African girl in tow, absolutely black, with a hot mouth, incredibly flat and narrow, with curly fuzz on her egg-shaped skull. And a name that was difficult to follow. You've not been to my place, the prince was saying, it's not far, a little apartment... a studio, really... our marriage is open... my son stays with his mother... that's where my car is... I had seen the photograph of his wife, nothing open there, more likely, the prince had been thrown out. *In vino veritas*, he mumbled and downed his glass. It was the last night of October, there was a farewell scent of warm foliage from open doors. The bar was floating. It was easy to believe that with a moon like that the Celtic unclean spirit brought over by the Pilgrim Fathers from the Old World would come alive for the one day in the year. Let's go to my place, the prince suggested. Let's get some drink and go. His nose had become entirely Celtic. I looked at my watch, it showed the same time as an hour ago.

The prince lived in Adams Morgan, which was on my way. We walked down a dark street, on the right lay black East-North, where they don't even have squirrels, probably because trees don't grow there. Though squirrels in Washington are like rats in the Bronx. A full moon, burbled the prince, one arm resting for support on his African beauty, the other clutching the paper bag with the bottles, Halloween, lunaholia. The African girl pointed at his feet, Who-oo-oo-ps! A pumpkin with cut-out eyes, nose and mouth was lying abandoned on the edge of the sidewalk. A candle still burned inside it. Do you know, whispered the prince, though the African girl probably wouldn't have understood anyway, I'm not terribly sure she's a girl. It might be a boy. Some sort of being. What do you think?

The prince's pad was one bedroom and half a bath, as they say here. A lair: bottles on the floor, shelves scattered with things, broken furniture, a dirty towel on the only table, a small easel in the middle of the room and a canvas with Levitan-esque daubings. The prince shoved the easel over to the wall, sat the African creature on the wreckage of the divan, put a record onto a crackly player. It was, I think, Rubashkin: Russian songs, the prince explained, opening a bottle. During the second bottle he fished out a folder with a manuscript. I put it under my arm and took my leave. The creature looked over my head. I found my way easily, but when I was crossing Duke Ellington Bridge, I heard from below, from the Zoo, the scream of a peacock. The keys were in place, but in the light of a streetlamp I discovered I'd lost my plastic cash card, which I'd only just got and which I was terribly proud of.

When I got into my room, I opened the blinds, the moon was suspended behind the glass, the Sheraton was a black cube, with only the occasional night light. The air conditioner was humming, though I thought I had switched it off before leaving. I turned on the wall lamp and lay down on the bed with the princess's manuscript. Her maiden name was simpler than her husband's, but none the less noble. First there were untrue descriptions of the garden she spent her childhood in, then a platonic, bicycle-powered, Nabokovian romance on the tree-lined avenues of the estate park, then leaving the family home for boarding school at the Smolny, and it was all redolent of that bitter-sweet Russian sadness, all those baskets and trunks packed and ready in the hallway. The name of the estate also whined and moaned quietly.

I skipped the part about her schoolgirl upsets, usually caused by a dry stick of a headmistress, and about her much more beautiful friend, who died of typhus in Bolshevik Petrograd before she was twenty. Her reminiscences of the First World War were much more mature, more sustained in a literary sense, and from them I gathered that the princess was a little younger than my own grandmother, who had also been a pupil at the Smolny and then, during the war, a nurse, we still had a photo in our family album of her in her uniform and white headgear with the black red cross.

I had a half of whisky hidden away, I made the effort, got up, found it in my bag, unscrewed the cap, took a swig, lay back down. In 1917 the future princess was in Kiev, and I greedily followed the details of the first love affair in her life — just like Bulgakov's Turbins, complete uncertainty, historic excesses and all. The boy came over as likeable, clear eyes, an idealist, news that he had been shot came through much later. They had to flee. Her uncle's estate near Kamenets-Podolsk. Nature. The manager, so polite until yesterday, now struts around the drawing room in dirty boots — the peasants are setting estates on fire — her two younger cousins are frightened to death, but even the steward gets skewered later on a rusty pitchfork.

The prince himself has not yet put in an appearance. Whisky between inebriation and sobriety disposes a person to tearfulness and bathos. So are we all of us, whichever side we live on, doomed to relive our memories of the deadly years of Russian killings? I was sobbing now and realised I wanted to go home, to Russia.

It was, to put it mildly, illogical. The more so since the prince had appeared by now — on one leg for some reason, he'd lost it fighting the Bolsheviks. Marriage, firstborn and flight to Galicia, then further, deeper into the backwoods. More children, Poland, an unknown forest where the prince worked either as a manager or a forester. Fighting back tears, I repeated to myself aloud the names of the wayside stations their transport passed through. One thought, mustn't get left behind, mustn't lose the place, must get to — nobody knew where they had to get to... I wanted to call Anna, but I remembered I mustn't do that. Anyway, what could she do to help me now...

When I woke up, I felt it was late. A young black had already dug a plastic cup out of a trash can and had sat on the kerb, head hung low and cup held out — by lunchtime it would be full of change. I called the prince to share my impressions. He sounded as though I had woken him, at any rate it took him quite a while to figure out what I was talking about. I promised to take the manuscript with me. He thanked me. He coughed for a long time into the receiver, I felt how dry his mouth must be. She's just this minute gone, said the prince, and do you know, she was a girl. And really sweet. We both agreed that an African girl was also not bad, not bad at all.

___To Paris___

*F*uck, fuck, fuck, muttered Michel, flapping his elbows against his plump flanks, a Jack Nicholson gesture. Even without doing that, though, he looked like a penguin: squat, round face with round glasses, a greying fifty-year-old penguin with a pigtail and a ring in his left ear. Just to one side of the garden where we were sitting, there was a railway track a dozen metres above the ground, and trains passed at odd intervals almost without noise. Weedy-looking roses poked upwards around the perimeter; crocus buds showed through the ground; the sun struck at an angle, dividing the garden into two equal triangles. I don't know why, but I experienced a quiet sense of exultation at the sight of this marvellous European morning.

Yesterday my hosts had met me at the airport — I hadn't anticipated such kindness, as I'd never met Michel before, and they brought me back to their townhouse. We dined in the kitchen, and went through to the sitting room to sample fruit beers made by Trappist monks. So as not to have to scramble up the steep wooden staircase, my host and I came out into this little garden to have a drink. You got into it from the kitchen, through a door that had been sealed up all winter. During one of our sessions, I managed to whisper to him that I didn't miss New York.

He understood me — we spoke in Russian, but he caught on quickly; we left my hostess and the children to get nostalgic about the States, and hit the Calvados in the kitchen. In honour of my visit Ritulya softened the strict regime on the consumption of spirits — abstinence during the week with a half bottle of Scotch on Saturdays — and Michel indulged with an easy conscience. Now — it was around ten in the morning — we were on our first snifter of cognac: fuck, fuck, fuck...

Ritulya and I had met quite by accident — in New York in an émigré household, and it was as if it was the most natural thing in the world for her: Kolya, we often used to talk about you — Gulya, Olga and I. You know Olga died.

Of course, I didn't know. If Ritulya and I had seen each other a couple of times when she was visiting Moscow, I'd not seen Olga once since saying good-bye at Sheremetyevo. But by a strange coincidence, over there, in the States, I'd read Dima's novel, which had come out in Paris a few years before. It was dedicated to Olga, still alive then. The book was full of bitterness, tears and stoic émigré attitudinising. But of our Yalta days, Dima hadn't written a word.

She had cancer, said Ritulya, that's what got our Olga. When she heard I was probably going to be in Europe in the spring she exclaimed: "But you can come and see us in Brussels! Oh, you'll like the one I've got now! Michel — he's really super!"

She practically hadn't changed. Maybe a little bit tubbier. Even her hair seemed to me dyed the same colour. Her American husband, like the previous French one, had been disposed of, and she had come to the States to arrange the divorce. She'd returned to Europe five years ago with two American children, one of whom had been in her belly and done the Paris-Yalta-Moscow tour all those years ago, and met up with Michel, who had in his turn dumped his English wife. Added together, the sum of their various children came to something like seven, and if you calculated the proportion of Russian blood, then it was three quarters between the two of them, if you count Russian-Jewish and Russian-Armenian as Russian. Michel's mother was Belgian, and his grandfather came from a family of pharmacists. Alas, there was nothing of the bourgeois left in Michel, and his cosmopolitan brood now spoke in a mix of English, French and Russian, and led a gypsy lifestyle. In Brussels I was able to observe teenagers at various stages — the English wife had left three of their four children for him to look after — come downstairs in the morning, sort of washed but completely unbrushed, to have breakfast in the kitchen, get themselves juice, milk or cocoa, tip themselves a bowl of cereal, open a bag of crisps, wander round eating a Mars bar and then disappear from the house one after the other. Responsibility for gathering together the dirty cups and dishes and putting them in the dishwasher had been placed on the shoulders of Michel. Well, he had spent his youth in Paris, knew Gulya and Olga when they were kids and Ritulya from when she was first married, and their two ships were destined to dock at the same port one day. Putting together what remained of the wreckage, they built an ark, rickety, yes, but sturdy enough to sail on together...

This fat slug starts drinking before breakfast, said Ritulya, leaning out of the kitchen, and the other was a drunk from the cradle... What are you going to eat?

At table we discussed our plans for the day. As a Belgian patriot, Michel felt duty bound to take me to Bruges. What the fuck does he want to see Bruges for, said Ritulya. I demonstrated my erudition by remarking that I knew the origin of the stock-exchange. Michel was impressed and touched and he poured another glass. "It is the very heart of the continent," I rambled on, "the place marking the boundary between Rome and the Reformation." And we could make a detour to Damme, said Michel. "The home of Eulenspiegel," said I. You Russians, Michel said with reverential irony, the Russians are the only people in the world who read so much! Besides, he said to Ritulya, we could drive on to La Kok, we have to do something about the cottage... Ritulya was dismissive: Do it by phone. Michel ignored her: they have incredible eels, he said, turning to me. Yes, but the price... said Ritulya. Those bloody Belgians take so much in taxes you can't afford to live. And all so they can build swanky autobahns... So, you're going to Rome? She was asking me.

"To Rome," I affirmed uncertainly.

"So, you'll have to go via Paris. Wait right there, I'll call Gulya, now."

"I don't have a visa," I said, stunned. "I mean, I flew into Belgium, because there's the least hassle with a Belgian visa."

"You awake, sweetheart? He wants to talk to you."

I took the phone. Hi, pussycat, I heard. That was definitely Gulya's voice. The same old Gulya with whom we'd hunted hidden treasure in a godforsaken dirty little town tucked beneath the hills. I even remembered the cat, the homeless stray, so keen to get out to a different world.

"Warn me when you're about to leave. If I can't be here myself, I'll leave the key with the concierge..."

Actually, what is the big deal about meeting friends many years later in a completely different part of the world? The world's a small place, and in fact what should really surprise you is something else: drinking for twenty-five years on and off with your old school friend, or sleeping with the same woman for years and years. Constant fidelity is much more astonishing than any indiscretion, coincidence is more the natural order of things than discharging a vow...

"And, listen, just who are you going to show that fucking visa to?" Ritulya asked me, when I replaced the receiver. Only now, when I looked at her, did I notice how much hunted melancholy there was in her perpetually extrovert good spirits...

We didn't go anywhere of course, and I spent the day wandering through the city. I strolled without purpose through the streets just breathing in the air; after tasting the paintings in the National Gallery I drank beer in one cafe, then in another. I watched, at a distance, the women, ordinary European women, and felt myself old and young all at once. Then I went to the station, where I studied the timetable long and carefully. From Liege to Paris the service was great. The trains were much less frequent in the other direction — Aachen. To Cologne, to Berlin, to Warsaw. The timetable didn't go beyond Warsaw. Warsaw was the end of the world I had been wandering through for a whole year.

Time to go home. The family was waiting dinner for me. Michel had evidently been making the most of my presence and had been at the Calvados in the afternoon. Ritulya and I sat in armchairs, he was on the sofa and within a minute his head was drooping. Ritulya rescued the glass that was ready to slip from his fingers onto the carpet. She told me she'd been to Russia recently. The first time for many years. How was her mother? Her mother had died while Ritulya was in America. Of cancer. Like Olga. I could imagine very clearly what it would have taken at that time to get a dying mother out of Russia to America.

"So I don't have anybody left over there anymore," said Ritulya.

"And do I?" I thought.

"Only Gulya in Paris," she added.

I wanted to ask why she'd gone to Russia, but didn't...

I left the following morning. It seemed Michel had grown out of the habit of drinking two evenings in a row. There was no question of taking me to Liege. I assured them I'd get there fine on the local train. I could get any train from there through to Paris. So Ritulya and Michel only took me as far as the station. The Liege train went in twenty minutes and Michel took us to the buffet. He ordered beer and french fries, which Belgians use to bring the calorific value of the beer up to scratch. It was one of my saddest leave-takings — God knows why. We really hardly knew each other, but when I leant out of the window as the train moved off — they kept standing there on the platform, and I thought that if I still knew how, I would probably have cried. For them, whose international children didn't understand a word of the language they preferred to have their arguments in, for me, for all our world, which is so small...

Not long afterwards I heard that Gulya died in a car crash a week after we spoke. She bumped into a boyfriend she hadn't seen in years. They had far too much to drink in a restaurant and on the way home had a head-on collision with a truck. Both were killed instantaneously. That was how I found out that Gulya had never learned to drive, he was at the wheel. So, if it had been me she was with that evening, it would never have happened, because Gulya and I would have had to take a taxi.

Return to Rome

We had left behind the acres of barrack-like multi-storey tenements, we had come into the city through the Belorussian gates, I had then walked slowly, unhurriedly down the wide street, when I was at last enfolded into the embrace of that beauty of a square, and the gaping windows, soot-blackened as if there'd been a fire, looked down from that familiar building — without stairs, terraces and statues, but with those moulded cornices with which facades were always embellished on structures erected during the time of the last of the Caesars. Lord, how my heart was thumping! There before me was the architecture I knew so intimately. A feeling of sadness overwhelmed me, a feeling familiar to anyone who has come home, when absolutely everything seems older, even emptier, and when every object you have known from your childhood speaks painfully.

I walked around my own dear piazza. The pavements and the underground pedestrian crossings were thronged with people, and with traders. Crowds of people of varying age, sex and background stood and sold Pepsi, spotlamps, children's felt boots, strings of sausages, second hand trousers, mayonnaise, women's lurex dresses, cucumber seeds, banana liqueur, a last year's _Playboy_, steel bolts, bottles of Zhigulyovskoe beer, coloured Yale sweatshirts, oven-ready pizzas, cheap paperbacks, chocolate bars, hand-knitted socks, no-lose lottery tickets, Russian porno videos, Fiat spare parts, chewing gum, dark glasses, pig's trotters, the writings of Jakob Boehm, figure skates, dried fish, tickets to the Operetta, lumps of sheep's cheese, a balalaika, basturma, size XL swim suits, Elephant brand Indian tea, communist leaflets, loose baranki, tins of instant coffee, drill sets, Mein Kampf, Adidas trainers, raw offal, men's gangster suits, children's boxed games, vodka in green bottles, brass pendant crucifixes, pairs of jeans, teddy bears, Chinese thermos flasks, loose mandarines, bottles of fake Opium perfume, packets of biscuits, antlers, a militiaman's hat, spaghetti in clear cellophane wrapping, vibrators using AAA batteries, matryoshki nesting dolls with masculine faces, glossy topless calendars, waffles, imitation crocodile ladies' evening shoes, baby cream, a competition penant with gold fringe, tampons, a painted rocking chair, a green jacket claiming to be Versacci, a set of crystal goblets, a tin of Syrian sausages and ladies' slippers with pompoms. Dark youths with gloomy faces offered to change money, even though there was a bureau de change nearby. Stunted girls, short-legged and low-arsed, aged about thirteen with the puffy faces of retards, offered to go round the corner with you and do the saxophone or faki-faki for a few dollars. I reacted like the foreigner, whose instinct is to inquire in bewilderment: but where is the ancient Third Rome?

In fact, the Third Rome lay before me. The walls I

had once known, now grimy and peeling, were plastered with signs in Latin script. Everything seemed to be covered with mould and dirt — the basilicas, desecrated decades ago, and crumbling palazzos. The Sandunvosky Public Baths, which like Diocletian's baths in Rome they wanted to turn into a museum, looked as though it's been drenched in a downpour of filth. I turned down a boulevard strewn with various cheap rubbish — empty Macdonalds milkshake cartons, Camel and Pegas packets, used condoms, torn Heineken boxes, motor oil cans, the remains of Christmas trees and the detritus of a holiday long past, pages of independent newspapers frozen here and there to the corrugated surfaces of wooden booths with rounded backs and paintwork which now looked more like a layer of stuck-on crushed Easter egg shells. I walked past two theatres — on my left and right — and came out to the monument that pisses in the rain. And stopped in confusion. I wasn't in a hurry any more, I could walk to the right, past the church where Pushkin, Horace's great successor, was married; I could proceed straight on in the direction of both Gogols; or I could turn left past the triumphant proletarian legionary clutching his phallus.

What I really ought to do was meet one of my compatriots, but I couldn't for the life of me think — who. I said to myself a hundred times: you're home. And that was all I could find to say to myself to explain the feelings of bewilderment, thrill and presentiment of fresh sadness that overwhelmed me.

Two sets of stone benches stood in semi-circles around the monument. I pulled the flap of my American overcoat under me and sat down. I lit a cigarette. This was the boulevard of my early childhood, my stupid adolescence, my youth. Were it not for the chilly April breeze, I would have sat here and waited until dusk and the ornate cast-iron lamps came on. I knew their smoky light. In the semi-gloom of the dying day it would only reach as far as the trembling June foliage of the nearest trees. In the midst of this vibrant warm fragrant half-light, it was good, all those years ago, to seek out the hot, damp hand of the young woman sitting next to you. I remembered her — her high Kalmyk cheekbones, her deep-set debauched eyes, her bright pouting lips and her darkly arching brows. She was an artist, had her hair cut like a boy's, she was called Sofi. That at least was how she called herself, but I suspected it was short for some other Tartar name.

We only knew each other vaguely, though I had fancied her for a long time from a distance. Then one June, we'd shared a table at the Actors' Club, and then gone to her studio. We'd drunk champagne, she'd mischievously ducked out of my embrace and said we'd sit out here, on the boulevard. And here she'd refused to kiss me, saying her son was wandering nearby.

She was rather fretful, and her mood seemed to me strangely exaggerated. All right, in her studio she could worry about him suddenly turning up, but why did we have to sit here, under the streetlamp, and not move further on into the shadows of the boulevard, already full of kisses and sighs. It seemed she was impatient to see him: was it maternal anxiety about what might happen to him out here on the boulevard?.. He did come, the son, two heads taller than her — she was tiny and frail — a pimply lout, who kept his slobbery mouth open. He looked half-witted to me, but she — she moved away from me, fussed, leapt to her feet, hugged him tenderly, and they whispered to each other. He went his own way and soon she left me.

Another time I also found myself in her studio by chance, there was a group of us, a bit drunk, and we'd gone there to round the evening off after the restaurant we'd been in closed. It was noisy, boozy, I lost sight of her though I hadn't abandoned the thought of scoring with her. The more so, since she'd been on her own at the restaurant, without a companion. I hunted for her on the divans, in the corners, in the vestibule, and ended up in the tiny kitchen, from where a door gave onto an equally minute shower room, converted from a store cupboard. I could hear sweet moans and indistinct whisperings coming from it, and I recognised her voice. I wanted to see who my rival was who had beaten me to it, and stood silent. Quite soon her son tumbled out, dribbling. The door was open a crack and I peeped round. She was looking at herself in the mirror and was beautiful. I saw the reflection of her face. Her hair was dishevelled, her face was red and glistened with sweat, her eyes clouded. Our eyes met in the mirror, she turned round and slammed the door. I bumped into her several times later by chance — either at a friend's place or having a drink, but then lost sight of her. And she slipped out of my mind.

Now I got up and walked to the side street opposite the cinema where the house she lived in should be. It was old then, in a bad state of repair and so all patchy in colour. To get to her studio, you had to go into the yard and up a back stairway. There was an archway through into the yard with a pool of black water standing in it, like in a stone canal. I made my way past somehow and thought I recognised the door I needed in a corner of the yard. Now I had to scramble up the dark stairs to the sixth floor, right under the roof, and I began to climb the crumbling steps, trying not to put any weight on the swaying metal banister, that looked about to give way at any moment. If I had the right one, the stairway should lead me straight to Sofi's studio. I leant against the wall and flicked my lighter: everything was as it should be, the door in front of me was the door that had had something painted on it in oils. I could hear music. I knocked. Once. Knocked again, I couldn't find the bell. Then I thumped harder with my fist, the door yielded and some half-naked tart darted back away from me like a bat. There was a cloying and distinct smell of sweet hashish. Sofi's son was standing blocking the way into the studio. The light was falling on me, his figure was only a silhouette, but even so you could see that he had turned into a waddling pot-bellied man over thirty. He didn't recognise me, though he was studying me hard, and I wasn't disguised as an old beggar.

"Who do you want?"

"Sofi."

"She's not here."

As he turned to look around the room, I could see his degenerate's receding chin was now adorned with wispy tufts of beard. His fat mouth was as slobbery as always.

"When will she be back?"

"Never," was the reply.

"Listen," I said, "I've got some presents for Sofi from abroad."

He leant towards me, because he was taller than me, and what I was saying evidently caught his attention.

"Give them to me," he said, "and I'll pass them on."

I took a step forward and he retreated. Sofi's studio looked like a crash pad: more or less human bodies scattered around, pointless music, the creature that opened the door was sitting on what had been a divan, wrapped in some kind of rag. Her face was puffy and had that washed-out bluish tinge of somebody coming down.

"So you'll be seeing her, then?"

"No," he said, "I mean, yes, I will. She's sick."

I fished out a packet of cigarettes, a lighter and a ten-dollar bill from my pocket. He immediately tried to take the money, but I moved my hand.

"Where is she?"

"In hospital. In a sanatorium, really. Out of town."

"You have the address?"

He went off, muttering, to a wrecked sideboard with one door hanging off, rooted around in it, then turned back to me, clutching a scrap of wrapping paper. He gave it to me, I handed him the ten dollars. The girl was watching us impassively, but not without a spark of intelligence. I threw her the cigarettes.

"How do you get there?"

"Dunno." He frowned, inspecting the money...

On the Arbat I bought a bunch of bananas and a bouquet of roses, pretty crumpled and faded, but with some remembrance of their original crimson colour. Five or six taxi drivers refused to take me, but the driver of a van did eventually, after some haggling over the price. When we left the city limits and were driving out along the highway he said: "It's not a sanatorium, though, I know all the sanatoriums".

About thirty kilometres further on we turned off the main road, waited for a long time at a level crossing, and then ten kilometres later turned down what had once been a tarred side road. We were surrounded by black abandoned fields with long wedges of dirty thawing snow. Crawling along the ruts, we reached a village. The driver wanted to ask the way, but every man we saw was drunk out of his skull. Finally, at the edge of the village we caught up with a middle-aged woman who looked fairly steady on her legs. She agreed to show us the way if we took her with us. When she squeezed in next to me I felt a strong fruity smell of muck coming from her padded jacket. She looked at me closely, or at the bananas and roses more like. Don't suppose your mum needs them there, she muttered, and I could barely make her out — she had almost no teeth. She soon asked us to stop and pointed the way: go down there, to the cowsheds, turn there...

A couple of kilometres further on we really did find the cowsheds — wooden barns with half-rotten shingle roofs, heaps of churned-up black soil in pens made from crooked saplings. The road forked, we turned right as the woman said. Soon we saw brick ruins up ahead. In front of the building, which had perhaps been a gentleman's country residence, a fairly decent-looking Moskvich was parked on its own. We stopped there, too. I got out of the vehicle. There was no sign on the building and some of the windows were boarded up with plywood. But where the glass was whole there were even floral pattern curtains. You could make out something going on behind them, and in a moment every window had an old woman's face looking at me. Finally a man in a padded jacket and muddy boots came out onto the porch. Who do you want? he asked impassively. I explained. The artist, you mean? Can't walk. I offered to come inside to see her. Can't do that. Visitors Saturdays only. I got out some money. All right, I'll take you, he said.

The windows were full of movement. Women, some of them not very old, were pushing each other out of the way and pointing at me. Some of them, I noticed with surprise, were wiping away tears. Time passed. My driver got out of the van and started kicking the wheels viciously, looking pointedly at his watch every so often. At last the door opened. The man held it open with his backside and tried to carry or drag something through it. Finally he managed to pull an object over the threshold, and I saw the high back of a wheelchair. The man brought the wheelchair out onto the porch and turned it around. The woman sitting in it had grey hair and a bloodless face, her immobile legs were covered by a dirty flannelette cover, a blouse was thrown around her shoulders, while the scarf tied under her chin was slipping towards the back of her head. It was Sofi. She looked at me almost with fear, without recognition, as her son had failed to recognise me. But then something moved in her face, and she covered her mouth with the palm of her hand so as not to scream. I went up to her, gave her the bananas and flowers, rested my hand on the back of the wheelchair. She burst into tears, but this did not stop her turning round towards the windows and look at her comrades with certain haughtiness. She made a theatrical and imperious gesture, as if dismissing the man. Just make it quick, he whispered, handing her over to me. I pushed the wheelchair to where Sofi directed me — around the corner of the building. She regained her composure, wiped away a tear and straightened her back. In one hand she clutched the bananas, with the other she lifted the wilting roses to her face.

But when we were out of sight of the denizens of this doleful place, she made a sign to stop. I looked at her face. Why do you look at me like that? She asked anxiously. Have I really altered that much?

Altered wasn't the word. There was nothing left of her. She was horribly thin, uncared for, and the special blue tinge at the temples, the special line of her sunken cheeks, the blackness round her eyes showed that she was probably not long for this world. "No, you're as beautiful as ever," I said, forcing myself to smile. She reached out to me, dropping the bouquet on her knee, but clumsily, so that the roses fell on the ground. I took her fingers, and she pulled my hand under her blouse. She made me squeeze her soft withered breast, and I had to lean closer to her. There was a sweet smell to her, like rotting straw, like stale perfume. She was looking at me very directly, unblinkingly, in intense expectation of something, and her Tartar eyes were like a saint's. I noticed a cheap gilt cross around her neck.

Suddenly I felt moisture on my fingers. I jerked my hand away involuntarily and saw that my whole palm was smeared with sticky woman's milk. Once again she smiled triumphantly and haughtily. And said with unexpected firmness: Kiss me. With a shudder I touched my mouth to her dry, bloodless lips, and her right hand pulled me down with unexpected strength. I noticed the nails of her left hand dug deeply into the green skin of the bananas. Pulling myself away with an effort, I bent down to gather the flowers. When I straightened up, she was sitting with her head thrown back, covering her eyes. I could hear my driver tooting the horn.

"Sofi," I called quietly, "Sofi, where are you?"

Glas 34: Strange Soviet Practices
a collection of short stories and documents
illustrating some typically Soviet phenomena

How was it possible that an entire country could live in mute fear?
Why did Soviet intellectuals denounce one another and conspire
with the authorities to brainwash ordinary people?
Why did Soviet submarines sink and
nuclear power stations explode?
This collection answers to some extent the questions
most often asked by people in the West about
the incomprehensible ways of the artificial and
inhuman Soviet system.

Set in 1937, Ilya **Zverev**'s "Sedov's Defense" is based on a real story involving a celebrated lawyer who managed to save four innocent people from death only to learn that several dozen others implicated in the case had been executed as a result of the acquittal.

No one has ever revealed the psychology of Soviet fear with such mercilessness towards the system and himself as Boris **Yampolsky**. In his "Confession" we see that the GULAG existed in people's souls as well.

The transcript of **Platonov**'s trial at the Soviet writers' Union reads as a scene from Orwell. Platonov's self-flagellation in front of a bunch of mediocrities whose names are long forgotten is a chilling evidence of the helplessness of art in conditions of all-round terror.

A former navel officer, Alexander **Pokrovsky** depicts the surreal and appallingly precarious world of a Soviet atomic submarine.

Vladimir **Kuzemko**'s "After the Blast", written in the wake of the Chernobyl disaster, is a satirical and frighteningly accurate account of the causes of the explosion and the consequences.